# THE Beautiful MESS

## AIMEE NICOLE WALKER

# THE *Beautiful* MESS

# *Chapter*
# ONE

KEEGAN'S HEART WAS IN HIS THROAT, PULSING IN TIME TO THE music blaring through the speakers. *Just breathe. In and out.* There was no reason to be nervous. Returning to the Thirsty Cowboy was his big idea, though his mission and sidekick vastly differed from his previous visit. Eighteen months ago, he'd thought men flocked to the bar for the drinks. He might've even asked if they served good food. His friends had colorfully explained that the patrons were there to quench a different thirst. And now, Keegan was there to do the same, and he'd brought Sven, the king of seduction, for guidance and moral support.

They'd chosen a table near the corner that let them observe a large expanse of the bar. Keegan's gaze kept returning to the couples on the dance floor, but he wouldn't let it linger for fear his memories of the one perfect dance he'd shared with Kerry Hart would ruin his chances of getting laid. After shooting down Sven's suggestions for twenty minutes, Keegan wondered if it was too late to save himself from a lifetime of longing. He compared each man to the one he'd never have, and they always fell short.

"Oh! What about him?" Sven gestured to a tall, dark-haired guy approaching the bar. A pale blue Henley stretched across an impressive chest, and dark-wash jeans hugged a nice ass. "He has a gorgeous smile, and look at those dimples. Bet he has a matching set just above that fine ass." Sven mimicked an alarm going off. "And I'm picking up big dick energy, even from this distance." Keegan wasn't sure what range Sven got with his big-dick detector, but he wasn't about to question the master's verdict. Sven waggled his brows at him and said, "I know you have a thing for dark-haired, brawny men."

It was the closest his friend had come to calling out Keegan's crush on Kerry, who also happened to be Sven's stepbrother. Lately, Keegan detected a little push in Kerry's direction from Sven and the rest of the Hart clan. The idea was ridiculous, especially since Sven had once cautioned him against falling for Kerry. Keegan would neither confirm nor deny his friend's suspicions. He tilted his head and considered the hot guy who leaned against the bar while waiting for the bartender. The man was fit and fine, for sure. He wore his dark hair short and neat, but the gelled strands didn't invite someone to touch them. Kerry was a few months past due for a haircut, but the longer curls framing his face were sexy and tempted Keegan to test their softness. Keegan usually loathed beards or facial hair, which should've been a point in the stranger's favor since he rocked a clean-shaven look. But Kerry's thick bristles made him look more like a plush-mouthed pirate and didn't remind Keegan of the bearded Salvation Anew members who'd wielded crushing slurs as painful as physical blows.

"Ahh. Have we found a winner?" Sven asked.

He hummed as if considering the question. The guy turned and scanned the room, and Keegan saw that his eyes were light, not black as pitch. Miriam—he'd stopped thinking of her as his mother—had warned him about black-eyed demons and the chaos they could cause during her fanatical religious teachings. He'd grown up looking for soul-snatching beasts around every corner, but it had taken Keegan twenty-three years of abuse and nearly two years of intense therapy to recognize the real monster had given birth to him. Keegan had since witnessed the visual representation of the black-eyed demons Miriam mentioned while watching reruns of *Supernatural*. Kerry's eyes weren't anything like those portrayed on the show, but Keegan was sure the man was on a first-name basis with chaos.

"Well?" Sven prompted.

"He's cute."

Sven growled and briefly hung his head before meeting Keegan's gaze. "Cute? Baby, no. We don't throw that word around unless we want to insult someone. Cute is for kittens and puppies. Cute is the kiss of death for a romantic endeavor."

"Oh." Keegan mentally added that to the list of things he didn't know or understand. Who the hell made up these dating rules, anyway? "Sorry."

Sven knocked his shoulder against Keegan's and patted his thigh under the table. "Not to worry. That's why I'm here, Goldilocks."

"*Goldilocks?*"

"Too big. Too hairy. Too horny."

Keegan snorted. "That isn't how the fairy tale goes, and I didn't say any of those things when I—"

"Rejected every eligible man in the building?" Sven asked.

"I…" The denial died on Keegan's tongue. He had dismissed every single suggestion with barely any consideration. Keegan forced his gaze back to the bar and was surprised to find the hot guy staring at him. The stranger winked, and Keegan sat taller despite his earlier dismissal. Keegan hoped his smile didn't look as forced as it felt. It certainly hadn't discouraged the man, who held their eye contact until the bartender arrived to take his drink order. Keegan sighed with relief and forced his attention back to Sven. "I'm trying."

"It's not too late for trivia night," Sven offered. He'd missed the exchange between Keegan and the stranger, or he would've jumped all over it. "If you're not ready for intimacy again, then you're not ready."

"I am." But he didn't want it with just anybody. He wanted it with—

"Kerry!" At first, he thought Sven had read his mind, but then his friend waved dramatically to get someone's attention.

Keegan turned his head and locked eyes on not just someone but *the one*. Shit! He'd come to the Thirsty Cowboy to get Kerry out of his head, but there he was, striding purposefully toward their table.

"Oh! Oh!" Sven cried excitedly and slapped Keegan's leg. "I think we've caught a live one. The guy from the bar is heading over," Sven said.

Keegan forced his gaze away from Kerry and saw that the hot guy from the bar was heading toward their table too. His stride was every bit as determined as Kerry's, and he had the advantage since he was closer. Kerry noticed the guy from the bar and must've recognized the man's intention because he lengthened his stride to arrive at the table simultaneously. Side by side, the similarities were startling, but the differences were glaring. One oozed seduction and warmth, while the other was a walking thundercloud.

The stranger smiled at Keegan and said, "Hi, I'm Ken."

"No, you're out of here," Kerry told him.

Ken turned to object until he saw the scowl on Kerry's face. "Bye."

Sven threw up his hands in frustration as Ken hightailed it to safety. "The cockblocker strikes again!"

Keegan wanted to ask Sven what he meant, but he couldn't look away from the dark gaze trained on him.

"What are you doing here?" Kerry growled.

"Um, duh," Sven said before Keegan could form a response. "We're here for the same reason as everyone else."

Kerry kept his eyes locked on Keegan and only managed a grunt. The sound triggered a primal response in Keegan's belly, and he fought the urge to squirm.

Sven touched Keegan's shoulder and said, "I'm showing Keegan the ropes."

Kerry narrowed his eyes, and a dark flush bloomed on his cheeks. "Ropes?"

"You know," Sven continued casually, unaware or uncaring of his brother's elevated tension. "I am going to teach Keegan how to seduce a man." Then he tsked, and Keegan knew without looking that Sven was raking a disapproving gaze over Keegan's wardrobe choices. He admired Sven's confidence in wearing crop tops and leather pants or booty shorts, but he hadn't reached that level of swagger and probably never would. Keegan wore a T-shirt a size too small and tight jeans to show off the physique he'd developed in the gym, and that would have to be enough. It had felt like a big step when he stood in front of his bedroom mirror at the ranch, but now he felt ridiculous.

"Seduce a man?" A strange energy snapped and crackled around Kerry as if he could conjure a thunderstorm at whim. At least he didn't double over and laugh at the notion of Keegan seducing someone.

"Ker Bear, no one is getting laid if you just stand here all night and repeat what I say. You look a little off. Are you okay?" Sven extended his leg under the table and pushed a chair toward his brother. "Maybe you should sit down." Keegan detected humor in his friend's voice, not concern, so he turned his head to study Sven. Pouty lips curved into a coy smile, and mischief twinkled in his cobalt eyes. "Why don't I go get you a drink from the bar while Keegan tells you all about how his therapist wants him to get laid?"

Kerry placed a beefy hand on the back of the chair and squinted at Keegan. "You want to say that again?"

Keegan swallowed hard. "I didn't say it. He did." He hooked his thumb and turned his head in Sven's direction, only to see him strolling across the room. "I didn't even hear him leave. He talks so much that I forget how stealthy he can be." Keegan couldn't say the same thing about the hulk, who pulled his chair away from the table with enough force to make its legs screech against the bar floor. Keegan winced and braved a look at Kerry, whose expression had grown impossibly darker. To lighten the mood, Keegan said, "The idea is ridiculous, right?"

Kerry dropped into the chair, placed his elbows on the table, and glared at Keegan as if he were public enemy number one. "Which one? That your therapist is acting like a pimp or that you've chosen Sven as your love guru?"

Something about Kerry's attitude rubbed him the wrong way. He knew the man was hurting. Hell, Kerry had recently learned the person who killed his sister twenty-five years ago was a woman he loved like family. But Keegan's days of being someone's punching bag were over. He straightened his spine and pulled his shoulders back. "Brendan isn't a pimp. He's someone who cares a great deal about my happiness and well-being. And who better than Sven to give me pointers on how to meet men?" Keegan notched his chin higher in a challenge. "Unless you'd like to volunteer as tribute. Is there something you'd like to teach me?"

Kerry's raven-black brows crept toward his hairline, and his mouth slanted into a smirk. Keegan's heart tripped over itself as he braced for a response. Had he crossed the line they'd been straddling since their first dance?

"*The Hunger Games?*" Kerry sidestepped the question, and Keegan felt like he dodged a bullet.

Keegan controlled his breathing so his relief wouldn't whoosh out of him in a dramatic exhale. He responded with the three-finger salute Katniss gave in the movies.

Kerry shook his head and sighed. "But you haven't watched *Jurassic Park.*"

"Nope." He knew the franchise was Kerry's favorite, but he wasn't sorry he prioritized *The Hunger Games*. Besides, he hoped to watch the dinosaur movies with Kerry someday, but it felt like he was waiting for an invitation that would never come. "Secular music, movies, and television were forbidden in my home, and I have to catch up on twenty-five years of pop culture. Cut me some slack."

Kerry crossed his arms over his chest. "I question your priorities."

"It seems like you have a lot of opinions about what I should do with my free time and my body," Keegan said.

Kerry's beautiful mouth formed a grim line as he stared at Keegan with a stormy expression. "The kitten has claws."

And Keegan would like to take them to Kerry's back as he—

"Here we go," Sven loudly announced as he *thunked* a frosty mug of beer onto the table hard enough to slosh some over the side. The intrusion made Keegan and Kerry jump like they'd gotten caught with their hands in the cookie jar.

Keegan watched the foam slowly glide down the side of the glass and had the strangest urge to lick it. He had little experience with beer, but he'd need to get acquainted with it if he wanted to play a significant role in Cash's future alehouse. Foam-licking wasn't included in the training his mentor had excitedly suggested to him a few weeks ago. Yet Keegan's tongue darted out and slowly swiped his bottom lip. A hoarse grunt came from across the table, and Keegan darted his gaze back to the brooding man whose onyx eyes seemed transfixed by the motion. Kerry blinked and shook his head as if to clear his thoughts or return from somewhere he hadn't meant to go.

But Keegan wasn't willing to relinquish the ground he'd made. "Kitten, huh? I guess it's an improvement over what you called me the first time we met here."

"Oh, this sounds titillating," Sven said, leaning in. "What did he call you?"

"Mind your own business," Kerry told Sven.

Keegan kept his gaze locked on Kerry when he answered his friend's question. "He said this meat market was no place for a little lamb like me. That was a long time ago, and as you've pointed out, I'm not the same person I was back then." The dance he'd shared with Kerry probably only lasted three minutes, but it changed his life. He doubted the encounter had even registered as a blip on Kerry's radar.

"God, this is good," Sven said. "Tell me more."

Kerry scowled at his brother. "Stay out of it. You've caused enough trouble tonight." He turned to Keegan and growled, "Dance with me."

Keegan faked a swoon in his chair and fanned his face with his hand. "How could I resist such a sweet invitation?"

Kerry stood up fast enough to nearly topple his chair. "Now, Kee. I want to talk to you and don't want *him* to overhear." He jabbed his finger in Sven's direction, and Keegan turned his head to catch his friend watching them with rapt attention. He'd placed his elbows on the table, laced his fingers together, and rested his chin on the bridge they made. The little shit didn't bother to fake his interest.

Sven batted his eyelashes. "Most people take it to the parking lot or restroom."

"That isn't the kind of talking I intend," Kerry growled. The king of laid-back charm exhibited a vastly different personality, and Keegan didn't know what to make of it.

"Pity, and since when have you danced to fast music?" Sven countered.

The current song ended, and a slow rhythm blared through the speakers before Kerry could form his answer. He triumphantly pointed both hands toward the ceiling as if his wishes alone conjured the switch.

Sven straightened in his chair and pulled a supersized fruity cocktail toward him. "It seems my work here is done," he said before pursing his lips around the straw and sucking hard. The provocative pose no doubt earned a collective groan from his fan club. "Have fun, boys."

Kerry shook his head and walked off without waiting to see if Keegan had followed. But, of course, he would. He sighed and pushed back from the table. It took everything in his power not to bound after him like a desperate little puppy. Keegan glanced over his shoulder and caught Sven watching them with a smug expression that halted him midstep. Not long ago, Sven cautioned Keegan to guard his heart around Kerry, and now his friend made shooing motions to encourage Keegan to follow Kerry onto the dance floor. Sven had told him Kerry would be tending bar at the Feisty Bull but hadn't seemed surprised when Kerry showed up. Keegan smelled a rat. Was that what Kerry had meant when he'd accused Sven of causing trouble?

"I look like a dumbass standing on the dance floor by myself," Kerry called out.

When Keegan turned back around, a slender guy with light brown hair had stepped into Kerry's personal space.

"That invitation wasn't for you," Keegan snarled, surprising himself with the ferocity in his voice. "Scram."

The guy curled up his fingers to mimic cat claws and said, "*Meow*."

Kerry seemed to get a big kick out of his feisty display if the massive smile on his face was any indication. "Even that guy knows you have claws."

"Don't get a big ego," Keegan said.

"Why not? Everything else on me is big."

Kerry looped his arms low around Keegan's waist and pulled him close. Too close. Keegan's nose nearly collided with Kerry's collarbone, but it allowed him to inhale Kerry's intoxicating scent without being a creeper. Keegan inhaled subtly to get another whiff of cedarwood, leather, and something smoky before he eased back a little and circled his arms around Kerry's neck. He willed himself not to take the bait with Kerry's comment on his size, but he couldn't help himself.

"Well, a guy your size would look ridiculous with little feet," Keegan quipped, refusing to feed into the man's inflated ego. "You'd tip over."

"Yeah, I was talking about my feet." Sarcasm dripped off his tongue, and Keegan longed to suck it off.

His recent thoughts about Kerry and their growing intensity rattled Keegan. It would only fluster him more to catalog the size of Kerry's features, such as the warm, large hands resting near the swells of Keegan's ass, the broad shoulders blocking out the rest of the room from his view, or Kerry's huge, cocky smile. The man knew the effect he had on other people, and the spreading warmth in Keegan's lower belly reminded him why he didn't want to focus on Kerry's powerful attributes, lest his mind wandered too far astray again. Instead, Keegan considered the similarities and differences between their first dance and this one.

Keegan's heart still tried to pound its way out of his chest, but he didn't let anxiety drown out all his other senses this time. He swayed naturally to the music rather than woodenly turning in a circle, keeping a foot of space between himself and the gentle giant. Kerry had pulled him flush against his body this time, and Keegan was more than happy to keep it that way. The heat and power radiating off Kerry were more intoxicating than Sven's enormous cocktail. Their changed physical dynamic was impressive, but the emotional shift was what kept Keegan awake, aching and longing late into the night. They were inexorably drawn to one another, but neither seemed willing to do anything about it.

The glimmer in Kerry's eyes changed from ornery to something else. Surprise? A different kind of awareness? It felt like Keegan should at least be able to recognize the response after years of intensive therapy, but the emotion eluded him. Kerry leaned in, and Keegan thought for a moment he might kiss him, but Kerry nuzzled his nose against Keegan's temple instead. Black dots danced before his eyes, and Keegan realized he was holding his breath. He inhaled deeply, and a lungful of oxygen cleared his vision.

Kerry lowered his mouth to Keegan's ear. "Eighteen months, three weeks, and two days."

The husky voice and Kerry's proximity made it hard for him to think. "Huh?"

Kerry pulled back and stared into his eyes. "You said our dance was a long time ago. It's been eighteen months, three weeks, and two days."

Hoping not to betray his shock, Keegan said, "You don't know the exact hour?"

Kerry lifted his arm and glanced at his watch. "Eighteen months, three weeks, two days, and twenty-two hours." When he returned his hand to Keegan's waist, it landed lower so that his fingertips dipped into Keegan's back pocket. "You aren't the same person I met back then, but this bar is still no place for you." The surly, arrogant remark almost ruined Kerry's stunning admission, and Keegan didn't think it was an accident.

"I don't agree." Keegan replayed the advice Sven had given him during their ride to the bar. He angled his head just so and peeked up at Kerry from beneath his eyelashes. He dragged his teeth over his bottom lip and barely resisted a giggle when Kerry's dark gaze dropped to his mouth. Feeling emboldened, Keegan raised his hand and twirled one of Kerry's curls around his finger. It was even softer than it looked. Kerry briefly closed his eyes, and his chest rose higher on his next inhale. His hand inched deeper into Keegan's pocket until his long fingers cupped Keegan's ass.

Kerry's dark eyes burned with intensity, even as he said, "Sven has taught you well, but those tricks won't work on me."

"Is that so?" Keegan asked. He slowly withdrew his finger from Kerry's hair and settled his hand over Kerry's racing heart.

"Yes."

"That's too bad," Keegan said, adding a heavy sigh for effect. "Maybe I should go find Ken and see how they work on him." He took a step back, and Kerry's hold tightened.

"We're not done talking," Kerry growled.

"Look who's turned into the Big Bad Wolf," Keegan teased. "Maybe you're not done talking, but I'm looking for something more than conversation tonight."

"God, I'm going to kill my brother," Kerry snarled.

Keegan loved how the men rarely referred to themselves as stepbrothers, but it wasn't the time to mention it, not with Kerry's penetrating stare boring holes into his skull. "Seems like a harsh penalty for helping a friend. If you want to be mad at anyone, you should be mad at me."

"I'm not angry. I just thought you were going to be at trivia night. Seeing you here caught me by surprise."

"And I thought you were tending bar," Keegan said. "I didn't expect to run into you either." They'd been manipulated by the master. Maybe he'd talked Kerry out of killing Sven so he could do it.

"I needed a break," Kerry said.

"From me?" The question was out before Keegan could stop it.

Black brows drew together in a scowl. "A break from you? No. I've been working extra shifts at the rescue station to cover vacations and paternity leave. Why would you ask me that?"

Keegan shrugged like the conversation didn't mean anything when it felt like he had so much riding on Kerry's answers. "I'm constantly underfoot. One of my best friends is your brother, and the other is married to your cousin." Keegan and Kerry had even been the best men at Rueben and Seth's wedding two weeks ago.

Kerry, Seth, and Sven's large, boisterous family had unofficially adopted Keegan into their clan and invited him to every family dinner and celebration. Kerry's mom was technically no longer a Hart since she remarried over twenty years ago, but apparently, the family's motto was "Once a Hart, always a Hart" because they held tight to their claim on her and welcomed Steven and Sven with open arms. And since Miriam had alienated their biological family with her extremist beliefs, Keegan found the Harts' inclusion both beautiful and addictive.

Kerry's thunderous expression returned. "What are you talking about?"

"First, I infiltrated your family, and now you won't be able to avoid me at the Feisty Bull since my first shift is tomorrow night." Working with their sommelier and hospitality crew would provide a lot of experience for the alehouse, so Keegan had jumped at the opportunity when Kerry's aunt and uncle offered him a job. Had that been a mistake?

"So, you're here to give me space and aren't trying to hook up with a stranger because your therapist suggested it?"

"More than one thing can be true," Keegan said.

"That isn't an answer," Kerry countered.

"Isn't it? And you haven't exactly answered my question either."

Kerry snorted and rolled his eyes. "I'm not here because I'm trying to avoid you. I don't think you've infiltrated my family."

Keegan swallowed hard. "I don't bother you?"

Kerry withdrew his hand from Keegan's pocket and settled it at his waist. "Oh, you very much do, but not the way you think." He cycled through a deep, slow breath before he spoke again. "I want to hear about your therapist's instructions."

Embarrassment heated Keegan's cheeks and made him look away. It was hard enough discussing it with Sven, who had zero boundaries, but he squared his shoulders and met Kerry's dark gaze. "When I started treatment, Brendan recommended I abstain from emotional and physical entanglements to focus on healing myself. I've made a lot of progress, and Brendan thinks I'm ready to get out there and—"

"Fuck?"

Keegan choked on his next breath. "Date. Meet guys. Embrace my queerness and freaking revel in it. I'll never accept my desires are normal if I don't immerse myself into healthy interactions."

"So fucking?" Kerry's one-track mind irritated him to no end.

"Isn't that part of healthy interactions?" Keegan fired back. "Or do you think I should spend the rest of my life lonely?"

Kerry's eyes narrowed, and his mouth thinned. "Of course not."

"I've suppressed my instincts and hated myself for far too long. I want to live and love. I want liberation, damn it, and I want to—"

"Fuck."

"Yes!" Keegan shouted. "I want to fuck!" Flames of humiliation licked up his neck and face, but Keegan was on a roll. "I want to wallow in a powerful orgasm and not weep in shame afterward. Do you have any idea how mortifying that is?"

Kerry stilled suddenly and lifted his hands to cup Keegan's face. His expression softened as he searched Keegan's eyes. The moment felt huge, like they stood at the precipice of something big, scary, and wonderful. Was Kerry going to kiss him? "Kee—"

Someone plowed into Kerry's back, breaking the intimate bubble they'd created on the dance floor. Kerry dropped his hands and turned to face their interloper.

"Dude," the stranger said, staggering a few steps backward. His

13

half-lidded eyes widened in alarm when he got a load of Kerry's dark expression. "Hey, are you Kerry Hart?"

"Yes."

The man's expression sobered immediately, and his posture went from relaxed and drunk to erect and astute. "Sorry about that." He extended his hand toward Kerry's, who reciprocated the gesture without question. But before their palms met, the guy pulled his free arm from around his back and slapped an envelope against Kerry's hand. "You've been served."

# Chapter
# TWO

KERRY'S FINGERS TIGHTENED REFLEXIVELY AROUND THE envelope, even as his brain tried to reject what was happening. The knot of dread festering in his gut for the past twenty months ruptured and sent poisonous bile spreading throughout his body. The urge to vomit overwhelmed him, but he kept his shit together. Kerry had mentally braced himself for the possibility of a lawsuit ever since Keith Bozeman's botched rescue attempt, but did it have to happen on the anniversary of his dad's death?

"Kerry." Keegan's tentative voice teased his ears seconds before a gentle touch landed on his shoulder.

The comforting gesture only amplified the tension gripping Kerry's body and reminded him of the mistake he'd nearly made. Kerry had been seconds away from kissing Keegan in the middle of the dance floor before the process server interrupted them. He glanced up from the envelope to see the man had already disappeared into the crowd, as if the dancers had swallowed him whole. Could they do the same for him?

Life had really fucked him over lately, and the bastard hadn't bothered to use lube. Kerry had only wanted to let off steam, forget his troubles, and hide from his sorrow. He'd planned to hook up with a guy who looked nothing like the one taking up too many of his thoughts. Keegan's remarks about infiltrating Kerry's life and his accusations of avoidance had landed too close for comfort. Admitting the truth would've hurt Keegan, and Kerry would rather let someone saw off his dick with a rusty, dull knife than hurt a person who'd become dear to him. So Kerry had settled for a half-truth he'd been willing to share. Keegan bothered him, just not in a way either of them were ready to handle. Even that had blown up in his face when their conversation veered into a territory that scraped his nerves raw and resulted in a near kiss.

"What the hell was that?" Sven asked angrily, pointing at the envelope.

"Whoa!" Keegan said. "How'd you get here so fast?"

"I saw that weirdo making his way toward you guys," Sven said. "One minute, he was striding purposefully through the bar as he searched the crowd, and the next, he was faking intoxication as he staggered toward you guys on the dance floor. I saw he had something in his hand, but I couldn't see what it was. I was out of my chair and halfway to you when the guy bumped into Kerry and handed him the envelope. Thank goodness the guy wasn't holding a weapon."

Kerry sighed and pulled away from Keegan's touch before he leaned into it. "This might be just as deadly," he groused. Kerry would survive a lawsuit, but Hart's Creek Rescue might not, and the business meant everything to him.

"Fucking Chuck," Sven snarled.

Just hearing his former employee's name was enough to make Kerry seethe with anger. He'd purchased the rescue business from Benny Johnson, a longtime family friend, after working for the man for fifteen years. Benny had hired Kerry after he graduated high school and taught him everything he'd learned about the business.

Kerry had worked his way up the ranks, getting promotions over guys who'd been there longer, which had ruffled a lot of feathers. The resentment had only grown when Benny chose Kerry to be his successor over Chuck Dahl, a hotheaded know-it-all who'd had a decade of seniority over Kerry. The curmudgeon liked to blab around town that Benny only chose Kerry because of his wealthy connections and easy access to the funds to buy the business. It was complete bullshit. The mountainside town and the surrounding county were named after his ancestor, but the bankers who approved his loan hadn't given a shit about that. They'd only cared about assets, credit scores, and the business plan to pay back the loan.

Kerry had kept Chuck on the crew after Benny's retirement, and the older man made him regret his kindness until the day Kerry had no choice but to fire him. Chuck had been surly and insubordinate on a good day and negligent and reckless on a bad one. And on the very worst day, all his negative personality traits had linked up to create a tsunami of suck, where Chuck the Fuck turned Keith Bozeman's routine vehicle crash rescue into a near catastrophe. Kerry thought he'd exercised perfect control afterward when he calmly told Chuck the Fuck to take a hike and never darken his doorstep again. He wished he could say that was the end of the saga, but the legal document in his hands said otherwise.

"Dad warned you this might happen, Ker Bear. Everything is going to work out just fine."

"Who's Chuck?" Keegan asked. "And what just happened?" Confusion pitched his voice higher, and Kerry knew he'd see worry brimming in Keegan's expressive hazel eyes if he turned and met his gaze. So he took a step away from temptation and then another until he was heading toward the door. The air in the room suddenly felt too thick to breathe, and his head throbbed in time with the music.

"Ker," Sven called out.

Kerry held up a hand, hoping it would stop Keegan and Sven from following, but he should've known better. He heard the murmur of their voices close behind him but couldn't make out the individual words. He suspected Sven was explaining the situation with Chuck the Cluster Fuck to Keegan, which was good since Kerry's brain cells were too scattered to form coherent words. Once he stepped outside the bar, Kerry halted his hasty escape, tilted his head back, and sucked in a lungful of crisp air, clearing his brain fog so he could focus better. Another deep breath and the throbbing in his temples eased. Stars twinkled like diamonds in the black velvet sky. The bone-rattling bass inside the bar became a mildly annoying background noise. Kerry ignored it along with the whispered exchange happening behind him and cycled through a few more breaths. Sven was right. Kerry had planned for this eventuality when it became clear that Bozeman hadn't accepted the insurance company's proposed settlements. Kerry's step-dad, Steven, was related to Vincent Marino, one of the most successful lawyers in Colorado. Steven received an endless amount of razzing from the family for having a cousin named Vinny, who was also an attorney. The family looked for any excuse to quote *My Cousin Vinny*. Maybe Kerry hadn't found himself in a backwoods town facing a potential death penalty, but that didn't ease the heaviness in his chest. He'd need his Vinny to pull out all the stops to clear his name too.

"And tonight of all nights," Sven said.

"What's significant about tonight?" Keegan asked.

Kerry wasn't going to talk about his father's death, and Sven would keep his mouth shut if he knew what was good for him. He turned and faced his stepbrother with a raised brow. "You're the only one I told about my plans tonight."

Sven gasped at the insinuation. "I'm appalled you could even think I'd betray you like that."

Keegan put both hands on his hips and turned to square off against Sven. "You told me Kerry was tending bar tonight."

Sven bit his bottom lip to fend off the sheepish smile forming, then arranged his features in a serene expression. "Did I? I must've gotten Kerry's schedule confused."

The showdown between friends promised to be an adorable diversion from his legal troubles and other woes, but Kerry couldn't afford to get distracted. "Hey," he said, pulling their focus to him. "I know damn well you wouldn't betray me like that, Sven. The process server probably followed me here." Kerry had just wanted to get even with him for meddling with his Friday plans. He knew damn well his brother would talk his way out of the corner he'd painted himself into, and Kerry didn't need to stick around to see it. "Which one of you is driving?"

Keegan raised his hand. "I am."

"Good." Kerry wouldn't have to worry about them getting home safely after Sven sucked down that massive cocktail. The bartenders at the Thirsty Cowboy loved Sven and used a heavy hand when mixing his drinks. Kerry turned his gaze to Keegan. The play of moonlight and shadows turned his handsome face into a work of art, accentuating his sharp cheekbones and full mouth. Hazel eyes shimmered with an emotion Kerry struggled to name, something melancholy that tugged at Kerry's heartstrings. "I don't say things unless I mean them, Kee. Don't hide from me."

Keegan swallowed hard and nodded.

Kerry released a soft growl and pulled the man into his arms for a hug. He pressed a soft kiss to Keegan's temple, then moved his mouth to Keegan's ear. "There's a lot more I want to say, but now isn't the time. Maybe we can chat tomorrow night."

Keegan tilted his head back to make eye contact. "I'd like that."

Kerry knew he should release the guy and step back, but he couldn't seem to resist the warmth radiating from both Keegan's body and gaze. "Maybe when Sven isn't around to cause trouble."

Keegan tensed in his embrace, and his expression cooled slightly. Kerry regretted ruining the moment by bringing up Sven's meddling. Then Keegan stepped back, forcing Kerry to lower his arms. Keegan turned to face Sven, giving Kerry his profile, but his irritation was still evident with the limited view. Kerry didn't know Keegan's full lips could form such a thin line. Kee's brow furrowed in what Kerry knew would be a deep V of disappointment. Sven widened his eyes with his trademarked mock innocence but still took a step back from potential danger. "I think you owe us an apology." Before Sven could play dumb, Keegan laid it all out for him. "You lied to me and manipulated Kerry into dancing with me."

Sven recovered quickly. "I didn't lie to you, Kee. I told you I suspected Kerry would end up tending bar." Sven aimed a pointed look at Kerry. "How many times have you pledged a night to yourself only to end up behind the bar at the Feisty Bull?"

*Too many to count.* He puffed out his cheeks and exhaled slowly. Sven had him dead to rights, but Kerry wasn't in a magnanimous mood to save his ass. "A few times."

"Ha!" Sven scoffed. "I'll let you have that one, even though we both know better."

"I don't think you can say you're showing me grace only to call bullshit in the next breath," Kerry replied. Yeah, he needed to make phone calls and get his legal shit sorted, but it was Friday night, and he wouldn't reach out to Vinny until a reasonable hour the next morning. He could afford to engage in verbal fencing with Sven and soak up a few more minutes of Keegan's warmth.

"Whatever," Sven said, waving off his objection with a flick of his wrist. "Now I have to address the second part of Keegan's claim." Sven pointed a long, elegant finger in Kerry's direction. "No one, and I mean not even divine intervention, gets this jackass to do a damn thing he doesn't want to do."

"Are you insulting my intelligence or comparing me to a male donkey?" Kerry asked.

"You are as stubborn as a mule," Sven replied. "A male mule is a jackass."

"Fair point." Kerry wouldn't bother to deny it.

"So, you agree that nothing I said or did convinced you to ask Keegan to dance with you," Sven said.

"He asked me to dance so we could talk away from you," Keegan insisted.

There was no way Kerry could let him go on believing that. "Nope." Sven and Keegan looked at him. The former smirked because he knew he was right. The latter wore a look of utter disbelief, and Kerry couldn't abide Keegan's self-doubt. "That was the excuse I gave because I wanted to dance with you again, Kee." A big part of him wanted to take the younger man by the hand and lead him back inside the bar to dance some more, which was why he took a few steps backward. Legal troubles were one thing, but matters of the heart were a completely different problem. "I say what I mean," he reminded Keegan. "You guys be careful going home," he said before turning and heading to his truck.

Once inside, Kerry tossed the envelope onto the passenger seat without reading it. He'd have time to obsess over every word later. Kerry checked the time and knew his stepfather would still be awake but didn't place the call until Sven and Keegan made it to their vehicle without incident. He started his truck engine and followed them out of the parking lot, then used his voice command feature to call Steven.

His stepfather answered on the second ring. "Is something wrong, Ker?" Steven's steady voice was like a balm for Kerry's shredded nerves. They'd had a rough time adapting to each other in the beginning, but Steven had won him over with unwavering patience, unshakable support, and unrivaled devotion to Kerry's mom. His gratitude for Steven's presence—then and now—choked him up a little, and he had to clear his throat before speaking.

"Just a court processor serving me legal papers at the local gay bar," Kerry said, leaving out the part where he'd been dancing with Keegan. His mother was the president of the Keegan Scott is Perfect for My Son Club, and he'd bet money that Sven phoned Lucinda as soon as Kerry was out of earshot. They would be insufferable after this.

"What?" Steven's outrage was probably more about the time

Kerry got served than where it had occurred. He was a card-carrying PFLAG member before Kerry officially came out, thanks to Steven Edward Ruehl Jr., dubbed Sven by a young second cousin who couldn't pronounce his name. His brother likely came out of the womb waving a rainbow flag, and Steven knew both his sons hung out at the Thirsty Cowboy. He preached safety, not censure. "I'm not saying that process servers don't have to get creative because some people are more slippery than others. But you have a business where you maintain regular hours, and you own a home. There's nothing elusive about you. The time and place of your serving feels very personal."

"My sexuality isn't a secret, and I used to be a frequent bar patron." Sven's comment replayed in his mind. Kerry had been noticeably absent from the bar for months. Nearly eighteen of them. He'd returned to the Thirsty Cowboy a few times since his first dance with Keegan, but he always left alone and unsatisfied. He'd only recently acknowledged to himself why hookups with random strangers no longer held appeal, and that was the change in demeanor Keegan had picked up on and misread. "And nobody has given me shit about being gay once I outgrew them." At least not to his face.

"It still feels like a personal dig," Steven said. "And that pisses me off almost as much as this lawsuit Chuck backed you into with his stupidity. What does the document claim?"

"I haven't opened the envelope yet."

"It's most likely a copy of the complaint and a summons that gives you the deadline to respond," Steven said. "Come over for breakfast in the morning. We can retreat to my home office afterward to review the document and call Vinny. The court will have allowed time for you to hire legal counsel, so there's no need to call him tonight."

"Sounds good to me." Though Kerry could think of better ways to bond with his stepfather.

Keegan turned right at a four-way intersection that would take him toward the town where Sven lived. Kerry's mountainside cabin was in the opposite direction, but he was tempted to follow Keegan to make sure they both got home safely. He signaled left but didn't make the turn until Keegan's taillights faded from view.

"Something just occurred to me," Steven said abruptly. "Why the hell didn't I think about it sooner?" Kerry knew his stepfather hadn't posed the question to him, so he waited for Steven to continue. "We should've called in your buddy Dominic. He's still a private detective, right?"

Kerry and Dominic Babb had been best friends since second grade when Dom's family moved to the area. They'd stayed tight, even though their busy lives pulled them in opposite directions as adults. "Yeah. He's moved back to the area. We keep talking about getting together, but it seems like he's always working on a case. He had a thriving agency in Denver and is trying to make a name for himself in Colorado Springs." The two cities were close geographically, but Dom told him the geopolitical climates put them in different galaxies. Kerry would have to take his word for it because he'd only lived in Hart's Creek. "Do you think I should call Dom and tell him what's going on?"

"Absolutely," Steven said. "The plaintiff might've had a general timeframe of when you'd get served, but it's unlikely he knew specific dates and times. It's possible he's living up a last hoorah before he's required to act beaten and broken for the court's sake." While it was true Chuck had exhibited a horrible lack of judgment at the crash site, Keith Bozeman had miraculously escaped serious injuries. Steven's remark sounded cynical, but spending three decades as a lawyer probably had that effect on a person.

"I'll call Dom in the morning."

"Call him now," Steven insisted. "There's no time to lose. Even if Bozeman knows you're getting served tonight, he won't expect you to take immediate action." Steven swore a blue streak. "I just realized what date it is. Kerry, I'm so sorry."

Kerry sighed heavily. "Me too," he said. "It's probably just a really shitty coincidence I got served on this anniversary, but it sucks. I'll call Dom as soon as we hang up."

"I'll let you get to it, then. Does eight o'clock work for breakfast?"

"Sounds perfect. See you then." Kerry said goodbye, then disconnected the call with a button on his steering wheel. He expected to get Dom's voicemail, but his friend answered on the second ring.

"Must be slim pickings at the Thirsty Cowboy if you're calling me at ten o'clock on a Friday night." Dom's lazy drawl made Kerry smile despite the turmoil filling his brain like fog again.

He lowered his window a few inches, hoping the fresh air would work its magic again. "Why does everyone assume I'm getting laid on a Friday night?" When he wasn't responding to emergency calls, Kerry spent most of his free time tending bar. Sure, the patrons flirted and slipped him their numbers, but he'd stopped taking them up on their offers months ago. Eighteen of them, to be exact. The brain fog lifted enough for him to picture shimmering hazel eyes in the moonlight. *Christ.* Kerry closed his window because pining for Keegan wasn't the clarity the moment called for.

"If you're breathing, some guy is trying to ride your dick," Dom said. And it had been that simple once, so why wasn't Kerry eager to get back to his old habits? "And to be frank," Dom continued, "there would be plenty of guys who'd totally go *Weekend at Bernie's* on you."

Kerry laughed at both the reference and the memory of watching the movie with Dom when they were teens. Dom had been delighted to think they'd take stiff dicks to the afterlife with them. The idea of someone riding his corpse's cock made Kerry shudder. "Fucking gross, dude."

"Sorry," Dom replied. "I'm just trying to stay awake on my current stakeout. A woman thinks her husband is cheating on her. I've been following this boring bastard for a few nights, and the only thing he's straying on is his wife's strict diet."

"Or he's picked up your tail," Kerry teased.

Dom snorted. "As if. No one sees me unless I want them to." Which was pretty impressive considering his size. He was only a few inches shorter than Kerry but just as broad. "Plus, I see the look of pure bliss when the guy bites into junk food. Pretty sure he just came in his pants at this Taco Bell. He ordered two large packs of those Cinnabon delights, and he's mowing through them. I think he's on number twenty out of twenty-four."

Kerry's stomach growled. "I could go for some of those about now." He'd tried to eat dinner before heading to the Thirsty Cowboy, but nothing sounded good. Suddenly, cinnamon sugar-coated donut holes stuffed with a gooey cream cheese icing center sounded amazing. Sharing them in bed with—

"Nope. Not going there." Kerry didn't realize he'd said the last part out loud until his friend chuckled.

"Didn't invite you, buddy." Dom yawned, and leather creaked on the other end of the connection. Kerry pictured Dom stretching in the nondescript minivan he used for stakeouts. "So, why are you calling me on a Friday night when you should be balls-deep into a firm, willing ass?"

Kerry locked his brain before any tempting images could form. "I need to hire you to investigate someone for me. It's really important, Dom."

"Are you home now?" Dom's voice shifted from a teasing best friend to a serious investigator in a heartbeat.

"Not for another fifteen minutes."

A persistent dinging came through the connection, followed by the familiar sound of an engine turning over. "I'm about ten minutes behind you."

"Don't you want to know what the investigation is about?" Kerry asked.

"You said you needed me, so I'm coming. I'll get the details when I arrive."

Kerry's throat tightened with emotion again, so his voice came out gruff when he spoke. "I don't expect you to bail on your case, Dom. I'm having breakfast at eight with Steven. You could—"

"Shut up," Dom growled. "You've never asked me for a fucking thing as long as I've known you." That couldn't be true. "Besides, we're long overdue to share a few beers and catch up. Tell your attack panther to behave."

Kerry snorted. Betty wasn't a panther, nor was she vicious. She was a calico-colored Maine coon cat, whose enormous size and panther-like prowess intimidated most people. Dom was all bluster now, but Betty would melt him into a puddle of goo when she curled up in his lap and purred loud enough to rattle the rafters. He would scratch her ears and coo to her within minutes of his arrival. "See you soon."

Kerry kept his window down for the duration of his drive home. The combination of road noise and cool air kept his mind from wandering back to the near kiss with Keegan. There would come a time later when Kerry could let his imagination and what-ifs run wild, but he needed to focus on saving his business. Betty met him at the front door. She stood on her hind legs and put her front paws on his abdomen, stretching to show her sleek magnificence. Betty's copper eyes perfectly matched the dark orange patches of fur that stood out in stark contrast to the black-and-white coat. If Kerry didn't know better, he'd think Betty's narrow-eyed gaze was a sign of judgment or disappointment. She was one hell of a hunter and never failed to capture her prey, and here Kerry had struck out again. He scoffed at his own ridiculousness. It wasn't like he brought his hookups home to meet his cat, which meant he'd projected his morose attitude onto his sweet lady.

Kerry gave her ears a vigorous scratching before moving farther into his house. He gazed around the two-story log cabin to make sure his home was at least presentable. No one would accuse him of being a slob, but the place could use some tidying up. With everything going on lately, cleaning had been the last thing on his mind. Kerry loaded the dirty dishes into the dishwasher and sorted through the mail and a little clutter on his countertops before wiping them down. He moved into the living room to straighten up the coffee and end tables and run his handheld vacuum over the leather furniture to remove cat hair. Betty sat on the throw blanket draped over the sofa and licked her crotch while monitoring him with his noise maker. The doorbell rang, and Kerry turned off the mini vacuum and headed toward the front door.

Dom stood on his porch with takeout from Taco Bell and a battered messenger bag slung over his shoulder. "Don't shoot, man," Dom said when he saw the vacuum in Kerry's hand. "I come bearing gifts. I heard the lust in your voice when you heard about the guy eating at Taco Bell. Some things never change." Dom gestured to the vacuum in Kerry's hand. "But some do."

"Get in here, fool."

Dom stepped into the house, and Kerry shut the front door behind him. They headed into the kitchen with Betty fast on their heels. Kerry returned the handheld vacuum to its charger and grabbed two beers from the refrigerator. Dom set the food and laptop bag on the table before pulling Kerry into a bear hug.

"It's been too long," Kerry told him when they pulled back.

"That it has," Dom said as he unpacked the bag of food. "I grabbed a little of everything because you sounded half-starved on the phone, and the smells coming from the place made my mouth water."

Kerry's stomach growled on cue, making Dom laugh. A white paw snuck up from under the table as Betty tried to snag some of their food. "I don't think so," Kerry said. He reached down and pulled her out from under the table. "You either behave, or I'll shut you in the laundry room."

Dom reached forward and let her sniff his fingers before moving in to scratch her ears. Betty fired up her engine and purred loudly. "If I could be sure I'd get a cat as perfect as you, I'd adopt one in a heartbeat. My ex is allergic to anything with fur, feathers, or scales, so pets were off-limits."

Dom had said little about his divorce, and Kerry hadn't pushed, though he was dying to know what happened there. Kerry had made it clear he was ready to listen anytime Dom wanted to talk and had left it at that. This was the first time Dom had mentioned his ex since he moved back to town, and Kerry took it as a good sign that he barely detected venom in Dom's voice.

Kerry gently turned Betty's head so he could look into her eyes once Dom returned his attention to sorting the food. "Can I trust you or not?" Betty narrowed her eyes as if she were on the verge of opening a can of whoop ass on him, so he released her. She huffed away from the table, leaped onto the back of the couch again, and resumed bathing her privates.

They dropped into chairs and attacked the food as if they hadn't eaten in weeks, so several minutes passed before either of them spoke again. Kerry settled back in his chair and sipped his beer as Dom pulled his laptop from his messenger bag.

"So, who do you need me to investigate?"

"Keith Bozeman," Kerry replied. "He's suing me for a botched rescue."

Dom's fingers flew over the keyboard as he typed. "What happened?"

"Do you remember me talking about Chuck Dahl?" Kerry asked.

Dom's fingers stilled, and he looked up. "Not that fuck again."

"Afraid so. Bozeman had lost control of his car and driven over the side of a ravine. I'd already answered a call and was in the field, so Chuck responded to Bozeman's accident. He'd radioed me with an update of the situation, and I'd instructed him to get the driver to safety first and then retrieve the vehicle."

Dom resumed typing. "That sounded like the sensible thing to do, but I take it Chuck disobeyed orders?"

"The idiot thought it would be working smarter to pull the car up the side of the hill with the crash victim inside it."

"Yikes," Dom said with a grimace.

"Yeah," Kerry agreed. "Dozens of things could go wrong in that scenario, but you only need one to cause a major clusterfuck. The crew shimmied down the hill and hooked the cables to the car. Chuck fired up the winch and started hauling it up the hillside. About halfway up, the rigging failed, and the car plummeted back down the ravine."

Dom flinched and sucked air through his teeth. "Oh damn."

"Uh-huh." Kerry tipped his bottle back but noticed it was empty. Dom hadn't even touched his beer yet. "You going to drink that?"

Dom stopped typing long enough to scoot the bottle toward Kerry. "You drink it. I'm on a case." He resumed typing for a few more minutes, then turned his laptop around to show Kerry a picture of a middle-aged man with dull blue eyes and thin dark hair with a receding hairline. His expression was pure annoyance as he stared at the camera. Must've been a long wait to get his driver's license renewed that day. "This Keith Bozeman?"

"Yep."

Dom pushed back his chair and stood up. "Let me see what I can find out."

Kerry stood too. "Right now?"

"Mr. Bozeman probably isn't aware you got served tonight. I want to see how he lives before and after he knows. I'd bet money he's desperate to live it up one last time."

"You sound as cynical as Steven."

Dom stowed his laptop in his messenger bag and zipped it before meeting Kerry's gaze. "You know firsthand how deceiving and manipulative people can be."

Kerry thought of Cynthia's betrayal and how scared his sister must've been in the last moments of her life. He fought back the rising bile in his throat. Thoughts of losing Natalie naturally led to the tragedy that followed. Kerry recalled the way his dad disappeared into himself, dying a little more each day until his broken heart gave out. He didn't want to go down that road either, so he pushed the pain away and latched onto the memory of Keegan's gorgeous face bathed in the moonlight. His silver lining. His horny little lamb.

"Whoa," Dom said, snapping Kerry back to reality. "Who are you thinking about right now?"

Kerry shook his head vigorously. "It's nothing. Just thinking about those Cinnabon Delights."

Dom chuckled. "Well, I'll leave you alone with them. Dim the lights and enjoy." He hooked an arm around Kerry's neck and hugged him again. "I'll be in touch soon."

"Thanks for dinner, Dom."

His friend waved as he headed to the door. He paused at the sofa to give Betty some love before heading out into the night. As tempting as the donut holes were, Kerry put them in the microwave for later. He needed to let off some steam, unwind before bed, and he really wanted to let his imagination and what-ifs run wild, preferably with his hand wrapped around his dick.

## *Chapter*
# THREE

**W**AS THE MUSIC SUPPOSED TO CALM THE ART CLASS OR put them into a trance? Or maybe Keegan owed his fugue-like state to a night of very little sleep and not to the combination of rain patter and melodic instruments. He'd gotten back to Redemption Ridge at a decent hour, thanks to the court processor, but he hadn't fallen asleep until a few hours before his alarm went off. Even then, his fitful slumber produced arousing dreams that stirred emotional and physical reactions best not remembered in a room full of people. He shouldn't recall his damp skin, the tangled sheets, or his hard-on pinned between his stomach and the mattress. But Keegan's mind went there, so the natural next memory was the way he'd eased that ache and the name he whispered as a rush of pleasure flooded his body.

"Yo, Kee," Rueben whispered into his right ear. "Are those blue balls symbolic of something?"

"Let me see," Sven said, muscling in from the left.

Keegan blinked to focus his eyes and nearly groaned when he saw the big, blue orbs he'd painted in the center of the canvas. He could barely recall picking up his brush, let alone choosing the three different shades of blue he'd turned into nearly perfect spheres.

Sven snorted. "It's definitely symbolic of his unrequited pining." He leaned closer and lowered his voice. "Whose balls are this symmetrical? One of mine is slightly larger than the other."

"Mine are the same size, but I swear my left buddy hangs a fraction lower than the right," Rueben said. "You hear ladies remark that their eyebrows don't have to be twins, just sisters. You think it's the same with our testicles? They don't have to be twins, just brothers?"

This time, Keegan groaned. Why had he invited these two goons to his first art therapy class? Because he freaking loved the men who'd do anything to make him laugh, such as the smiley face Rueben painted on the right blue ball.

"No way Keegan's *brothers* are smiling," Sven countered. He leaned in and painted a frowning face on the left ball.

"This looks like a social commentary about playing favorites," Rueben said.

"One brother got all the affection while the other got ignored," Sven agreed. "Must show them both equal love."

Someone cleared their throat toward the front of the class, and Keegan locked eyes with the instructor, Melinda. Her expression was a mixture of the two emotions Rueben and Sven painted. Her mouth turned down at the corners, but her eyes sparkled with good humor.

"Sorry," he mouthed before shooing his friends back to their canvases.

Their first session turned out to be a freestyle paint instead of a guided practice. Melinda had pinned several inspiration images at the front of the class, but none of them resembled his blue balls, Sven's colorful sailboat, or Rueben's lakeside landscape. Keegan easily recognized Rue's setting as Seth's fishing cabin but had never heard Sven mention anything about sailboats.

"Do you like to sail?" Keegan asked.

Sven smiled ruefully but didn't look away from his project. "Never been. It's just a series of easy shapes I can connect and turn into something close to art." He brushed more sunny yellow paint on a sail to give it a deeper color. "And my mom collected sailboats. Her grandmother had grown up in Martha's Vineyard, and my mom talked about us vacationing there someday. But money was tight after my parents got divorced, and then…"

Sven's mother had died of cancer when he was eight, which was right about the time his father remarried. He'd moved in with Steven, Lucinda, and Kerry. Sven once referred to that period as a family of fractured souls trying their best to exist in a world that wanted them to suck up their grief and move on. Lucinda and Kerry's entire world had been turned upside down just two years prior when Natalie's murder destroyed their family. His mother's brief sickness and death shattered Sven, and Steven was trying to be the stalwart rock for everyone to lean on. The environment was ripe with potential pitfalls and land mines, but they'd navigated through the storm and came out stronger on the other side. Keegan had been in their midst enough to recognize genuine love when he saw it.

"Maybe we should plan a trip to Martha's Vineyard for next summer," Keegan suggested.

Sven turned and smiled at him. "I'd love that, but you'll be busy planning your honeymoon."

Keegan rolled his eyes and turned his attention to his canvas. He would not continue the conversation they'd had the previous night. Sven was convinced Kerry had developed feelings for Keegan, but he couldn't afford to entertain the notion. Keegan's subconscious lacked the same discipline and had turned his dreams into vivid images of what Kerry's love could look like. But he was awake and in control of his thoughts, so Keegan reached deep for his determination and studied his painting. What exactly was he going to do with his blue balls? Um, do about them? Keegan's focus teetered and nearly pitched his mind back into the gutter.

"Excuse me," Rueben said, leaning into his personal space again. "Did I hear something about a honeymoon?"

"No," Keegan growled.

"Yes," Sven countered. He moved in closer until Keegan was once again sandwiched between them. "You should've seen them last night." Sven's voice took on a dreamy quality, and his eyelids lowered to half-mast.

Rue narrowed his eyes and glared at Keegan. "You're dating someone and didn't tell me."

"Nope," Keegan said. "Sven has turned into a delusional matchmaker while you weren't looking."

"I am not the one with blinders on," Sven countered. "Kerry was seconds away from kissing our sweet Keegan in the middle of the dance floor."

"Kerry who?" Rueben asked. "*Hart?*"

"I don't know another Kerry." Too late, Keegan realized his answer sounded like an admission.

"Aha!" Sven exclaimed, causing everyone in the class to turn in their direction. "You admit he was about to kiss you."

"Chill, dude." Keegan added a soft elbow jab to Sven's ribs with his whispered admonishment. "And Kerry wasn't on the verge of kissing me." Except maybe he had been. Keegan recalled the warmth of Kerry's hands against his face and the smoldering intensity sizzling in his dark gaze. "Nothing happened."

"Yet," Sven countered in a singsong voice.

Rue's quirked eyebrow expressed his curiosity, but his dark eyes glittered with fierce protectiveness. "You sound too breathy, so it definitely had to be something."

"Something hot," Sven said, fanning himself.

Keegan turned an annoyed glare on his friend. "Knock it off."

"What happened to you warning Keegan away from Kerry?" Rueben asked. "Didn't you tell us that Kerry has built vast walls around his heart and employs a miniature dragon to patrol them?"

Sven scoffed. "I doubt I said that exactly."

"Close enough," Keegan said. "The implication was clear."

"So, what's changed?" Rueben asked.

Sven cocked his head and pursed his lips as he considered the question. Keegan tried not to let on just how invested he was by the answer. "It's not a specific thing." Keegan hated the way his heart sank, and he hoped his disappointment didn't show. "It's this collective energy of actions and reactions whenever Kee enters the room. You're too wrapped up in Seth to attend family dinners right now, but you and my cousin are missing out on one hell of a saga."

Rueben assessed Keegan with twinkling eyes. "Is that so?"

"Nope," Keegan said.

"The temperature goes up twenty degrees whenever Keegan and Kerry are in the same room," Sven said.

Keegan's foolish heart soared like a balloon on the breeze. He tried to grab the string before his daydreaming carried it too far away, but it only floated higher. "You're ridiculous." But had he meant Sven's assumptions or his foolish heart?

Rue waved off Keegan's denial. "Continue. I want to hear specifics."

"First, Kerry does an impression of a meerkat whenever Keegan arrives," Sven said. "His head pops up, and he goes on high alert, looking left and right with quick, jerky motions." He demonstrated what he meant and winked at Keegan. "Listen, I'm telling this in terms Rueben can understand."

Keegan laughed at the reminder of his first visit to the Thirsty Cowboy, where he'd not only danced with Kerry but got to see Sven in action for the first time. Rueben had hilariously narrated Sven's flirtations like they were wildlife encounters occurring in a *National Geographic* documentary. Sven was the gazelle who masterfully seduced the hunky lion. Kerry had asked Keegan to dance before he got to witness the outcome of the conquest. Keegan had asked Sven about it during their drive home last night, and he'd learned that the lion had fallen prey to Kerry's cockblocking antics.

"Let the gazelle talk," Rue said.

"It's like his every sense is tuned in to where Keegan is and what he's doing," Sven said.

"I think I'd know if that was the case," Keegan argued.

But Sven continued talking as if he hadn't heard Keegan's protest. "The rest of the room fades away as Kerry tracks his every move. He laughs when Keegan laughs and smiles when Keegan smiles."

"Christ," Keegan groaned. "I'm really concerned about your observational skills. Pretty sure those are grimaces."

"Nothing wrong with my eyesight or perceptions," Sven replied before returning his attention to Rueben. "And the look on Kerry's face whenever Lucinda wraps her arms around Kee. I'm telling you, that big, growly bear melts because Kerry adores his mother. And guess who Mama Lulu loves?" Sven pointed at Keegan.

"He's growly like the Big Bad Wolf," Keegan corrected absently. He would not touch the other parts with a ten-foot pole.

"Huh?" Sven and Rueben asked.

Well, damn. He couldn't pretend he hadn't said it or easily explain his comment away. Luckily for him, Melinda announced that their class was over.

"You can leave your paintings on the easel to dry," she said. "I'll stow them in the back room, and we can pick up where we left off next time."

She instructed them on how to clean their brushes and tidy their stations before leaving. Multiple sinks lined one wall, but there weren't enough for them to wash up at the same time. A petite, perky brunette stopped Sven to ask where he'd bought his hot pink T-shirt with the word "fabulous" bedazzled across the chest. Keegan took advantage of the distraction and moved to the line farthest away from where Sven chatted with the woman. He wasn't upset with his friend, but he needed time to recover from Sven's outlandish claims. Kerry was fond of him, and sometimes he flirted, but that was it. Right?

"You okay, Kee?" Rueben asked.

"I painted a metaphorical representation of my pathetic pining during art therapy, so I don't reckon I am okay."

Rue's smile was sympathetic. "How'd you end up dancing with Kerry? I thought you were going to trivia night."

"That was the plan until I'd told Sven some things Brendan recommended at my last therapy session."

The lithe blond appeared by their side as if summoned and waggled his brows. "Brendan wants Keegan to get laid." At least he had the good grace to whisper. "And I had a plan to make it happen."

Rueben's expression was a mixture of amusement and horror. "This sounds like a long story."

"The longest," Keegan replied.

"Which is why we're going to mosey on down to the diner," Sven announced. "We can grab a bite to eat while I spill the scalding hot tea."

"Isn't this Keegan's story to tell?" Rue asked.

Sven cocked his head and briefly tapped a finger against his full lips. "We'll tag team."

Rue's brow shot up. "Was that part of your master plan last night?"

The question earned a wicked grin and a shoulder shimmy from Sven. "Well, I did agree to show him the ropes. I had meant to take a hands-on approach, but I hadn't considered a three—"

"No," Keegan said, holding up his hand to ward off whatever else Sven was about to say.

"—some," Sven finished anyway. "Especially since the intended target was Kerry." He scrunched up his face in disgust. "Biology doesn't make family, and Kerry is my brother. I don't judge others, but there's no way I would—"

Rue slapped a hand over Sven's mouth. Their friend continued to talk, but his muffled words were inaudible. "I know that beautiful brain of yours has a filter. Try using it, okay?" Sven nodded vigorously, and Rue released him. "Let's clean our brushes and head to the diner."

It was too early in the spring to draw many tourists, but the locals had packed the diner for lunch. Several heads turned in their direction, and Keegan couldn't help feeling like everyone in the restaurant knew his personal business after he sat down for an in-depth web series interview with Rory for the ranch's YouTube channel. Spilling the details of his time with the cult had been one of the hardest things he'd ever done, but it was a cathartic process and his only avenue for closure since most of his assailants were dead. The lone survivor pleaded guilty to his crimes against Keegan, but they got swallowed up by the bigger atrocities Reggie Ulrich committed.

Keegan's impact statement at sentencing had barely registered as a blip on the radar, even though it had been the scariest moment of his life. He'd felt cheated afterward and wanted an outlet to vent his sorrow and rage. Rory had provided that safe space and patiently guided him through his story. Keegan just hadn't expected anyone to watch it, let alone half a million people in less than a month. It unnerved him that everyone in the diner might know the abuse he suffered from Miriam and the people she'd entrusted to "cure" Keegan of his homosexuality. But he was more than his trauma. Keegan Scott was a fucking survivor, and it didn't matter what anyone else thought. He was learning to love himself more and more every day.

Rueben clapped him on the shoulder. "I spot a table in the back corner."

Keegan notched his chin up higher and led the way. Rueben slid into the booth beside him, and Sven sat opposite them. They made idle chitchat until their server took their lunch orders. Then Sven started with his animated recap of their night at the Thirsty Cowboy. It was Keegan's story to tell, but he preferred to sit back and let the master entertain him. He only had to interrupt a few times to scale back Sven's boldest exaggerations.

Rue listened with rapt attention until the story came to a dramatic end. "Holy crap."

"Wait," Keegan interjected. "Kerry did not kiss me passionately under the moonlight before we parted ways. He barely brushed his lips against my temple." The gesture had been brief, but Keegan felt the resulting tingle for hours.

"I have never seen Kerry give such a tender gesture to anyone outside our family," Sven argued.

Keegan swallowed hard as he floundered for a response. Luckily, their server returned with the food. Sven dug into his bowl of Aztec chicken chili with reckless abandon, so Keegan pivoted the conversation to safer subjects. "Have you heard anything else about the lawsuit?"

Sven shook his head, then swallowed his food. "I haven't talked to my dad yet this morning, but I'm confident that Kerry will come out of this unscathed."

"Why is someone suing Kerry?" Rueben asked.

Keegan had also gotten that story during the drive home but didn't feel qualified to answer questions. He'd also learned what Sven had meant about his "tonight of all nights" reference. Kerry getting served on the anniversary of his dad's death was terrible. Keegan wished he could rewind to the previous night and hug Kerry tighter.

"Now that I can tell you." Sven made him wait while he dipped a wedge of grilled cheese sandwich into his soup and ate a bite. Then he launched into a detailed account of an accident like Rueben's, though the location wasn't as harrowing. Rue gasped when he heard about the equipment malfunction and the car plummeting back down the ravine.

"With the guy in the vehicle?" Rue sounded as appalled as Keegan felt. "And since Kerry owns the company, he's responsible for his employee's actions."

"Yep," Sven said. "It doesn't matter that Chuck disobeyed company procedure and direct orders. Kerry's ass is on the line."

"And what a fine ass it is." Keegan didn't realize he'd spoken his thought out loud until Sven's mouth curved into the wickedest grin Keegan had ever seen. The Cheshire Cat and the Grinch had nothing on this guy. "Just don't, okay?"

Sven held up both hands as if in surrender, but Keegan knew better than to fall for it. His friend would strike as soon as Keegan let his guard down.

"What's Kerry going to do?" Rueben asked.

Sven told him about a cousin named Vinny who practiced that type of law, which Rueben found hilarious.

"I don't get it," Keegan said, looking between his grinning friends.

"And we need to expedite your pop culture education," Rueben said. "That's a classic movie that everyone needs to see." Sven and Rueben bounced movie quotes back and forth, and Keegan had to admit he was intrigued.

"I've got time to kill before my first shift at the Feisty Bull starts," Keegan said. Sven was all for movie time, but Rueben grimaced. "It's okay if you have plans with Seth."

The remark only seemed to make Rueben feel guiltier. "I don't feel like we get to spend much time together outside of work."

Keegan missed hanging out with Rueben too, but he was happy for his best friend. "You came to art therapy with me today, and I really appreciate it."

Rue bumped his shoulder against Keegan's. "I had fun, and I'm looking forward to going with you again." Rue leaned over and lowered his voice. "It's interesting to see what your subconscious confesses through your paintings." Rue jabbed a finger at Sven. "And you!"

Sven clutched his chest and batted his long eyelashes. "Me?"

"Yes, you," Rue said. "Let Keegan make his own decisions and steer his own course. He's had enough people trying to control and manipulate his journey to last him three lifetimes. Kee doesn't need that from you." When Sven protested, Rueben cut him off with a wave. "What feels helpful to you might feel stifling to him."

Sven searched Keegan's eyes for several moments, sighed, and nodded his agreement. "I'll be on my best behavior from now on." A tiny smile tugged at his lips. "Besides, the train has left the station and is chugging full steam ahead to happily ever after."

Keegan's heart thundered like a locomotive at the mere thought of something special brewing between Kerry and him. The good intentions he gripped in his hand turned to sand and sifted through his fingers.

Rueben blew out a breath and shook his head. "I tried, Kee."

"And I appreciate the effort." Keegan wouldn't hold his breath that Sven's ceasefire would last long.

The diner door opened, and Lucinda walked to the front counter, where a server greeted her with a smile. Kerry didn't look a thing like his petite, blonde mother, but Natalie had been her spitting image. The server pointed to their table, and Lucinda followed her gesture. Her light blue eyes met Keegan's and lit up with recognition seconds before she headed toward their table.

Rueben whistled softly. "Wow, she is happy to see you."

Sven turned his upper body to see who Rueben was talking about, then smiled smugly. "Told you so."

"My boys," Lucinda said, opening her arms wide, though they would've slid out of the booth to hug her without the encouragement. "You've made my day." She hugged Sven first and ensured he was enjoying a much-deserved day off. Sven worked as a stylist at Lucinda's salon, and his services were in high demand. He only allowed himself one Saturday off a month, and Keegan was humbled that Sven had spent it with him at art therapy. "Rue," she exclaimed, cupping his face. "You get more handsome every time I see you. Marriage really suits you." Then, it was Keegan's turn to say hello. "Keegan," Lucinda said reverently. She took his hands in hers and squeezed. "I love you so much it hurts sometimes."

Emotion clogged Keegan's throat. If he could have torn his gaze away from Lucinda's, Keegan knew Sven would be wearing a smug expression. "I love you too."

"You better, because I'm keeping you," Lucinda said before she dropped his hands. "I better pick up my carryout order and head back to the salon. My break between clients isn't very long today."

"Are there any updates on Kerry's lawsuit?" Rue asked.

She smiled and kissed his cheek. "Steven and Kerry were holed up in the war room when I left. I know they have Dom working on the case since they can't see Vinny until Monday. Kerry texted me a little while ago and said he was headed to the rescue station to stay busy. That's better for him than watching a *Jurassic Park* movie marathon and eating his weight in buttered popcorn and M&M's."

Sven visibly tensed, and the smugness drained from his expression. "Did you say Dom?"

Lucinda looked at him with a puzzled expression. "Surely you haven't forgotten Kerry's best friend. You used to follow them around like a little puppy."

Sven smiled, but the gesture looked forced. "Of course I do."

"Dom went over to Kerry's house last night as soon as he heard about the lawsuit." She reached for Keegan's hand again. "I'm so glad my son has such wonderful people in his life."

That time, Keegan caught Sven's smug expression. He was tempted to ask questions about this Dom guy just to wipe the arrogance off Sven's face. Maybe he should bring the guy up every time Sven poked his nose into Keegan's business.

"Are you coming to family dinner tomorrow night?" Lucinda asked Keegan.

"Um, I'm not sure." Despite Kerry's denial, Keegan still felt like he was underfoot. Kerry needed one Keegan-free zone in his life.

"He'll be there," Sven said.

Lucinda's light blue eyes twinkled merrily. "Maybe the newlyweds will join us," she said to Rueben.

"Maybe," he replied noncommittally.

She kissed the air, spun on her heels, and strolled to the counter, where her order waited for her. Lucinda paid for her meal and waggled her fingers in their direction as she headed back out the door.

"Mama Lulu is planning your wedding to her son," Sven announced.

"She is not." Keegan looked to Rueben for help, but his best friend only shrugged. "Are you guys finished eating, or do you want dessert?"

None of them had room for sweets, so they headed up to the

counter to pay for their meals. Keegan went first and stepped aside after he finished to make room for the others. The owners had hung a corkboard by the register so local businesses could advertise their goods and services. One colorful ad caught Keegan's eye, and his stomach dropped when he recognized the name at the top. "Dahl Rescue and Retrieval," he read aloud.

Sven snapped his head around so fast it was a wonder he didn't wrench his neck. "What the—" He let out a gasp when he saw the ad. "You've got to be kidding me. Fucking Chuck." He finished up his transaction, then stomped over to the board and ripped the ad right off. "I don't fucking think so. Come on." He shoved the door open and hauled ass down the sidewalk without making sure Keegan and Rueben followed.

"He's my ride," Keegan said. He'd ridden to town with Rueben, but Sven volunteered to drive him home afterward so Rueben wouldn't have to double back before going home to his husband.

"I can run you back to the ranch if you don't want to get caught up in Sven's crazy schemes," Rueben offered.

"And miss all the fun?" Keegan replied. "I'm sure it will be fine."

Rueben's widened expression said, "Famous last words," but he told Keegan to call him later and tell him what happened.

Keegan nodded before hustling out of the diner. He caught up to Sven just as he reached his vehicle. "Where are we going?"

Sven stopped at the driver's door and held up the ad he swiped off the board. "To the rescue station."

"We're going to confront Chuck Dahl?" Keegan asked.

Sven pursed his lips as he opened the door. "Why didn't I think of that?" He shook his head. "Hell no. Kerry would kill us. We're going to Hart's Creek Rescue to make sure Kerry knows about this. The timing of the lawsuit and Chuck's new business can't be a coincidence."

Sven got in the car and closed the door, but Keegan didn't budge. He ached to see Kerry and make sure he was doing okay, but not so soon after a night of vivid dreams. And definitely not with Sven's tantalizing words still filling his head with hopes he couldn't afford to cling to. Rueben stepped out of the diner down the street. It wasn't too late to call out to him and catch a ride to the ranch. Keegan could regroup and recharge before facing Kerry later that afternoon when he started his first shift at the Feisty Bull. Rueben looked in his direction and stopped. He must've sensed Keegan's internal struggle because Rue headed toward him.

The passenger window of Sven's car rolled down, and his friend leaned over the console to look at him. "Are you coming, gorgeous?"

When had Keegan ever missed an opportunity to lay eyes on Kerry Hart? And if Sven was right, Keegan would get to lay his hands on him someday. He waved goodbye to Rue and reached for the door handle. Surviving was great, but Keegan's stubborn heart insisted that Kerry was the key to thriving.

## *Chapter*
# FOUR

**K**ERRY'S FIST LANDED WITH A LOUD *THUD*, AND SHOCK WAVES reverberated up his arm. Picturing Chuck's face on the punching bag suddenly wasn't enough to ease his tension. Kerry wanted a real confrontation with the man, which only added to his stress. He'd always been big for his age, so his dad had taught him alternative ways of dealing with his emotions besides getting into fights. Kerry's means of letting off steam changed over the years, depending on the circumstance. Fucking was out of the question since the only man he wanted was the one he couldn't—*shouldn't*—have.

Kerry had witnessed Keegan's wistful expression while watching Seth and Rueben fall in love and start a life together. It was plain that Kee wanted those deeper connections for himself, and Kerry avoided emotional entanglements like his life depended on it. But Keegan wasn't the only one caught up in the bliss radiating from the newlyweds. Kerry likened it to a toxic cloud from a chemical spill, slowly enveloping and tainting everyone within its reach. Christ, he sounded cynical as fuck, but who could blame him?

Cynthia had destroyed Kerry's family when she killed Natalie in a fit of selfish rage twenty-five years ago. He'd no longer caught his parents slow dancing in the living room after they thought he'd gone to sleep. They'd stopped reaching for one another as if pulled together by a magnetic force. Hell, they'd rarely been in the same room together after Natalie died. Graham Hart had blamed himself for the death of his only daughter and had withdrawn to someplace Lucinda and Kerry couldn't follow or weren't welcome. His big, strapping father had wasted away in front of his eyes, surrendering to his grief one minute at a time until the clock stopped ticking and Graham's broken heart stopped beating. Kerry had come home from school and found Graham in his recliner, resting peacefully for the first time since Natalie's death. And Kerry had known why before he touched his dad's cold hand. In less than a year, he'd lost his sister and his father, and Kerry's world had never looked the same again.

They hadn't known the truth of Cynthia's treachery until recently. All this time, his family had treated her as one of their own. Kerry viewed her as a sister because that's how Natalie thought of her. She joined them to celebrate Natalie's life on every birthday or memorial of her death, and Kerry hadn't fully processed her treachery yet. He acknowledged it verbally but hadn't allowed himself a healthy emotional outlet to let off steam. The lawsuit Chuck caused was another result of Kerry showing kindness to someone who didn't deserve it and only added to the pressure building inside him. So yeah, he had trust issues, but for the first time in his adult life, Kerry resented the barriers he'd constructed to protect himself. But not enough to let his guard down and let Keegan in. Getting involved with Keegan was the last thing he should do, even if it was what he wanted most. To fall into those welcoming arms and lose himself in Kee's gorgeous hazel eyes and sexy body would be—

Kerry drove his fist into the punching bag before he could finish the thought. Then he followed that up with a series of waist-high rapid jabs as if he had Chuck Dahl pinned against the ropes and was pummeling his stomach. Kerry finished the sequence with a powerful knee jab that would've finished his opponent and dropped him to the mat. Tension still rode him like a vicious jockey, so Kerry figuratively stood Chuck back up and started the cycle all over again, alternating punches, jabs, and kicks like his life depended on it. His sanity and livelihood sure as hell relied on him to keep his shit together. He could not afford to turn into a human powder keg.

Kerry had tried his best to set the pending lawsuit aside and go about his work. They'd had the usual wrecker service calls, which made up the bulk of their work. They had the equipment to assist both private passenger and commercial vehicles in all terrains, which was important in Colorado mountain towns. Hart's Creek Rescue also partnered with insurance companies to answer roadside assistance calls, handling everything from keys locked in vehicles to disabled cars and trucks. They were uniquely positioned to assist with the more dangerous rescues and recoveries where vehicles went off the roads and into ravines or worse. People treated posted speed limits and treacherous passing signs like mere suggestions, so there'd never be a shortage of calls for them to answer.

He'd earned a sterling reputation for being prompt, professional, and safe, so local and state law enforcement agencies offered him lucrative contracts to be their primary responder. And it would all be in peril if the lawsuit caused his clients to lose confidence in his work. Would Kerry have to resort to taking the bank repossession jobs he'd always refused? The idea of capitalizing on someone's financial woes had never sat right with him, and those situations could get dicey. He'd heard some awful war stories from others in the business and preferred to keep out of those situations. Kerry had been fortunate enough to afford his overhead without taking on those jobs. He'd built a state-of-the-art facility, offering his employees comfortable amenities for those working overnight shifts, including the gym where he worked off his frustrations. Would he lose it all if Bozeman won his lawsuit?

Kerry landed one last blow and stepped back from the swinging punching bag, his chest heaving from the exertion. The exercise finally settled the anxiety pinballing in his brain. The tension in his body was no longer from stress but from awakening every muscle in his body. His shoulders and biceps burned, and his legs trembled, but he embraced the discomfort. He'd handled his stress in a healthy way that didn't hurt anyone, though his knuckles would probably protest since he'd barely taped his hands.

The door opened suddenly and slammed against an interior wall. Sven rushed into the room, clutching a piece of paper and looking wildly around the room. Kerry wasn't used to seeing his brother in a frantic state and immediately went on high alert. Keegan entered at a slower pace but looked just as frazzled until he caught sight of Kerry. Hazel eyes widened in surprise before roaming over Kerry's seminude body. The perusal seemed to last forever, and Kerry felt it as strongly as a physical caress. Keegan's attention seemed riveted to the myriads of tattoos decorating his skin. Kerry's body tensed and flexed under the attention as a primal yearning gripped him by the balls. When Keegan's eyes finally met his again, Kerry saw the same longing burning in his gaze.

Sven mumbled something inaudible before clearing his throat. "Should I leave you two alone, or can we figure out how we're going to shut Chuck the Fuck down?"

The question doused Kerry's desire like a bucket of ice water, but it restored his clarity and purpose. Tearing his gaze away from Keegan's, Kerry gave Sven his full attention. "What are you talking about?"

Sven marched across the gym and shoved a piece of paper at him. "I find the timing of this new venture very suspect."

Kerry looked down at the document. Most of his brain cells were still angling for time alone with Keegan, so it took a few seconds for him to compute the words on the page. "Are you fucking kidding me?"

"Nope," Sven said. "Keegan found it hanging up at the diner. What are you going to do about this?"

Kerry read the advertisement that boasted Chuck had the most experience in the business, which was at least true for the tri-county area they served. He hadn't proclaimed to be the safest, and he'd avoided using libelous adjectives or phrasing. It still grated on Kerry's nerves. "There's nothing I can do about this."

"Come on, Kerry," Sven argued. "This guy just happens to start a new company around the time Bozeman sues."

Kerry snapped his head up to meet Sven's fiery gaze. "You think they're in cahoots?"

Sven's eyebrows shot up. "You don't?"

Every gain he'd made from his workout disappeared. The anxiety he'd barely suppressed reared its ugly head. Only the monster had grown bigger and stronger this time with Sven's suspicions fertilizing his unrest. "I agree something smells fishy."

Sven scrunched up his face. "Smells fishy? Is this an episode of *Scooby-Doo*?"

"Sven," Keegan admonished. "Be nice."

Kerry slid his gaze over to Keegan, but his little lamb was too busy checking out Kerry's chest to notice. The urge to flex his pecs like a douchebag was strong, but he resisted. Keegan must've sensed his attention because he jerked his head up and met Kerry's gaze. An adorable blush bloomed across his cheeks, and his full lips parted on a sigh.

"No," Sven snapped. "*Nice* is what got Kerry into this mess. We need to be vicious and go after the threat with relentless fury." He released a long, frustrated groan, but Kerry couldn't tear his gaze away from Keegan's. His discarded T-shirt hit him in the face, breaking the spell Kerry had been under. "Put that back on and dial down your pheromones."

Kerry chuckled, though nothing about his life was funny. He used Sven's comedic interlude to pull himself together. By the time he put his shirt on, Keegan had turned away to study the gym setup. "You're right," Kerry said.

"Of course I am." Sven preened for a few seconds before sobering. "About which part? You're going to unleash vicious fury?"

Kerry chuckled and shook his head. "What good would that do? A furious reaction is sloppy and a waste of time. I need to be strategic and precise. Like a surgeon."

"We're not going to neuter him," Sven argued. "Although…"

"Kerry is right."

The trio turned to see who'd interrupted them. Dominic stood in the open doorway wearing the same clothes from the previous evening and carrying his messenger bag. Either he wore the same outfit every day, or he hadn't been home yet. Kerry was going with door number two and added guilt to the cocktail of emotions burning a hole in his stomach lining.

"I'll take it from here." Dom strode across the gym with a swagger that matched his confident remark.

Sven narrowed his eyes. Kerry knew he hated being dismissed or ignored almost as much as he resented Kerry for cockblocking his attempt to seduce Dom at the Thirsty Cowboy on the same night Kerry met Keegan.

"Why should I trust Kerry's future in your hands?" Sven demanded.

Dom smirked as he joined them, staying just out of clawing range. "You sure wanted my hands all over you not that long ago."

Sven snorted. "As if. You would've been lucky to make it past first base."

"Oh my god!" Keegan turned big hazel eyes on Sven. "He's the lion from the Thirsty Cowboy."

"Mmhmm." Sven's eyes flashed with irritation when he looked at Kerry. Clearly, his brother still held a grudge about his interference.

"Lion?" Dom asked.

Keegan recapped the story of Rueben's playful narrations, and Dom seemed to get a kick out of the comparison. He raked his gaze over Sven and said, "A gazelle, huh?"

"Graceful and beautiful," Sven said smugly.

"And still shopping in the twink department," Dom said. "Aren't you a little old for crop tops?"

Sven's cobalt eyes shimmered with wicked delight, and his mouth twisted into a smirk. He was about to unleash one hell of a snappy comeback, and Kerry was certain it would contain details from their encounter that he didn't want to know.

"Whoa!" Kerry said, stepping between them. "Let's not hit below the belt," he told his friend.

Dom held up his hand. "Sorry, Stevie. Maybe I'm just jealous because my midsection has gone to hell while your body is banging." He cut his eyes to Kerry and grimaced. "Sorry."

Sven normally would've been pissed at anyone calling him Stevie beyond the age of twelve, but the compliment seemed to soothe his ruffled feathers. "I'm sorry too. There's no one better than you to have Kerry's back at a time like this."

Kerry was on the verge of patting himself on the back when Dom turned his full attention to Keegan with a spark of interest in his gaze.

"I don't believe we've met," Dom said, a seductive smile curving his lips.

Keegan had been watching Dom and Sven's byplay like a tennis match. His gaze widened when he realized he'd gained the lion's attention. "Hi. I'm—"

Sven slapped his hand against Keegan's shoulder. "Time to go. Dom and Kerry don't need our help." Sven propelled Keegan toward the door.

"You could at least introduce me to your friend," Dom called after them. His lips curved into a smile until he turned his head and met Kerry's gaze.

"Don't," he growled.

Dom's eyes widened. "What?"

"Keegan isn't for you." Kerry dropped his gaze to avoid the knowing look in his friend's eyes. He went to work, removing the tape from his hands instead.

"Man, I didn't realize you were dating him. Sorry. I just flirted with Keegan to irritate Sven."

Kerry had congratulated himself for preventing what he'd been certain was a mistake eighteen months ago. Dom and Sven hadn't seen each other for several years and hadn't recognized one another. Dom had been in the middle of a nasty divorce and wasn't in the right headspace. The situation had "recipe for disaster" written all over it, and Kerry had put a stop to it before things advanced too far. Now, he suspected he'd only created an unresolved sexual tension situation between them. He pulled the last bit of tape off and dropped it into the trash can. He flexed his fingers to get the blood circulating freely and met Dom's curious gaze. "We're not dating. It's just…" His voice trailed off as he considered what to say. Declaring Keegan as vulnerable felt like betrayal, and Kerry couldn't form the words. "Just don't, man."

Dom held up his hands in surrender. "I hear you." He cocked his head to the side as he lowered his arms. "That snarly growl you used sounds pretty possessive. Pretty sure at least some part of you has staked a claim on that cutie."

Kerry didn't dignify the comment with a remark. He thrust Chuck's flyer at him instead. "Sven thinks Chuck and Keith Bozeman are working together to ruin my company."

"Yeah, I overheard most of your conversation. You were too busy gawking at the guy you don't date to notice I'd entered the gym."

"Why are you provoking me?" Kerry asked.

Dom chuckled and shook his head. "I'm only speaking the truth. That's never bothered you in the past."

Kerry almost didn't recognize himself lately. He wasn't used to feeling possessive over a guy, but he'd snarled at that Ken from the bar and then treated Dom's harmless observations as threats. He cycled through a deep breath as he thought about his options. Maybe his problem was that he didn't have a single person in his life he could talk to about Keegan without them getting matchmaking ideas. "Fine. I want him. I want Keegan more than my next breath, but I can't have him."

"Why?"

Kerry shook his head. "You didn't come here to talk about my shitty love life."

Dom's brow shot up. "Since when do you have a love life?"

"Sex life," Kerry amended. "Same thing."

"A person can have sex without love, as you damn well know," Dom said. He settled his big hand on Kerry's shoulder. "Seems like you need to get something off your chest. You can trust me, Ker."

"I know." And he did, but Kerry couldn't talk about what he didn't yet fully understand. "Right now, winning my lawsuit and preventing Chuck from stealing all my business has to take precedence."

Dom grinned wickedly. "Do you know what's better than winning a lawsuit?"

"Building a time machine so I can go back and prevent this clusterfuck from happening?" Hell, if Dom could do that, Kerry would go back twenty-five years and save his sister and father. But then he couldn't imagine his life without Steven and Sven in it. He couldn't go back and change one thing without impacting dozens or possibly hundreds of others. Had he not learned anything from watching *Back to the Future*? A wiser man would reference complex theories and multiple concurrent universes, but there was a reason people complimented Kerry on his looks and physique. He relied on a different kind of intelligence that rarely let him down. But when it did, he ended up getting sued.

"I can't procure a time machine, but I think it might be the next best thing," Dom replied.

"Consider me intrigued. Let's take this to my office."

Dom followed him out of the gym and down the long corridor. The doors to the left and right opened to private spaces for his overnight crew to use between calls. Some questioned the expense and extravagance of keeping the rescue staffed twenty-four hours a day, but those people had likely never found themselves in a perilous situation where minutes mattered. Yes, he could've hired a dispatch service to field the calls and alert the responders on call, but that meant his crew would either have to take their service trucks home, or they'd have to drive to the station, pick up their rigs, and then proceed to the accident. No one wanted to be trapped in a disabled vehicle for a minute longer than they had to, especially if that vehicle was in a perilous spot. He'd invested time and money to provide the best environment for his employees and offer an incomparable service to the community. The desire to protect everything he'd built surged to the forefront of Kerry's mind, enabling him to push away thoughts of anything else.

Kerry opened his office door at the end of the hall and switched on the light. Something about the space had always brought him peace, even on the most stressful days. Maybe it was the family photographs hanging on the wall or tucked into the gaps in his bookshelves. Perhaps the cool tones of the slate-blue paint color soothed his nerves. Kerry figured it had more to do with the pride he felt every time he stepped into his office. This was something he'd built through grit and determination. He gestured toward the coffeepot and minifridge. "Care for something to drink?"

"I've far exceeded my caffeine limit, but I'll take a bottle of water if you have one," Dom said.

Kerry retrieved two bottles and handed one to Dom before sitting behind his desk. Dom sipped his water and perused the photographs on the shelves for a few moments before pointing to a photo of them from their youth football days.

"Who are these studs?" Dom asked.

Kerry chuckled. "We thought we were big shit, didn't we?"

Dom nodded and stared at the photograph again. Lucinda had taken the image right after they'd won the Super Bowl game for their age group. Dom and Kerry, the two football captains, hoisted the trophy between them, their grins stretching from ear to ear. Those innocent boys didn't have a care in the world. All their youthful dreams had come true on the gridiron, and they couldn't imagine the cruel twists ahead of them. "We thought we'd go pro." And one of them nearly had.

Dom had entered their junior year as one of the top-rated high school quarterback prospects in the country. All the top colleges had been vying for his attention, but Dom hadn't let the attention go to his head. His singular focus had been winning games because the rest would fall into place. He hadn't partied or even dated. The one time he'd made an exception to partying after a game had resulted in the end of his dream. A vehicle went left of center, and Dom swerved to miss it. The other car clipped his bumper and spun him out on rain-slick roads. Dom's car went off the side of the road and traveled down a steep embankment. A tree limb smashed through the windshield and impaled Dom's shoulder, pinning him to the seat until a rescue crew could extricate him from the vehicle.

The car that caused the accident hadn't stopped, so Dom's wasn't found until his missed curfew triggered a search party. He'd sat in the car for hours and lost a lot of blood. He'd had multiple surgeries on his shoulder to improve its function, but his throwing arm was never the same. His football career ended, and so had his dream of playing professional ball. If Dom was resentful, he'd never let on. But the way he kept staring at the photo made it clear the hurt was still there.

Dom turned suddenly and dropped into a seat in front of Kerry's desk. He set the bottle of water down and removed his laptop from his messenger bag. Dom opened the computer and started typing. "I won't say the information I've uncovered so far will guarantee Bozeman will drop the lawsuit, but it's enough to make him reconsider. I'm emailing the file to you now, and you'll want to forward this to your attorney." Dom pushed a button on his keyboard and grinned evilly. "I still have more avenues I can explore if they think it's necessary."

Kerry's spirits lifted as his desktop pinged with an inbox alert. "What's in the file?"

Dom's grin grew impossibly more wicked. "I started with a search of his financials because it tells you a lot about a person."

"But how'd you do that? I only gave you his name?"

"It's my business to find the things people don't want you to know," Dom replied. "Don't worry. I get my information legally. Once I have his name and address, it's easy to find the other information I need to run a credit check." He let out a whistle. "Bozeman is a bozo with his finances. His negative equity is in the mid-six figures. I'm talking maxed-out credit cards, overextended lines of credit, a mortgage teetering on foreclosure, and a car that got repossessed just this morning." Dom nodded toward Kerry's computer. "I've included photographs of him literally chasing the tow truck in his bathrobe." Dom grimaced and fidgeted in his chair. "Dude needs to learn to cinch his belt tighter. Anyone in his neighborhood who was awake at six this morning got to see Bozeman's cock and balls bouncing as he sprinted down the middle of the street."

Kerry had been reaching for his mouse to open his email, but he recoiled. "Dude! I don't want to see naked pictures of Keith Bozeman."

Dom chuckled at his distress. "The mad dash down the road was enough to question Bozeman's claims of diminished physical activity." The downright devilish gleam in Dom's green eyes did nothing to erase the ick factor. Kerry was a big fan of cock and balls, but not those belonging to the man suing him. He had standards and wasn't that hard up, for fuck's sake. "And those weren't the first nude shots I took of Mr. Can No Longer Please His Partner."

Kerry had called Dom after he and Steven thoroughly reviewed the lawsuit paperwork. His friend had sounded amused at the time, but Kerry's spiraling mind hadn't let him linger on the reaction and ask questions. This time, Kerry scooted his chair back from his desk.

Dom cackled, leaned back in his chair, and regaled Kerry with everything that he'd witnessed during his stakeout. "His frolicking began in the hot tub and ended up on the patio table. And I got crystal clear pictures since the moon was full." Dom paused for effect with a cheeky grin. "And I mean both the one in the sky and the white ass pounding away at the girlfriend who'd supposedly broken up with him when he couldn't get an erection after the accident."

"Yeah, I figured out what you meant." The rest of Dom's statement registered, and Kerry sat up straighter. "Wait. How do you know the woman he was with was the same girlfriend who supposedly dumped him?"

Dom snorted. "Any amateur sleuth with a Facebook account could've figured that out. There are thousands of photos of them together going back nearly five years. I captured screenshots before they could delete the evidence of what they'd been up to since the accident."

"Which was?"

"Ski trips, mountain hikes, and skydiving, to name a few," Dom replied. "These two are very active." He wiggled his brows suggestively. Kerry didn't want his thoughts to go there, but Dom's mouth was moving before Kerry could stop him. "She has an OnlyFans account for their more intimate moments on the trips. Bozeman has a thing for water. Bet he gets aroused just firing up the dishwasher."

"Gross," Kerry said.

"I'm not out to harm the woman's reputation, so I applied a filter in the photographs on the videos. No one will see her private bits, but you'll definitely get a gist of what's going on." Dom snickered and shook his head. "I also documented her loading the trunk of her car with her belongings from Bozeman's house this morning. If anyone inspected the house, it's doubtful they'd see any sign of her existence. My photographs and the recent lease agreement I located should take care of proving they had not broken up, as Bozo claimed."

Kerry's hope soared. "You've got proof that his biggest claims are bullshit. That should force Bozeman to drop the suit and accept the settlement my insurance company offered him. I can't believe he thinks he can get away with this."

Dom didn't react to his remark with equal enthusiasm, which tempered Kerry's excitement. "Desperate men do stupid things. Bozeman probably thinks you'll be quick with a settlement offer to make it all go away. Most civil cases never reach a courtroom. I don't know what will happen when your attorney reveals what you know. Stay alert and watch what you do and say. Bozeman might have someone keeping an eye on you too, which is how they knew where to serve your papers."

"I rarely go to the Thirsty Cowboy anymore," Kerry said. "Last night was a fluke." Kerry's gaze landed on the flyer Sven had given him. Or someone with outdated information tipped Bozeman off about Kerry. He leaned forward and tapped the piece of paper. "About this…"

Dom snatched the ad off the desk and tucked it into his messenger bag with his laptop before getting to his feet. "I'll see what I can find out." He nodded toward Kerry's computer. "Let me know what your lawyer says on Monday."

Kerry stood up, rounded the desk, and hugged his friend. "Thanks, brother. I owe you."

Dom saluted him with two fingers and headed for the door. He stopped with his hand on the knob and looked over his shoulder. "Hey, Ker. Stop living in emotional purgatory and take a chance on the cute guy that makes you all growly."

Kerry's heart skipped a beat. "I don't know who you're talking about."

Dom sighed, shook his head, and left Kerry to his own thoughts, which unsurprisingly turned toward the hazel-eyed hottie who'd enthralled him from the jump.

## *Chapter*
# FIVE

KEEGAN'S HANDS SHOOK AS HE PULLED HIS T-SHIRT OFF. NOT because he was afraid but because the act of undressing reminded him of seeing Kerry's naked, sweaty chest. He'd somehow stayed busy enough not to dwell on the interaction all day long. His reprieve ended when he arrived at the Feisty Bull early to get a tour and a basic rundown on his game plan before his shift started. Most new hires began in specific positions, but he was there to learn all aspects of hospitality. Keegan didn't know where they'd start him, but he'd hoped it would be in the kitchen so he wouldn't gawk at Kerry all night long and remember his bare, slick skin and all those intriguing tattoos. His fingers itched to trace the dark lines and follow them wherever Kerry allowed. The restaurant manager had handed him black slacks and a red dress shirt with the Feisty Bull logo embroidered in black. It was the uniform for the front of the house, though some wore it better than others. Keegan ran his fingertips over the fabric and recalled the way Kerry's shirts stretched over his powerful chest and thick arms. He imagined stripping the fabric off him and letting it fall to the floor.

*And then what?* Would he ever be brave enough to physically go where his mind frequently traveled? Keegan would never claim to be an expert at relationships, but even he'd recognized the desire burning in Kerry's dark gaze that afternoon. He'd expected Sven to razz him about it, but he'd been too distracted by the surprise visitor. Any attempt to learn more about Dom was met with grumbling responses Keegan couldn't decipher, which only made him more curious. Sven seemed like a completely different person around Kerry's friend. His flirty, devil-may-care attitude disappeared in an instant, and Sven became more antagonistic, especially when Dom turned his charm in Keegan's direction. It had taken a solid hour for Sven's fabulous attitude to return. It was clearly a sore spot, and he wasn't about to poke it, though his friend wouldn't offer him the same grace.

Sven wasn't the only one rattled by Dom's flirtations. The glower Kerry had sent his friend made the thundercloud expression from the bar look like rainbows and sunshine. Desire and jealousy meant Kerry wanted him. Keegan would admit that, at least to himself, but that didn't help him figure out what to do with the knowledge. His new thrive mentality didn't come with an instruction manual. This was when Keegan needed to think like Sven. He'd know when to push and when to pull back to achieve the desired reaction. A knock sounded on the employee changing room door just as Keegan pushed his jeans down his thighs.

"Hey, Kee. You in there?" Kerry's voice made Keegan's breath catch. The gasp was audible in the small room, but could Kerry hear it through the door? The silence stretched on for only a few seconds, but it was long enough to trigger an avalanche of emotions, each one gaining strength as they tore down the mountain. Lust, longing, loneliness, and fear jockeyed for who'd come out on top when they reached the bottom. "It's Kerry."

As if his identity needed clarification. That delicious voice came to Keegan in his sleep and whispered the wickedest things. Lust was the victor when the landslide ended, burying his doubt and willingness to play it safe. Keegan knew exactly what to do. "Give me a sec," he called out as he shoved his jeans down his legs and kicked them aside. A quick glance at his body made Keegan extremely proud of the muscle and definition he'd added since moving to the ranch. His gaze landed on his white socks, which were the furthest thing from the sexy impression he wanted to make. Keegan stripped them off, then crossed to the door before he or Kerry could change their mind about this impromptu meeting. He took a deep breath for courage as he unlocked the door and pulled it open. "Hey. You're here early." Keegan's casual voice made it seem like he greeted people in his underwear all the time.

"I, uh..." Dark eyes devoured the bare skin on display.

Keegan placed his hand on the doorframe and let the big guy look his fill while he studied the reactions his near nudity triggered in Kerry. That big, beautiful body was pulled tight enough to snap, and a dark blush dusted Kerry's cheeks. Full lips moved but formed no words, and Keegan momentarily worried he'd gone too far until those wicked, dark eyes snapped up to meet his again. "Did you want to talk to me?" Keegan prompted.

"Talk?" Kerry's raspy voice hinted that talking wasn't the action on his mind.

Keegan had come too far to give up, so he doubled down by stepping back in invitation for Kerry to enter the small room. "What else could you want me for?" The teasing lilt in his voice was new, but he loved the reaction it got.

Kerry swallowed hard and even shook his head a little, as if to pull himself together, but his gaze remained dazed and ravenous. "Uh, talking. Sure. That's what I want."

Keegan let go of the door, turned his back, and sauntered farther into the room. Kerry's options were to catch the door and come in or wait in the hallway until he finished dressing. Keegan's actions said he didn't care either way, but his pounding heart betrayed the truth. Luckily, he didn't have to wait long to find out which option Kerry chose. The door thudded against Kerry's hand, and Keegan glanced over his shoulder as Kerry pushed it open and stepped into the small space. At best, three normal-sized people could get dressed in the room without bumping into each other. With Kerry inside, it felt like just enough space for them to grind up against each other. Keegan waited to feel the press of Kerry's body against his, but it didn't come. He turned and found the man leaning on the far side of the locker row. Pity, but Keegan was on a roll and had no intention of easing up on the gas.

He reached into his borrowed locker and turned to face Kerry. "So talk."

Kerry crossed his arms over his chest, the action making his biceps bulge beneath his red dress shirt. Keegan wanted to wear that one instead of the shirt hanging up in his locker. It would be warm and smell sexy and smoky like Kerry. Rueben had talked about wearing Seth's shirts occasionally and the closeness it evoked. Keegan could pretend it was a hug and not a simple piece of fabric. That thought teetered on desperation, and he clawed it back before it could kill his vibe. Keegan wanted to seduce Kerry with a glance, not remind him of an ASPCA commercial of a pitiful puppy in need of rescue.

"Get dressed." Kerry's voice sounded thicker, harder, not unlike the reaction it triggered in Keegan's black boxers.

Tilting his head to the side, Keegan curved his lips into what he hoped was a seductive smile. "You didn't want me to return the favor?"

Black brows knitted over a hungry gaze that traveled the length of Keegan's body once more. "Favor?"

"I got to ogle your body today, so it's only fair you get to see mine. Keeps the playing field level."

Kerry's eyes snapped back to meet his as he straightened to his full height and stalked a few steps closer. Unfortunately, he stopped before he got within touching range. "Playing? Is that what we're doing?"

"Is that what you want to do?" Keegan asked.

Kerry's nostrils flared with a deep inhale. "Fire. That's what you're playing with."

Flames of lust licked a path up Keegan's body until he was fully engulfed. An alarm went off in his brain, cautioning him not to provoke someone as large as Kerry Hart, but Keegan shut it down. Kerry was nothing like the monsters who'd hurt him. The knowledge added fuel to the fire instead of dousing it. "Why? You said you just came in here to talk." He took a few steps toward Kerry, daring him to back up. The big guy held his ground, but Keegan saw the indecision in his expressive gaze. So, he stopped again but well within Kerry's reach. Then, he lobbed a verbal volley back onto his side of the court. "Is there something else you have in mind?"

Kerry's arms fell to his sides, and Keegan stiffened with anticipation. Maybe he misunderstood Keegan's reaction because Kerry shoved his hands in his front pockets. "What I want to do and what I will do aren't the same thing."

Insecurity clawed through his newfound confidence and made him want to reach for his clothes. The last thing he wanted to see was pity or disgust in Kerry's gaze. The urge to lower his eyes was strong, but he forced himself to maintain eye contact. Brendan taught him how to view situations with his eyes and not the perceptions he projected onto everyone. It was challenging to do at the best of times, but practicing the technique nearly nude with Kerry felt impossible. Yet, he dug in and forced his own perceptions away and relied on his senses. Kerry's chest rose and fell with fast breaths, and his pulse hammered against his neck. His masculine scent was stronger in the cramped space, either from the internal heat making Kerry's eyes sparkle like black diamonds or because he'd put cologne on before coming to work.

"What do you want to do?" Keegan took the few remaining steps to bridge the gap between them, stopping just a few scant inches from Kerry's body.

Big hands came up and rested on Keegan's hips, fingers pressing deep. "Don't," Kerry said, even as he pulled Keegan closer.

"Don't?" Keegan prodded.

"Start things you can't finish."

Keegan quirked a brow and glanced down to where their

midsections pressed together. He was hard as hell, and there was no way Kerry missed it, just as he was fully aware of Kerry's arousal. "Are you carrying around a lead pipe in there?"

"I'm serious, Kee. I can't hurt you."

"That's why they make lube, big guy."

The remark earned a small smile, but it didn't linger on Kerry's sensuous mouth. "I want you, and it would be foolish to deny it at this point." Kerry's fingers flexed on his hips as he heaved a sigh. "We don't want the same things."

"Two straining erections say otherwise." Later, he'd be equal parts mortified and impressed by his fortitude. Desperation led the charge because he was terrified his opportunity would slip away. "What is it you think I want from you? Marriage?" He waited for a horrified shudder to rack the big body pressed against his, but it never came. Keegan placed his hand on Kerry's chest and slid it upward until his fingers brushed up against silky curls. "Part of embracing my sexuality is getting familiar with my body and what pleases me. Thoughts of you bring me great pleasure, and I can promise you that marriage, babies, and happily ever after aren't included in my fantasies about you when I'm riding a dildo."

Kerry's lips parted, and a tortured gasp escaped. "I don't believe you."

"You want video proof with narration of every thought that crosses my mind?" He wouldn't do it, but Kerry's blistering curse made the idea tempting. "Or are you so arrogant that you think every person who fucks you also wants to marry you?"

"No, of course not."

"So, it's just me? You think I'm so pitiful that I will cling to any man who throws me a pity fuck?" Keegan's desire was taking a darker turn.

Kerry's restraint broke, and he pushed Keegan against a locker, pinning him with his massive body. Keegan had a momentary flash of fear, but it died when Kerry tenderly cupped his face. "You ever think I'm the one who doubts his ability?"

"Not for once." The idea was absurd.

"Well, you should," Kerry replied. Hungry eyes searched Keegan's face. Would Kerry kiss him? "I'm not built for happily ever after, Keegan. I don't want that. I know what it's like to love someone with your whole heart only to have them ripped away from you. I've seen what pinning your hopes and dreams on someone else can do. I never want to feel that level of desolation again. You are the first person to come along and test my resolve."

"And that's why you could so easily rattle off the length of time between our dances?"

"Yes." Kerry took a deep breath, and he dreaded what would come next. "But it doesn't change how I feel, and sometimes I resent the hold you have on me."

Keegan's heart sank, and his show of sexy bravado melted like an ice cream cone in August. The urge to get away, to hide and cover his body, rose swiftly, triggering fear and humiliation. He pushed against Kerry's broad chest, and he stepped back without hesitation. "I'm sorry. I know what you've lost, and I should've respected your boundaries."

Kerry turned his back on him and strode a few steps away, stopping abruptly and running both hands through his hair. He turned back around on a frustrated growl and returned to Keegan, but he didn't reach for him. "I don't want your apology. I want you to understand where I'm coming from. I care about you a lot, Keegan. You radiate warmth that draws me near, and you smell like sunshine. You've become my happy place, even if against my will." Kerry tried to smile to lighten the mood, but it fell flat. "You light up the world around you, and I never want to be just another asshole who dims your brilliance."

He closed his eyes and shook his head. Kerry's expression was that of a tortured man when he met Keegan's gaze again. "This is hard for me to say, but it's necessary. You deserve someone who will love you like Seth loves Rueben. I want you to find that guy because I can never be that for you." Kerry's breath hitched as he leaned his forehead against Keegan's. "But you won't find that kind of devotion at the Thirsty Cowboy or by looking in my direction. I don't want to be someone who breaks your heart, so please don't ask that of me."

The anguish in Kerry's eyes flayed Keegan to the bone. His honesty had cost him so much, and Keegan wouldn't be just another person who crushed Kerry's spirit. There was only one thing for him to do. "I won't."

They stayed that way for a few more glorious moments before Kerry eased back. "I'll see you out there."

He left without a backward glance, and Keegan had to remind himself several times throughout his shift not to look in Kerry's direction. Not when he shadowed Allison at the hostess station and learned the ins and outs of the seating charts and the booking software. The Feisty Bull accepted reservations, but the bulk of their patronage came from walk-ins. Keegan wasn't at all surprised when the entire ranch showed up to support him on his first night. He got a little flustered, knowing Cash was observing his interactions with the patrons. But his mentor's watchful gaze wasn't what made Keegan's hands shake when he switched from shadowing the hostess to a server midway through his shift. There was no one better to observe than Nate, but serving tables included many trips to the bar to place drink orders. Keegan avoided Kerry whenever he could by giving his drink orders to Ryder, and he avoided Kerry's gaze whenever the other bartender was busy. That was what Kerry claimed to want, but the intensity of his stare increased with each passing hour until Keegan thought he'd go nuts before the last customers cleared out.

The entire crew gathered at the bar to share a single drink of their choice to celebrate a successful night. It was a welcome reward after hustling for hours, but it didn't signal the end of their work. They needed to restore the restaurant to pristine order before they could leave, and the crew worked like a well-oiled machine to get it done efficiently. Keegan felt like a wrench in the cog, but he was grateful to everyone for either their time or instruction.

"The night's still young," Allison said when a group of them exited the restaurant through the back door. "Who's up for pizza?"

Keegan was dead on his feet. He hadn't slept well the previous night, and it felt like he'd been put through an emotional gauntlet from the moment his feet touched the floor that morning. But pizza sounded amazing, and he didn't want to be alone with his thoughts yet. "I'm in."

"Mind if I get a ride with you?" Nate asked. "I rode with Kelly, but she needs to head home. She has church choir practice before the service."

"Sure," Keegan said. "I'm just over there." He pointed toward the Redemption Ridge truck Cash let him drive.

"Hey, Keegan." Kerry's voice rang out from behind him. "Can we talk a minute?"

Several pairs of eyes shifted to Keegan, so he worked hard to conceal his dread. He clicked a button on the key fob. "Go ahead and get in," he told Nate. "This won't take long."

Nate darted a glance between Keegan and Kerry, then furrowed his brow. "Is everything okay? I couldn't help but notice you kind of avoided Kerry tonight."

Well, darn. So much for not being obvious. "Everything is fine. I'm sure he wants to ask me something about Sven." Nate sent one last questioning look in Kerry's direction before he walked away. Keegan pivoted and made his way to where Kerry stood next to the building. The area was heavily shadowed and kind of creepy, but he wasn't scared. Much. "Hey," he said casually.

"What the hell was that back in there?" Kerry's voice was low and gruff. He gestured toward the building in case Keegan needed clarification.

Keegan had thought his emotional tank was empty when he stepped outside, but Kerry's surly attitude reignited his spark. He straightened his shoulders and notched his chin higher. "I gave you what you wanted, Kerry. You said you didn't want me to look in your direction."

Kerry growled his frustration. "I didn't mean ever. I just don't want you to look at me with those bedroom eyes."

"I don't even know what that is, so I best keep my gaze averted."

"Please don't," Kerry said.

"Please don't what? You tell me not to look at you but then get upset when I do what you ask. Do you even hear yourself?"

"I know," Kerry groaned. "You're right. I'm sorry. I just don't want hard feelings between us. My family adores you, and they'd never forgive me if you stopped coming around because I'm an asshole."

"You're not an asshole," Keegan said. But he intended to scale back his time with the Hart clan. He would miss them like crazy, but his mental health wouldn't survive their matchmaking attempts. Keegan didn't really believe Kerry's standing with his family was in jeopardy, but his concern seemed sincere. "Everything will be okay. Tonight was just…raw. I'll see you around."

"Christ," Kerry bit out. "I recognize a brush-off when I hear it."

Keegan forced a laugh. "Don't be ridiculous."

"So, you'll be at dinner tomorrow night?" Kerry pressed.

"Unless something comes up." And it would.

Kerry huffed out a sigh. "Fine. Be careful tonight, okay?"

"I'll practice defensive driving and make sure I have Tums on hand for potential heartburn from eating greasy pizza late at night." He glanced over toward the truck where Nate waited. "And I don't think my co-pilot is into me, if that's what you're thinking."

Kerry hooked his finger in the open V of Keegan's dress shirt and released him as soon as their skin connected. That brief touch of bare skin was enough to transport him right back to the tiny locker room, where he came so close to knowing what Kerry tasted like. "Everyone is into you."

Along with the memory came the brief resurrection of his confidence. "Well, maybe this night will end better than I hoped. See you later."

Kerry called out his name before he made it three steps, but Keegan didn't slow his stride. Keep him guessing. That's what Sven would do.

# *Chapter*
## SIX

KERRY CHECKED HIS WATCH AGAIN, BUT IT WAS ONLY THREE minutes later than the last time he looked. The air stirred beside him, and he caught a whiff of Sven's cologne. Kerry braced himself for a confrontation with his brother, but Sven remained silent. He should've embraced the quiet, but it only unsettled Kerry more than the clock creeping closer to six with no sign of Keegan. He'd known the little minx wouldn't show, but he couldn't stop himself from hoping Keegan would change his mind. And what kind of dickhead did that make him? He'd warned Keegan away, pulled him closer, and then pushed him away again. When Keegan had done precisely what he'd asked, Kerry had gotten his feelings hurt. Yeah, he hadn't meant Keegan should never look at him again, but the previous shift at the Feisty Bull was torturous. The last thing he'd ever wanted to do was hurt Keegan, but he'd done it anyway.

So much for honesty being the best policy. Not to sound like Jack Nicholson, but sometimes people couldn't handle the truth. Better to find out now before things got too deep with Keegan. Who the fuck was he trying to kid? That ship had already sailed. And Sven still stood beside him, an unusually silent sentinel who somehow still radiated enough sass to get under his skin. "What?" Kerry snarled as he turned to face his brother. "You've never been this quiet a day in your life."

Sven's serene countenance was even more suspicious than his silence. The man didn't do calm. That could only mean Sven had a secret knowledge of something, and he planned to wield it like a weapon. His brother was as lethal as a rapier, cutting and deadly when he needed to be, and Kerry had a feeling he was about to bleed badly.

"It's nearly dinnertime, and Keegan isn't here yet," Lucinda said. "It's not like him to be late." For Lucinda, on time was late. When she said dinner would be served at six o'clock, she meant people should arrive a minimum of thirty minutes earlier.

Sven's expression reminded him of the viral meme of a little girl smiling wickedly as a building burns in the background. Christ, he hoped his mother's fire extinguisher hadn't expired. Kerry shook his head to discourage his brother, but when had that ever stopped him? "Keegan isn't coming tonight."

The disappointment was a palpable thing in the room. Did Keegan have a clue just how much Kerry's family adored him? Not likely. And Kerry would not pile guilt onto Keegan's surprisingly toned shoulders. The guy hid a rocking body beneath his modest clothes. Walking away from that temptation in the locker room had been one of the hardest things Kerry had ever done. Sven raised a brow to bait Kerry, daring him to ask where Keegan was or why he wasn't coming. No way. He'd be in the doghouse for sure if Lucinda and his aunts thought Kerry had scared Keegan off. Thank goodness the newlyweds were still too enamored with one another to attend the family dinners, or Rueben would help Sven lead the charge.

"Why not?" Lucinda didn't bother to hide her disappointment.

Sven kept his gaze locked on Kerry. "He met someone."

70

"Ohhhh," came the collective reply from many in the room. A few others asked who it was, how they'd met and when.

Not Lucinda. She marched right up to Kerry and placed both hands on her hips. "Do you know anything about this?"

Both her expression and tone transported him back to when he was a seven-year-old boy with major-league ambitions. Seth had pitched a strike right over the makeshift home plate, and Kerry had hit the game-winning grand slam…right through the family room window. He'd been too stunned to run and hide like Seth had, so he literally got caught red-handed, still holding the bat. Lucinda had struck the same pose and asked the same question. He hadn't been smart enough to save his ass back then, but he could talk his way out of nearly any situation as an adult. "I only know that he went to get pizza after his shift last night."

"With who?" Debbie asked.

"Nate and a few others," Kerry replied. He'd only sensed platonic vibes between Nate and Keegan, but he must've misread the situation. His mopey mood threatened to turn downright mean.

"Nate's a good kid," Debbie said. His aunt and uncle didn't have kids of their own and doted on their staff like family. "I've never seen him flirt with Kerry, so I didn't think he was interested in guys."

Sven snorted. "Not every gay or bi man wants to take this big lug to beg."

Kerry arched a brow and pinned his brother with his patented "you wanna bet" look.

"I can't speak to Nate's sexual orientation, but he's not the guy Keegan is going on a date with tomorrow night." Sven explained that the crew had driven to Colorado Springs for pizza, where Nate ran into an old high school buddy who was also there with some friends. "A friend of Nate's buddy took a real shine to our sweet Keegan. He bailed on his group to hang out with the Feisty Bull crew and get to know Kee better. His name is Danny, and he's really cute. They exchanged phone numbers and have been chatting and texting ever since. They would've gone out tonight, but Danny had prior commitments."

"I still don't understand why Keegan couldn't join us, then." Lucinda huffed a resigned sigh before heading to her kitchen.

"Did you have to break her heart?" Kerry asked quietly when they were alone.

"Did you have to break his?" Sven countered.

Kerry's stomach dropped. "How much did he tell you about our conversation?"

"Aha!" Sven said. "I knew something must've happened during his shift at the Feisty Bull."

Kerry gestured with his hands for Sven to keep his voice down. "How?"

"Because Danny wouldn't have stood a chance otherwise," Sven said. "Keegan wouldn't have given the guy his phone number, let alone stay up until two in the morning texting him."

That punched Kerry in the gut. "Sounds like they made a serious connection."

"What happened between you two last night?" Sven pushed.

"None of your business," Kerry replied, earning a scowl.

"You're both idiots." Before Kerry could defend himself, Sven pointed to Kerry's face. "You should see how mad you are that Keegan is going out with someone else. It's almost the same response you had to finding out Keegan was hoping to pick up for a guy at the bar on Friday."

Had that encounter really only happened two nights ago? It felt like at least three lifetimes had passed. "You're wrong."

Sven crossed his arms over his chest. "Guess we'll find out, won't we?"

Lucinda dashed out of the kitchen, wiping her hands on a towel. "He's here!"

Kerry didn't bother to ask who she was talking about because only Keegan triggered that kind of response lately. "Should we be jealous or offended that our mother is happier to see Keegan than us?"

Sven nudged him with his elbow. "You should see that dorky smile on your face. You adore seeing your mom fret and fuss over Keegan."

Kerry glanced across the room and caught his reflection in a mirror. Yeah, he was rocking the biggest, dorkiest smile. "Because Keegan deserves the attention. He soaks it up like a sponge."

Sven's sigh indicated he thought Kerry was the dullest tool in the shed. "Keep telling yourself that."

Lucinda didn't rush onto the porch, but she opened the door before he could ring the bell. She threw her arms around Keegan as if she hadn't seen him in ages. "I'm so glad you could make it. Family dinners just wouldn't be the same without you."

The sentiment echoed in Kerry's brain, and he nodded before he could stop himself. He hoped everyone was too busy watching his mother squeeze Keegan like a starving python to notice, but he should've known better. Sven snorted, and Aunt Deb winked at him. Just great. The announcement that Keegan had met someone hadn't dampened Kerry's craving or diminished his family's matchmaking schemes.

"Honey," Steven said gently. "Keegan's turning blue. Maybe you should loosen your hold or let him go."

Lucinda ignored her husband and, if anything, held on tighter. Keegan didn't seem to mind and, if anything, hugged her just as tightly. "I made your favorites."

Keegan pulled back but didn't drop his arms. "It's not my birthday."

"Every day is a reason to celebrate you." Lucinda patted his cheek before she completely relinquished her grip on him. "Something told me you could use the comfort food. Am I wrong?"

Kerry braced himself for Keegan to do or say anything that would give their conflict away. A simple glance in his direction would be all anyone needed to leap to conclusions. Keegan just smiled. "Everything is fine. I'm just a little tired."

"Because you stayed up late talking to a guy," Aunt Deb teased. "Sven told us what he knew about Danny."

Keegan scanned the room until he found Sven. "Really? Is nothing sacred?" And since the brothers stood together, Keegan's hazel gaze slid to Kerry next. His expression wasn't chilly, but it lacked the warmth

73

Kerry had gotten used to and now craved. Keegan looked between the brothers, then narrowed his eyes slightly. Was he still raw from their conversations at the Feisty Bull last night, or did he wonder what Sven had told him? "Hey, Ker." Keegan's voice lacked its usual warmth, but Kerry was grateful he hadn't outright ignored him.

"Hey." Christ, he sounded like Eeyore. Kerry wanted to get Keegan alone to clear the air, but Lucinda looped her arm through Keegan's and led him into the kitchen under the guise of getting his help. She wanted the hot gossip on the new man to assess his risk to the happily ever after she envisioned for Keegan and Kerry.

Sven waited until Lucinda and Keegan were out of the room before he turned and glared at him. "You better fix whatever you fucked up."

"I—" That was as far as he got before Sven cut him off.

"Don't waste your breath. That special sparkle Keegan gets whenever he looks at you is missing."

Kerry's chest felt tight, and regret burned a trail from his stomach to his throat. He wanted something cold to drink to soothe the ache, and he needed Keegan's warmth again. He could find both those things in the kitchen, but he'd have to go through Lucinda first. *Fuck it.* Kerry released a low growl and crossed the room.

"What does Danny do?" Lucinda was asking when Kerry stepped into the kitchen.

"Hey, Ma," Kerry said before Keegan could answer. "Can I borrow Keegan for a few minutes?"

When she turned around, she wore the smuggest smile he'd ever seen on her face. "Take as long as you need, dear." She set her potholders on the counter and turned off the stove. "Dinner can wait."

He wanted to ask since when but didn't dare. Lucinda shot him a warning glare on her way out of the kitchen. Kerry waited a heartbeat before he crossed the room. He wanted to crowd Keegan against the counter and cup his face, so Kerry stopped a few feet away and tucked his hands inside his front pockets. "Hey."

"Hey." Keegan bit his bottom lip and shook his head. "I think we already said that."

Kerry nodded, suddenly at a loss for words. He might not be as vocal as Sven, but he never lacked something to say. "I want to tell you how sorry I am about the way things went down last night."

"So say it," Sven said from the other side of the kitchen wall.

"Sven!" Aunt Debbie cried. "Get back in here and leave them alone!"

"Damn it," Sven groused.

Kerry looked over his shoulder and considered waiting until they were alone again, but that hadn't worked so well for him. Maybe having an audience nearby would help him keep his sanity. "I find myself in troubled waters, and I'm not sure how to navigate them."

Keegan's posture softened, and he eased a little closer. "That makes two of us."

"I'm sorry for saying anything that upset or confused you."

"So you're not sorry for thinking those things, but you're sorry for saying them." Keegan pursed his lips and nodded. "Good to know."

A snarl of frustration caught in Kerry's throat, and he swallowed it down. He took a deep breath to settle his nerves. There were all kinds of delicious aromas in the kitchen, but Keegan's signature sunshine scent was his favorite. "Yeah, look, I am sorry for thinking stupid shit too. I didn't mean to imply that I'm some massive force of masculinity you can't resist. I don't think one night in my bed will keep you jonesing for more for the rest of your life."

Keegan barked out a short laugh, lowered his head, and pinched the bridge of his nose. "You're not helping."

Kerry stepped back and pondered what he'd said wrong this time. "I should just stop talking. I can never say the right things around you."

Keegan cocked his head and studied him. "It never used to be that way. Why is it different now?"

All Kerry could do was shrug. "Troubled waters."

Keegan nodded. "Think maybe we could build a bridge and get over them?"

Kerry didn't really have a choice if he wanted to keep Keegan in his life. "Definitely." His answer earned a genuine smile, and the pressure in Kerry's chest eased up. He'd just have to fake his enthusiasm about Keegan's big date.

"We better get back out there. It's probably taken all of them to hold Sven back," Keegan teased.

More than one pair of feet fought for traction on the other side of the kitchen wall as nosy family members scampered away before getting caught. Kerry would place money on the culprits being Sven, Debbie, and Lucinda, but the busybodies were too fast for him to catch. Everyone looked deep in conversation by the time they rejoined the family in the living room.

Lucinda searched their expressions as she stood up. "Guess I'll finish putting dinner together," she said.

"I'll help," Keegan said.

"Me too," Sven and Debbie echoed.

"I need help setting the table," Lucinda told them.

"Fine," Debbie said, "but I'll need you to speak up so I can hear your conversation. Years in the restaurant business has left me hard of hearing." Kerry snorted. She could hear a frog fart from two thousand yards away. "I heard that, Kerry," she said to prove his point.

Keegan's favorite meal was Kerry's too. The chicken and stuffing casserole was something his mom had learned to throw together quickly on a busy weeknight, but the dish tasted like it had taken all day to make. She always served it with mashed potatoes, steamed vegetables, and buttery rolls. Normally Kerry savored every bite, but he didn't taste a single thing as he hung on every word his family drew from Keegan's beautiful mouth.

"His name is Danny Rodgers," Keegan said.

Sven leaned in close and whispered, "Have Dom run a background check."

"You ask him," Kerry fired back.

Oblivious to their conversation, Keegan continued. "He's a few years older than me and works in insurance sales."

"Half a step above a used car salesman," Deb whispered from Kerry's other side. "You still have a chance."

Kerry shoved a large forkful of casserole in his mouth instead of replying to her.

"He wants to have four kids, two dogs, and a cat," Keegan said.

And Kerry's food lodged in his throat. He coughed until his eyes watered and his nose ran, but he finally dislodged the lump and swallowed it. Sven pounded on his back while Deb handed him a glass of water. "I'm fine," he rasped between sips. "You can stop using this as an excuse to hit me."

"I should get one of Lucinda's cast-iron skillets," Sven countered.

"Oh dear," Lucinda said. "I hope I shredded the chicken well enough."

"It's fine, Ma," Kerry replied, then drained the glass of water. "I know better than to hoover my food. It's just so delicious." And he was horrible about eating well during the rest of the week. Kerry gestured at Keegan. "I'm sorry I interrupted. You were telling us your plans to have four kids, two dogs, and a cat with Danny."

Keegan narrowed his eyes, and his face turned a darker shade of pink. "That's not what I said."

Food forgotten, Kerry leaned back in his chair. "I'm a little surprised big topics like kids and pets came up so soon. Didn't you just meet the guy last night?" He knew it was the wrong thing to say when Keegan's eyes snapped with irritation.

"Why does it matter to you?"

Kerry shrugged his shoulder like he didn't have a vested interest in Keegan's answers. "Just seems soon."

"So, you're saying one or both of us is desperate?" Keegan asked.

"I don't think that's what he meant, honey." Lucinda pinned her son with a dark scowl. "Right, Kerry?"

"It sure sounded like that's what Kerry meant," Sven said. That little shit was enjoying every bit of Kerry's comeuppance.

"I just want you to be careful," Kerry said.

"Because I'm pathetic and stupid in addition to desperate?" Keegan asked.

Kerry pushed back from the table and put his hands up in the air. "Whoa. I didn't say any of those things."

"But you thought about them, right?" Keegan pressed.

Kerry sighed and stood up. "I think I'll head back to the station and catch up on some paperwork."

"Kerry, no," Lucinda said. "This is a simple misunderstanding that you and Keegan should work through."

"Preferably right here," Debbie said.

Kerry looked at Keegan. He was only three chairs down, but he might as well have been sitting on the opposite side of the Grand Canyon. Maybe building a bridge was impossible after all. "I hope Danny turns out to be everything you want him to be because you deserve the best." He picked his plate up and took it to the kitchen, where he fed the leftovers into the garbage disposal. The whir of its small engine and running water covered the sound of his mother following him, but Kerry sensed her presence. He rinsed off the plate, set it in the sink, and turned off the faucet. When he turned around, Lucinda was spooning food into containers. Kerry knew it wasn't because she was eager for him to leave. His mother just knew there was no changing his mind once he'd made it.

"I made pineapple upside-down cake for dessert," she said. "Would you like a few slices?"

"I'd take the entire cake if you let me." A few slices of that and some good bourbon ought to make the night a lot better. Maybe if he drank enough, he'd get some sleep.

Lucinda looked over her shoulder and smiled. "If I had a backup plan for dessert, I'd let you have the whole thing." She turned back around to her task, her movements concise and sure.

78

"I meant what I said. Keegan deserves the best."

She stilled for a moment but didn't turn around. After a few seconds, she resumed packing enough food to feed an army. "He does," she said. "You and I just don't agree on who the best person is for Keegan."

"Ma, I told you I'm not made for relationships."

"And I told you a long time ago that you'd change your mind when you met the right person."

"You did," he agreed.

"I knew Keegan was that special someone the first time Sven brought him home to meet our family. You come alive, and you navigate toward him like he's a beacon pulling you out of the dark."

"Ma, you've read too many romance novels," Kerry said.

"And you haven't read enough," she countered. "I'm right, and we both know it."

"I don't want the kids and dogs, and I already have the most perfect cat."

"Keegan didn't say he wanted any of those things," Lucinda pointed out. "You have jumped to many conclusions about Keegan, my love. You've made decisions for a person who's spent a lifetime under someone else's thumb. Freedom of choice is the most important thing to him, and you must respect that."

"Even when he could make the wrong one?"

She turned and faced Kerry, cupping his face with both hands. "That's all part of life. Loving and losing are two sides of the same coin. You can't have one without the other. You can build walls around your heart and play it safe, but that's not living. It's a slow death from joy deprivation. You deserve better, Kerry. You deserve the best."

"I'm a hot mess, Ma."

"You're a beautiful mess, and I love you more than you will ever know." She sighed and lowered her hands. "I just wish I'd been firmer about therapy after Natalie and your dad died. I should've tried harder." Lucinda's eyes filled with tears, and her lips quivered. "I'm sorry I let you down."

"Mom, you did everything right. You took me to see a therapist. It's not your fault I refused to talk to her." He'd lost count of the times they'd had the same conversation. Kerry didn't know if his argument wasn't strong enough or if she just brushed it aside. He wasn't the only stubborn one in their family, but Kerry wouldn't give up until his mother forgave herself. "You didn't let me down. Look at the incredible example you set for me. You worked hard to keep Natalie's memory alive through good deeds and your crusade for justice. The salon is more than just a place for your clients to get their hair or nails done. It's a loving community where you lift each other up. You were brave enough to risk love again and found Steven. I got an amazing role model and a bonus brother out of the deal. My faults are my own."

And he was the only one who could repair them. Until he met Keegan, Kerry wasn't interested in self-reflection, healing, and growth. He liked his simple life, and no one had challenged him to do better or want more. And now that he'd met that someone, it could be too late because he wasn't brave enough to admit it.

"We'll just have to agree to disagree." Lucinda gave her standard reply to his rebuttal. Occasionally, she used her position as his mother to override him. "Are you sure you have to leave?"

He didn't have to go, but it was for the best. The people in the other room might be his family, but Keegan needed them more at the moment. And Kerry really just needed a quiet place to think, and no one would ever describe their family dinners as peaceful. "I'm not going far, and I will be back." It might've sounded trite to some, but Lucinda needed to hear it. Mothers who lost a child to sudden and unspeakable death needed more from their surviving children, and Kerry would gladly give it.

Lucinda searched his gaze for a few seconds before she nodded and retrieved the bag of food she'd packed for him. "Maybe we can have lunch this week. Just the two of us."

Kerry accepted the food and kissed her cheek. "I'd love that. Name the time and place, and I'll be there."

He left through the utility room door on the side of the house to avoid any awkwardness, but escaping without another confrontation wasn't in the cards. Sven leaned against the driver's-side door of Kerry's truck. He could easily overpower his brother and make his escape, but he wouldn't, and Sven knew it. Kerry was raised to be aware of his size and strength compared to others, and Sven would press any advantage he could get.

"I'm not running," Kerry said. "Just retreating to reboot. I'm exhausted."

Sven sniffed the air over the bag. "Do I smell pineapple?" Kerry was tempted to barter the dessert for his freedom, but his brother spoke again before he could make the offer. "I'm worried about Kee." Sven's solemn voice matched his expression. "Really worried about him." The emphasis was overkill, but that should've been Sven's middle name instead of Edward. He did nothing in half measures. "This thing with Danny is too fast. I mean, what dude discusses future children and pets within the first twenty-four hours of meeting someone?" Sven didn't pause long enough for him to answer, choosing to charge ahead with his concerns, spitting them out like rapid machine gun fire. "I tell you, Ker. I have a really bad feeling about this. I think Danny is telling Keegan whatever he wants to hear so he'll let his guard down."

Kerry was riddled with doubt and guilt by the time he finally halted his diatribe, but he remembered what his mother had said about Keegan's need to be in control and make his own choices. He repeated her pearls of wisdom for Sven and earned a scowl.

"Well, fuck." Sven dropped his gaze to his feet and kicked a piece of gravel. "She's right. But how do we make sure he's safe? We don't want your *little lamb* to stumble into an eager butcher."

Kerry felt the same fears and frustrations but didn't have a solution. "Other than follow him around, what can you do?" Kerry asked.

Sven straightened, and his eyes widened. "That's exactly what I'll do. Getting Keegan to tell me where they're going on their date will be a cinch. Then I can just discreetly follow to make sure Danny Boy doesn't get out of line." He launched himself away from Kerry's truck and headed toward the house.

"Whoa, wait!" Kerry called. "I didn't intend that as a serious suggestion."

"You're a genius!" Sven fired back.

His brother didn't have a discreet bone in his body. Sven lived for standing out, so there was no way Keegan wouldn't notice the tail. This would come back on Kerry. He could see it now. Keegan would confront Sven, and his brother would throw him under the bus. Then Keegan would…what? Seek him out for a confrontation? Get curious about Kerry's intentions? Would that be a bad thing? *Yes!* Kerry wrenched his truck door open and climbed inside. He needed to discourage Keegan's crush, not encourage it. Sven's plan spelled absolute disaster. If he were smart, he'd give Keegan a heads-up. But Kerry was worried too, and Sven's intentions were good. So he fired up his truck and drove home to Betty, bourbon, and a crushing hangover if he weren't careful.

Kerry had set his alarm ninety minutes earlier than usual. He'd planned to put himself through a grueling workout in his home gym to reduce his anxiety before his appointment with Vinny. His pounding head and queasy stomach made exercise difficult, but he managed to sweat out some of his misery. Pain meds, a hot shower, and strong coffee helped him feel almost human by the time he pulled out of his driveway.

Vinny Marino looked nothing like Joe Pesci's character in *My Cousin Vinny*, but they both had swagger. The attorney greeted Kerry and Steven warmly and offered hugs instead of handshakes. The man's suit probably cost more than all of Kerry's clothes combined, but he wore it well. Vinny looked to be in his midforties, but Kerry knew he was pushing sixty at least. They spent several minutes catching up while sipping expensive-tasting coffee before Vinny set his cup down on the desk and got down to business.

"I reviewed the information Steven emailed me this weekend. Your investigator is incredible," Vinny said with a cocky smile. "I've known the plaintiff's counsel for many years, and I thought it was only fair to let Roger know I am going to represent you. I didn't reveal my hand, but I let him know in no uncertain terms that their client will not win. I also clarified that we would not make a settlement offer."

"And?" Kerry asked hopefully.

Vinny sighed and shook his head. "Roger didn't heed my warning, so he'll have to find out the hard way. Your options are to file a response to dispute the allegations or countersue. Either way, we enter the discovery phase, where I gather the evidence and witnesses we will need. I figure opposing counsel will drag this out until depositions, which should take place about four weeks after I file our response or countersuit. The deposition is where I'll go hard, and they'll fold like a weak-ass house of cards."

The attorney's comment buoyed Kerry's confidence, but he wanted to maintain a grip on reality. "You sound certain."

"Because I am. I've won cases with a lot less evidence than Dominic Babb provided you. A good investigator is priceless. Do you think he'd be interested in doing some work for me?"

The pivot in conversation caught Kerry off guard, but it also elated him. "Definitely."

Vinny pulled a legal pad and pen from his desk and slid them to Kerry. "Would you mind providing his contact information?"

Kerry didn't bother checking with Dom first. He knew how hard his friend was working to build up his clientele. Landing a successful lawyer like Vinny could be a lucrative arrangement with infinite possibilities. He jotted Dom's phone number and email down for Vinny without hesitation, though he'd give Dom a heads-up once they left. "You said something about a countersuit? Is that what you recommend?"

"Yes, I do. I think you should sue for a dollar," Vinny said. "It sends a powerful message. At first, Bozeman will think it's a weak counter-suit, but then I'll clarify that he will also pay all your legal fees when you win. I'm not charging you a penny for this, but he doesn't need to know that. And his attorney sure as hell knows how much someone with my experience charges."

"So, you're saying my son has nothing to worry about, Vin?" Steven asked.

"That's exactly what I'm saying." Vinny turned his attention to Kerry. "Do not lose another moment to worrying about this case. If this man is stupid enough to take this all the way to court, I will make him regret the day he was born."

Kerry slapped his hands against his thighs. "That about settles it, then."

"Only thing left is the crying. His," Vinny clarified with a wink. "You've already provided all your documentation on the accident and a list of witnesses who were on the scene and can confirm that Chuck Dahl acted in the opposite manner you instructed him during Mr. Bozeman's rescue. I will contact your insurance company to obtain documentation on their negotiations with Mr. Bozeman. They will have done an ex-tremely thorough investigation into the matter. We've already hit the ground running on this, so I'll be in contact when I need more infor-mation or have an update to share."

"I can't thank you enough, Vin," Steven said.

"This is what I do." He smiled at Kerry and said, "I hope you feel better about the situation."

"Immeasurably so," Kerry replied.

They left the office a few minutes later. Steven offered to buy Kerry breakfast, but he was eager to get back to a normal routine. Caffeine and Vinny's assurances had worked miracles, and time was wasting. The two men hugged before parting ways, and Kerry headed to the station. He called Dom to give him a heads-up, but Vinny had beat him to the punch.

"Do you know what this could do for my business?" Dom asked.

"Great things, I hope."

"His assistant is sending over a contract and information on a case Vinny wants me to start on right away. I can't thank you enough."

"Your work created the opportunity. I just provided your contact information. I'm really happy for you."

They chatted for a few more minutes so Kerry could tell Dom what Vinny said about his case. They promised to meet up soon for a steak dinner before disconnecting. Kerry almost felt like a new man when he strolled into his station. The crew whistled when they caught sight of him in a suit.

"This old thing?" Kerry asked as he continued to his office.

He kept spare uniforms at the station for emergencies but decided not to change unless he needed to respond to a call. The suit made him feel like a boss, and he needed the boost after weeks of floundering. Kerry sighed when he saw the mountain of paperwork on his desk. His role at Hart's Creek Rescue had become more administrative over the past few years as he'd expanded the business and hired additional crew. He'd fallen behind miserably on his paperwork and was determined to set things right.

Kerry removed his jacket, rolled up his sleeves, and got to work prioritizing the outstanding tasks. Facing the music was overwhelming at first, but he found a rhythm in no time. Kerry started with the outstanding renewal contracts because they were the rescue's primary source of income. Those agreements cemented Hart's Creek Rescue as the first responders to accidents and rescues, and he was fortunate to work with nearly every municipality in the tri-county area, as well as state-funded entities. Kerry sent the renewal documents out ninety days before the existing contracts expired, then followed up forty-five days later. It was common for the municipalities and state to wait until the last minute, so Kerry wasn't initially alarmed that three renewal contracts were still pending until he saw how close they were cutting it. Two of them still had three weeks until their contracts expired, but he only had ten days left to secure Hart's Creek Township's renewal.

Kerry tried to track down the three entities by phone but didn't have much luck. Township trustees managed the municipalities, but it was rarely their primary jobs. Kerry left messages and sent emails, hoping he'd hear back from them soon, and continued working through the mess he'd made.

One of the crew brought him lunch, and he took breaks to stretch, snack, and hydrate throughout the afternoon. Around three o'clock, Kerry received an email from Frank Tallus, a trustee for Hart's Creek Township, in response to the renewal contracts. Dread knotted his stomach when Frank admitted they were considering other service providers. One of the trustees raised nepotism claims, pointing out that they shouldn't just choose Kerry because of his lineage or relation to the county sheriff.

"Fuck!" Kerry snarled. This had Chuck's fingerprints all over it. The timing of his newly formed company and the renewal holdouts couldn't be a coincidence. He took a deep breath and wrote a respectful reply to Frank's email, signing off with his hope that they'd continue to work together. He jotted a follow-up in his calendar so he could make a last pitch to Frank before the contract expired.

Kerry wanted to give in to his temper, pause to pound the punching bag for an hour, but he directed his focus to getting caught up. Before he knew it, dinnertime arrived. Kerry thought longingly of the leftovers waiting for him at home, but he'd made great strides and didn't want to ease off the throttle. He jumped when his phone vibrated with a text message from Sven around seven o'clock. Kerry's heart raced when he recalled his brother's plans for Monday night.

*At the Thirsty Cowboy. I really don't like this Danny guy. Need backup. Now!*

Kerry was out of his chair and heading to the door before he finished reading the message. *On my way*, he typed. Sven was many things. Dramatic was one of them, but he wouldn't trigger unnecessary panic. If Sven said something was off about Danny, then Kerry believed him. The drive to the bar only took fifteen minutes, but his mind spun countless possibilities—each one worse than the next. Sven had texted him up-dates, which he checked as soon as he parked in the crowded lot. The number of thirsty cowboys at such an early hour on a Monday was sur-prising. Equally concerning was the attention Kerry got when he strolled over to Sven's table. If his brother hadn't texted him with his location, Kerry would've struggled to recognize him. Hell, he didn't even know Sven owned a regular ball cap that didn't have sequins or glitter on it. The black-framed glasses were a nice touch, and his dowdy, oversized shirt and baggy jeans hid the assets he typically showed off at the bar.

Kerry's attire must've equally distracted Sven. "Did you come from a funeral?"

"I had a meeting with Vinny about the lawsuit," Kerry replied.

"Oh my god! I forgot all about that," Sven said, then gestured across the room to where Keegan sat with a dark-haired guy close to his age. Danny was deep in conversation with a couple sitting across from them while he absently stroked Keegan's hair, shoulders, and arm. "He looks miserable. Every time he stands up to leave, Danny places a hand on his leg. Do something."

"I will not storm over there and yank Keegan out of his embrace." Though that was exactly what he wanted to do.

Before Kerry could formulate a plan, Keegan scooted his chair back and stood up. Danny had reached for him, but Keegan evaded his touch. His little lamb said something to the table before heading to the bathroom. Danny watched Keegan go with a telling glint in his eyes that made Kerry's stomach curdle. The tablemates said something Danny found hilarious, but he never tore his gaze away from Keegan. When Danny stood up to follow, Kerry was moving too. The distance between them was too great for Kerry to intercept Danny, but he should only be a few steps behind. Unfortunately, that was all the head start Dickhead Danny needed.

"I said no, Danny." Keegan's distressed voice rang down the hall-way, and Kerry ran the last few steps, his mind spinning with horrible possibilities.

"You little cocktease," came the angry reply. "You should consider yourself lucky—"

Kerry pushed through the door hard enough to make it slam against the interior wall, cutting off the rest of what Danny had to say. He'd crowded Keegan against the sink but luckily hadn't put his hands on him. Scared hazel eyes met Kerry's, then widened in surprise.

Danny had his back to Kerry and hadn't turned to see who'd entered. "Go away, man. Me and my guy need a minute."

Kerry had spent a lifetime trying not to make people feel uncomfortable about his size, but he embraced his brawniness with fervor and pushed that strength into his voice. "Step away from him if you want to leave this place alive."

# Chapter
# SEVEN

K EEGAN HAD JUST BEEN ABOUT TO DRIVE HIS KNEE BETWEEN
Danny's legs when the bathroom door flew open and crashed
against the wall with a loud *bang*. A supersized man in a suit
barged into the room with a murderous expression on his face. Wait!
Keegan knew those eyes, but he'd never seen them burn with rage. And
he'd never seen Kerry all dressed up. What the hell was going on?

Danny pressed closer against Keegan, making a knee to the groin
nearly impossible, but it wouldn't matter. Kerry was there and appeared
to be seconds away from removing Danny's limbs one by one. He'd even
said as much when the fool in front of him tried to brush Kerry away
like an annoying gnat. Danny had rolled his eyes when Kerry issued
his commanding threat.

"Look, pal." Danny angled his upper body to address his doom
face-to-face and froze.

Kerry looked impossibly big in that tiny space. Like *Reacher* kind
of big. And not that lean Tom Cruise, but the other hulking Alan guy

from the Amazon Prime show. Kerry looked imposing, but he wasn't taut. Fighters knew better than to tense up because it slowed their reactions. Owen had taught him that during boxing lessons, which he'd failed to implement when Danny crowded him against the sink. Kerry had relaxed into the moment and was prepared to cause some serious damage on his behalf. Humiliation might come later when he thought of Kerry riding to the rescue like Keegan was a damsel in distress, but right then, he was just so damn grateful.

Danny sidestepped to get away from Keegan and turned his body to keep Kerry in his sights. He put his hands up to show he wasn't a threat and eased toward the door. "This is just a big misunderstanding."

Kerry was not appeased in the least. He eased closer to the door, blocking Danny's path. "When someone tells you no, you stop. Period. Do you fucking hear me?" Kerry's voice was cold and hard, something Keegan never imagined. "There is no forcing your will on someone else and then justifying your actions afterward. No fucking means no."

Danny nodded vigorously. "I got it, man. No means no."

"If I find out you've forgotten, I will track you down and make you pay, Danny Rodgers." The asshole's eyes widened when he realized Kerry knew his name, and he darted for freedom when Kerry stepped aside to unblock the doorway. "And lose Keegan's number, asshole!" Kerry yelled after him.

It was just the two of them, and Keegan didn't know what to say, so he went with the first thing that popped into his mind. "This is a new look."

Kerry closed his eyes and shook his head. "You've been spending too much time with Sven if the first thing you comment on is my outfit." He muscled the bathroom door shut before closing the gap between them. Kerry paused just outside Keegan's touching zone and opened his arms in invitation.

Keegan launched himself against Kerry's chest hard enough to make him stagger back a half step. Muscular arms enfolded him in the biggest, safest hug he'd ever known. Keegan melted into his embrace and pressed his forehead against Kerry's chest. "I'm so glad to see you." He closed his eyes and cycled through some breaths to calm his racing heart. Kerry's nearness made the latter part a challenge. "I want you to know I was about to knee that asshole in the balls when you rode to my rescue."

A chuckle rumbled through Kerry's chest. "I have no doubt."

Keegan lifted his head and met Kerry's gaze. The rage he'd witnessed earlier was gone, and he was afraid to assign a name to the warmth shimmering there. "You must think I really am desperate and dumb."

Kerry slowly lifted his hands to cup Keegan's face but stopped before making contact. "May I?" He wanted to be annoyed by the hesitance and gentle handling, but Keegan had to admit it was exactly what he needed at the moment. He leaned into one warm palm, and Kerry closed in with the other. "I have never thought those things about you. I think you're—"

The bathroom door banged open again, and the two of them jerked apart and faced the new intruder. A guy wearing slouchy clothes, a ball cap, and black-framed glasses entered the room. He placed one hand on his heart and the other on the wall. He panted like he'd run a mile. "Christ! That asshole nearly ran me over with his eagerness to get away."

Keegan recognized the voice right away, but it didn't belong to the dude in the room. "Sven?" *Wait a minute.* He'd never seen Kerry in business attire, and Sven never wore dull, oversized clothes. He sure as hell wouldn't wear anything to mess up his hair. All the relief he'd felt from Kerry's rebuttal faded. What were these two doing there, and why were they dressed weirdly? "What the hell is going on?"

A lull washed over the cramped space for a few seconds. Then Kerry and Sven spoke at once, talking over each other, verbally and physically pointing at each other. Keegan couldn't make out much of what was said, but the wild gesturing and arguing broke the tightness in his chest. A giggle-snort burst from his mouth, catching the brothers' attention. They turned and looked at him with matching quizzical expressions that triggered a fit of laughter. Whatever the reason for Kerry's and Sven's attire or presence didn't matter because their actions came from a good place. He'd get the truth out of them, but it didn't have to be in the sketchy bathroom of a gay bar. Keegan couldn't imagine taking his pants down to piss in there, let alone bend over and offer his ass. He'd only fled to the bathroom to figure out a way to extricate himself from the disastrous date without causing a scene.

"Way to go," Sven said to Kerry. "You broke him."

"I did not," Kerry argued. "He's just releasing tension. Ever heard of people laughing at a funeral?"

"Danny came close to needing a funeral a few minutes ago," Keegan said.

Sven narrowed his eyes. "What the hell did that fucker do? It's not too late to kill him? We'll hide the body where no one will find him, and I bet no one reports him missing."

"Take it down a notch, *Dateline*," Keegan said.

"Dude," Kerry scoffed. "You're winded just from hustling down a small hallway. You think you're going to sprint out to the parking lot and catch him before he drives off?"

"To avenge Keegan's honor? Hell yeah, I could."

The brothers bumped fists, united once again. Keegan got so caught up in the sweetness that it took him a few seconds to realize they were both watching him with concerned expressions.

"I'm fine, guys." The date had been a disaster from the jump, but the aftermath was…beautiful.

Kerry held out his hand, and Keegan took it. "Let's get out of here."

Sven flapped his hand in front of his face like he got a whiff of something horrible. "No doubt. Drinks are on me." He opened the door and stepped into the hallway. But when Keegan moved to follow, Kerry tugged on their joined hands to stop him.

"I meant let's leave the bar," Kerry said.

"And go where?"

"Anywhere you want, but I was thinking my place."

Keegan could only blink for a few seconds. "Together?"

Kerry laughed and cupped Keegan's face with his free hand. "Yes, together. We need to talk."

"Talk?" He tried not to sound disappointed.

Kerry swallowed hard. "And I really want to hold you and kiss you, if that's okay—"

Keegan darted toward the door, hauling Kerry behind him. Delicious chuckles met his enthusiasm. "I met Danny here, so my truck is outside. That's one smart thing I did tonight." Time would tell if going home with Kerry would fall into the same category.

"This way," Kerry said once they stepped into the hall. He nodded his head toward the door at the end of the corridor marked as an exit.

Keegan wondered how often Kerry had left through that door with his hookups, but he didn't let the thought ruin his good mood. "Should we tell Sven we're leaving?"

"He'll figure it out." Kerry squeezed his hand, then added, "I'll text him right before we pull out."

Keegan would've preferred to ride with Kerry, but he didn't want to leave the ranch truck behind. The ordeal with Salvation Anew was finally behind them, but why risk drawing attention or retaliation from bitter followers? Kerry didn't release his hand until they reached Keegan's truck. He fished out the key fob and unlocked the door.

"I'll be right behind you," Kerry said.

Keegan didn't need to ask where Kerry lived. He'd passed his gorgeous log cabin every time he visited Seth and Rueben. This would be the first time Keegan stepped inside Kerry's house, and the thrill of that blocked out any of the nerves he'd normally experience. Keegan moved to open the door, but Kerry stood in his way.

"Are you sure about this?" Kerry asked. "I don't want to pressure you."

Keegan cupped his neck and pressed his lips to Kerry's. "I'm not going home with you because you saved the day and I owe you. Talking is the last thing I want to do with you right now, though I understand it's necessary."

Kerry's cheeks flushed with warmth, and his eyes darkened. "Sounds like you have big plans for me."

"I've had big plans for you since the day we met." The moment called for complete honesty, so he added, "But tonight proved that I may not be as ready for intimacy again as I'd thought."

Kerry brushed his thumb over Keegan's cheek. "I will happily wait for as long as you need me to."

A rush of euphoria made Keegan light-headed, and he swayed for a minute.

"Are you okay to drive? I can call Seth and Rueben to come over and pick up your truck."

Keegan shook his head. "I'm fine. I think maybe your words gave me a mini orgasm or something."

Kerry's lips curved into a wicked smile, and he shook his head. "Little lamb, there will be no thinking involved. You'll know when I give you an orgasm, and there won't be anything miniature about it."

Keegan needed to brace his hand against the truck door. "Go now before we get in trouble."

Kerry laughed before he pressed a quick kiss to Keegan's forehead. "Drive carefully."

Keegan climbed into the cab and locked his door. He waited for Kerry to get into his truck before he started the engine and eased out of the parking spot. As promised, Kerry followed him at a safe distance. His presence was there but not looming or threatening. Keegan didn't replay their conversation or relive anything that had happened. He sure as hell didn't let his imagination run wild on what could happen once they reached Kerry's house. Keegan kept his thoughts on the drive and his senses on high alert while navigating the winding mountain road. He breathed a sigh of relief once he pulled into Kerry's driveway, but the reprieve only lasted until Kerry parked beside him. Keegan had wanted this for so long, and now he feared he might blow it. His thoughts whirled, and he kind of zoned out until a knock sounded on the driver's side window. Keegan blinked Kerry's worried face into focus and smiled. He'd rather take a swing and miss than wonder forever what could've happened if he'd just been brave enough. Keegan killed the engine and got out of the truck.

"Are you—"

Keegan pressed his lips to Kerry's, preventing him from asking him one more time if he was sure about something. He didn't linger long and smiled at the big man's bemused expression.

"I was going to ask if you're hungry, but okay," Kerry said.

Keegan's eyes widened, and heat spread across his chest, neck, and face. "I'm an idiot. I thought you were worried I'd changed my—"

It was Kerry's turn to cut him off with a kiss. He added a hint of tongue against Keegan's lips before retreating. "You were right. I was going to ask if you'd changed your mind. I shouldn't have teased you."

"We won't get much talking done if we're constantly tiptoeing around each other," Keegan said. "Let's agree here and now that I will tell you if something is bothering me or doesn't feel right. You won't need to guess, second-guess, and double-check all the time."

"Fine," Kerry said before adding a caveat. "As long as you know that you always have a choice. When you're ready to explore intimacy, I will never take your consent for granted."

Keegan's yearning for the man just increased tenfold. "Thank you."

Kerry gestured his head toward the house, a stunning two-story log cabin nestled amidst dense trees. The stark black roof, window trim, and porch gave the home a modern feel. The combination of the dark building materials might've looked ominous if not for the soft gray stones in the chimney and the surrounding lush green landscape. The windows along the front of the home were tall and wide to let maximum sunlight into the rooms, and the upper-story windows featured curved arches at the top, breaking up the masculine vibe with a touch of whimsy. The house matched the man—big, imposing, but with surprising touches of tenderness. "Let's take this inside. I want you to meet Betty."

Disappointment washed over Keegan as he fell into step with Kerry. He'd really hoped they'd be alone. "Who's Betty?"

"My cat."

A few minutes later, Keegan's eyes widened when a massive calico beast rose from the back of the leather sofa and stretched its long, sleek body. Keegan pointed and said, "That's not a cat."

Kerry chuckled before making the universal clicking noise with his tongue that cats seem to recognize. Just one and the enormous beast leaped to the ground and prowled toward them. "This is my Betty."

Keegan was too mesmerized by her magnificence to be afraid. His mother had never permitted pets, and his only interactions were with the felines on the ranch. Those pampered pets looked nothing like Betty. She reached the men and wove around Kerry's legs, purring her greeting. This he was familiar with. "What kind of cat is Betty?"

"She's a Maine coon," Kerry replied. He slapped his hands against his thighs, and the cat stood on her back haunches and stretched up to rest her front paws on his stomach. Kerry scratched her ears vigorously and made some sort of cooing noise at her. "She's just a big baby house cat," he told Keegan. "Nothing to fear from my girl." The cat turned her brilliant orange eyes on Keegan and studied him until Kerry hit a delightful spot. Betty closed her eyes and purred louder, leaning into the touch.

Keegan had never been more envious of anything or anyone as he was Betty just then. "She's magnificent." The cat's eyes opened wide, as if she'd forgotten all about his intrusion. He couldn't blame her. She dropped back on all fours and closed the short distance between them. Keegan leaned forward a little and extended his hand so she could sniff him, though he didn't know if that was proper protocol. Betty angled her head and rubbed her cheek against his outstretched fingers. Her fur was as silky as it looked. "Wow," Keegan gushed. "Your eyes are the same color as your orange spots. I wouldn't believe you are real if I wasn't touching you."

Kerry made a humming sound and pulled Keegan's attention away from the cat. "I feel the same way about you."

Keegan straightened and dropped his hand to his side. "But you're not touching me." The flirty response had rolled right off his tongue, and his chest swelled with pride when Kerry's nostrils flared.

"Are you hungry?"

*Meow.*

"Not you, little lady. You're always ready to eat. How about you?" Kerry asked.

Keegan arched a brow. "Hungry for what?"

Kerry chuckled and ran a hand through his waves. The gesture brought Keegan's attention to the rolled-up sleeves that showed off powerful forearms. The stark white fabric made Kerry's tattoos stand out and reminded Keegan of the artwork hidden under the shirt. The urge to trace the intricate dark lines returned with vigor, and Kerry's reactions spurred him on to be even bolder.

"Conversation?" Keegan hedged. "Companionship? Kissing? Maybe some exploratory touching?"

"Dinner." Kerry's voice sounded as gravelly as his driveway. "Have you eaten? I have a ton of leftovers from last night."

Had that family dinner fiasco really been just yesterday? The reminder killed Keegan's flirty mood. A dozen apologies flittered through his head, and he needed to voice at least one of them to ease his conscience. "About dinner last night. I am really sorry—"

Kerry cupped his neck and silenced his apology with a quick kiss. "Don't be sorry for standing up for yourself. I'm the one who needs to apologize. I needled you out of petty jealousy, and I'm sorry."

"But I ran you out of your mother's house," Keegan protested. "I am horrified by my behavior. I projected all my fears and insecurities onto you. And maybe I was acting desperately and stupidly because the red flags with Danny were there. He was moving too fast and saying all the right things, so I ignored the warnings in my head that he was too good to be true."

Kerry shook his head. "I didn't leave because of anything you did or said. I was running from my feelings for you." He sighed heavily and said, "And if I had been completely honest with you on Saturday night, you wouldn't have met Danny."

Keegan cocked his head to the side. "Why do you say that?"

Kerry closed the distance between them but was careful not to crowd Keegan. "Because you would've come home with me instead of going to the pizza place with Nate."

Keegan wanted to tease Kerry about his arrogant assumptions, but all he managed was a breathy "Oh."

Kerry scrunched his handsome face into a dark scowl. "And speaking of Nate, I'm going to have a talk with him about the friends he keeps."

Keegan settled his hand on Kerry's chest. "This isn't Nate's fault. He met Danny the same night I did. He isn't responsible for a friend of a friend's behavior."

"Danny has potential predator written all over him."

Keegan shuddered to think what might've happened. He'd planned to kick Danny in the balls and use the skills Owen had taught him to defend himself, but what if Danny had been armed with a date rape drug? He could've had a weapon on him that Keegan hadn't known about. The encounter could've gone a dozen different ways, and he was so grateful for the outcome.

"Thank you for following me." Keegan rubbed his hand over Kerry's dress shirt. "How did you end up in the position to rescue me? You and Sven talked over one another back at the bar, and I only picked up bits and pieces. I'm dying to know the full story." There was no doubt he'd get the most accurate version from Kerry, though he had every intention of getting Sven's side for pure entertainment value once he could look back on the night without cringing.

"Let me feed you first, then I'll tell you everything you want to know," Kerry said.

"Tell me *while* you feed me so we don't get distracted by other things."

Kerry arched a brow. "Other things?"

"The real things we're both hungry for. The kissing and touching." Keegan had thought he was ready for more, but a single date with Danny had him questioning so much. Not his sexuality, at least. He was primed and ready to embrace that, so why had he frozen up when Danny dialed up the heat on his flirtations? He'd been charmed by him when all they'd done was talk or text, but that had all changed the moment Danny laid a hand on him. And that was before Danny became aggressive. What had gone wrong?

Kerry groaned and tugged Keegan through the open floor plan to the kitchen at the back of the house. "I'm trying to be good."

And Keegan had his answer. The in-person date forced him to acknowledge that Danny wasn't the man he wanted. Flirting was one thing, but he hadn't wanted anything deeper with the guy, not even a kiss. It was Kerry or bust for him, which meant Keegan had a big decision to make. He could tiptoe around and hope things worked out, or he could fight for what he wanted. Surviving versus thriving. Yeah, there was no real choice to make. "Who the hell asked you to do that?" Keegan teased.

"I demand it of myself." Kerry stopped next to the kitchen island and turned to face him. "This is too important for me to fuck up."

Keegan threatened to melt right there. "Will you tell me one thing right now?"

"Anything."

"Back in the bathroom, I said that you must think I'm desperate and dumb. You replied that you didn't think either of those things, but Sven barged into the room before you could say what you think of me. That exchange felt like it was gearing up to be the most honest conversation we'd ever had, and we didn't get to finish it."

Kerry slid his arms around Keegan's waist and tugged him into his powerful embrace. "I was going to say I think you're beautiful and perfect and so fucking brave. Sometimes I think you're too good for this twisted world. That I could cause you a moment of hurt fucking kills me, Kee. You make me want…things. Things I never considered for myself. You terrify me."

"Me?"

"Yes, you." Kerry lowered his head and nuzzled his nose at Keegan's temple. "Losing my sister to a murderer and my father to grief didn't kill me. It set me back a lot, but I built a fortress around my heart and moved forward as best I could. And then you came along and…"

Keegan tilted his head back and stared into those dark, bottomless eyes. "Fed snacks to your dragon and sneaked past your defenses." He cocked his head to the side and considered. "I at least crossed the crocodile-infested moat, but I don't think I've cleared the drawbridge."

Kerry chuckled. "You've battered my portcullis until it's a misshapen hunk of metal."

"How?" The mere idea was laughable.

"By breathing."

Keegan snorted. "If it were that easy, some young buck would've come along and stolen your heart a long time ago."

"It took the right guy," Kerry said.

"Feels like we're venturing way off topic," Keegan teased.

"Or maybe hearing that I think you're extremely rare and precious makes you uncomfortable."

"A diamond of the first water?" Keegan asked, though he didn't know where he'd heard that reference. The ranch was on a *Bridgerton* and Regency-era kick, so that was probably his source of reference.

Kerry placed his hand under Keegan's chin and notched it higher so they were staring into one another's eyes again. The intensity in Kerry's expression made Keegan's pulse leap. Damn, this guy really knew how to wreak havoc on his nervous system. "We're really running the gamut of historical references."

"And getting further off topic." Keegan slid a hand up Kerry's neck and curled a silky lock of hair around his finger. "Let's agree about a few things to make both our lives easier."

"Okay. You go first."

"We're intensely attracted to one another," Keegan said.

Kerry's hands inched lower until his fingertips brushed the upper swells of Keegan's ass cheeks. "Abso-fucking-lutely."

"Your turn," Keegan prodded.

Kerry remained silent long enough for Keegan's nerve to waver. But then he raised a hand and traced the curve of Keegan's face with a finger. "We both want to explore these feelings to see where it can take us."

Keegan silently urged himself to remain calm and cool. *Don't blow it now, Kee.* But being bold and honest was what had finally led to this moment. Keegan placed his hand over Kerry's heart. "Let me in. At least unlock the door and give me a chance to walk through it."

Kerry's response was a yielding moan, followed by an impassioned kiss that rocked Keegan to his core. The first press of lips ignited a spark in his belly that turned into an inferno when Kerry slipped his tongue into Keegan's mouth. He'd been kissed before, but nothing had ever felt like this. Kerry licked into his mouth, teasing and sucking on Keegan's tongue and eliciting the neediest moans that only seemed to add gasoline to the fire burning in his veins. The fear he'd felt with Danny was nowhere in sight. Instead of clamoring to get away from Kerry's touch, Keegan had to restrain himself from climbing him like a tree.

Maybe Kerry sensed his need because the next thing Keegan knew, his feet were off the ground, and his ass landed on the kitchen island. Kerry cradled Keegan's head with one large hand and rested the other on Keegan's thigh. Parting his legs and making room for Kerry seemed as natural as breathing, and fuck, they notched together so perfectly. Desire pooled in Keegan's core, spreading out until every pore and hair follicle was on fire for the man between his legs. Kerry moved his hand from Keegan's thigh to his ass, scooting him closer until they were groin to groin, hard and aching for one another.

Keegan wasn't sure where to put his hands since he'd told Kerry sex was off the menu for the moment. He didn't want to be the tease Danny had accused him of being. The thought dampened the moment a little, and Kerry must've heard the hitch in his breath. He eased back and searched Keegan's gaze.

"Too much, too fast?" Kerry asked.

Keegan bit his bottom lip and shook his head. When he didn't an-swer right away, Kerry reached out and gently rescued the abused flesh from his teeth. "I…um…didn't want to put out mixed signals. And…"

Kerry's eyes darkened with something like malice, but Keegan knew it wasn't directed at him. "I'm nothing like that asshole. If you ever want me to stop, I'm stopping. Period. And for the record, a person may change their mind at any time. Maybe you green-light me right up through penetration but decide it's too much. No means no. Stop means stop. I will be your safe place, Kee."

Relief flooded Keegan's system, and tears filled his eyes. "But what about your pleasure? I feel how hard you are. I don't want you aching and miserable."

Kerry brushed away the few tears that escaped Keegan's eyes. Then he raised his right hand. "I've been making do with my bestie since we met. We can get by for as long as you need."

Delicious images of Kerry pleasuring himself sprang to mind, and Keegan couldn't contain his moan. "Damn, that's hot."

Kerry nuzzled his nose against Keegan's neck. "I'll let you watch anytime you want."

Keegan tried to scoot off the island, but Kerry stopped him with a dark chuckle. "Food and talking first."

"We are talking," Keegan said. He reached over and snagged a shiny red apple from the fruit bowl. He crunched into it and offered it to Kerry for a bite, but he pressed his tongue inside Keegan's mouth and stole his bite instead. Dark eyes crackled with smug pride as Kerry chewed and swallowed the apple.

Kerry held the fruit up to Keegan's mouth, but he wanted to taste the apple on Kerry's lips. Keegan cupped his neck and pulled him down for another deep kiss. The sweet, crisp fruit juice made Keegan's mouth water and his hunger grow. The apple fell to the island and rolled to the floor. Keegan and Kerry simultaneously reached for each other, their hands shifting, seeking, and exploring over their clothes.

Kerry eased his mouth free, then immediately kissed a path down Keegan's neck toward his collarbone. Keegan angled his head back to give him access and grabbed a fistful of Kerry's hair. It would be so easy to lie back on the island and surrender to the feeling surging inside him, and he was mere seconds away from doing that when Kerry abruptly pulled back.

"Huh-uh," Kerry said. "I promised to feed you, and I said we'd talk."

"I had fruit for dinner, and there's nothing else we need to discuss right now." Keegan pointed to Kerry and said, "You want this." Then he pointed at himself. "And I want this. That's all we need right now."

Kerry's stomach growled pitifully in rebuttal. And if he was honest, Keegan would admit he was hungry too. Kerry stepped back between Keegan's thighs and captured his lips for a sweet but too-short kiss. "Let me feed you."

Keegan pursed his lips like he was mulling it over. Then he straightened up and smiled wickedly. "Fine, but I want the show you promised me."

"The show?"

Keegan made a fist but didn't have to gesture crudely for Kerry to get the point. "You know the one."

A dark blush swept over Kerry's tanned cheeks. "I'll give you the best show you've ever seen." It was Keegan's turn to blush, and Kerry smiled at his reaction. "Don't go anywhere. I might need kisses to tide me over until after we eat."

"Maybe for your opening act, you can tell me just how you and Sven came to be at the bar tonight," Keegan said.

As Kerry pulled leftovers from the refrigerator, he told Keegan about the conversation he had with Sven at his truck the previous night. "I didn't mean to imply he should actually follow you."

"He didn't misunderstand what you said," Keegan said.

"I'm trying to be gracious," Kerry replied before explaining Sven's frantic text from the bar. "I didn't know he'd dressed down, and I almost didn't recognize him in that getup." While the chicken and stuffing casserole reheated in the microwave, Kerry returned to the island to snag a few kisses. When the appliance beeped, Kerry captured one last kiss before returning to his task. The chicken came out, and the potatoes went in. "Do you want vegetables too?"

Keegan shook his head. "I'm sure Sven didn't expect you to be dressed up either," he said. "You look so handsome, but you always do, no matter what you're wearing." Keegan thought about Kerry wearing nothing but a pair of gym shorts, and it wasn't hard to picture him in boxers...or nothing at all.

"I wanted to look presentable when meeting with Vinny about the lawsuit. Then I threw myself into work and didn't make time to change."

"But did you eat?" Keegan asked.

"The crew brought me lunch, but I worked through dinner. I've procrastinated on paperwork for too long and needed to dig myself out of the hole. I made a big dent today, and I feel productive." Kerry stepped between Keegan's thighs and cupped his face. "Not as good as this makes me feel, though."

"Thank you for riding to the rescue," Keegan said.

Kerry brushed back the hair from Keegan's forehead and traced the shell of his ear. "I'll always be there for you. No matter what."

The microwave dinged, and Keegan was ready to forget all about food until he remembered the way Kerry's stomach had growled.

Kerry retrieved the mashed potatoes, gave it a vigorous stir, and looked down into the bowl. "Maybe I should reheat these a little longer."

"I'd eat them frozen if it means your shirt comes off faster."

Kerry's head snapped up, and a wicked smile spread across his handsome face. "Yeah?" He set the bowl on the counter and went to work on his shirt buttons. "You can gawk while I heat them up some more." Kerry peeled the shirt off and tossed it on the island but remained out of touching range.

Keegan watched the play of muscles under that gorgeous, inked skin as Kerry put the dish back in the microwave and shut the door. Either it took more muscles than he realized to push buttons on an appliance, or Kerry was flexing for show. Keegan just knew he wanted to touch that warm skin. "Come over here."

Kerry looked over his shoulder, a hint of a wicked smile curving his lips. "Huh-uh. I'll burn the potatoes."

"Then they likely didn't need to go back in the microwave," Keegan said. "Come over here." When Kerry didn't make a move to comply, Keegan pulled his shirt over his head and dropped it on the island.

*Ding.* "Dinner's ready."

Kerry made no move to open the microwave. He stalked the short distance between them and gathered Keegan in his arms. Kerry's body heat enveloped him as his kiss devoured Keegan's mouth. Their hands moved again, sliding over bare skin and taut muscles. Keegan learned the sharp curve of Kerry's shoulder blades and the smooth flesh between them. He traced the lines of ink he couldn't see and learned the surprising places that made Kerry gasp, like the sensitive skin under his armpits or the area just under his rib cage. Keegan wanted to move his hands around to learn the curve of Kerry's chest, but he didn't want to draw away from him to have room for exploration. Damn, he could really get used to having Kerry's body against his, over his, and hopefully inside his soon.

As if the universe had plans to fuck him over, a phone rang shrilly from the vicinity of Kerry's pants.

A savage growl erupted from Kerry's lips when he broke their kiss. "No, no, no." He took a few breaths while the phone rang a second and third time. Kerry lifted the phone from his pocket and accepted the call. "Hart." His gruff voice betrayed his displeasure, and Keegan felt sorry for the person on the other end of the connection. "Holy shit, Curtis." Kerry stepped away from Keegan and headed out of the room. "I need to change clothes, but I'll be there as soon as possible." Kerry disappeared out of sight, but Keegan could easily hear his end of the conversation as Kerry gathered more information on his way upstairs. "I'm only twenty minutes away." Kerry continued discussing the equipment and tools he wanted on site.

Keegan grabbed his shirt and pulled it on over his head, and then he returned the leftovers to the refrigerator. Kerry returned to the kitchen by the time he finished, and he looked at Keegan with genuine regret. "Maybe the universe is telling us something," Keegan said.

"The universe is telling us that semitruck drivers shouldn't drink their weight in beer and then get behind the wheel of a deadly weapon," Kerry said. A wry expression formed on his handsome face. "Bet good ole Frank wishes he hadn't sent me that email this afternoon."

"Sounds like an interesting story."

"And I'll tell you all about it later." Kerry snagged Keegan around the waist and pulled him in close for a quick kiss. "You and I are just getting started. I'll call you later if I finish the job at a decent time."

"Bye, Betty," Keegan called out. "It was nice meeting you." She cracked open one eye but otherwise didn't acknowledge him. "She hates me."

Kerry chuckled. "Betty's crazy about you. She just might not know it yet." He walked Keegan to his truck and kissed him one last time. "Be careful going home."

"You be careful too." Keegan got in his truck but poked his head back out and hollered, "And make sure you eat something."

He waited for Kerry to back out first before following. When Kerry reached the road, he turned on the emergency light bar on top of his truck. Keegan followed at a slower pace, and it wasn't long before Kerry's truck disappeared. He hoped the interruption wasn't an omen of things to come.

# *Chapter*
# EIGHT

ONLY THE MAGNITUDE OF THE EMERGENCY CALL KEPT Kerry's thoughts from wandering to Keegan and the scary territory they'd entered. An inebriated semitruck driver had fallen asleep while driving over a busy bridge. He'd jerked awake when the front right side of his bumper scraped along the side of the bridge, overcorrected, and lost control of the semitruck hauling a trailer full of goods. He'd gone left of center and crashed through the steel-enforced concrete barrier rail on the opposite side of the bridge. The only thing that kept the truck from plummeting hundreds of feet into the river below was the trailer wedged between the bridge's steel cantilever arms. According to Curtis, his crew captain, the truck cab was dangling over the side of the bridge. Rescuing the driver meant lowering someone down to the driver's-side door and hauling the man back up. Kerry was that someone.

It seemed ole Frank Tallus wasn't so damn concerned about nepotism when his new buddy Chuck couldn't get the job done. Frank had given him a bullshit excuse just hours ago about why Hart's Creek Township was looking at other companies to fill their contractual needs. Now wasn't the time for Kerry to point out the error of Frank's ways, but they'd definitely have a lot to discuss after he got the driver to safety and his team prevented the semi from plunging into the river. Traffic was backed up for a few miles, but Kerry's emergency lights and assistance from responding officers helped him get to the barricaded bridge without incident. Several news vans were parked nearby, and their crews were giving live reports. The number of officers and crew on the bridge testified to the severity of the ordeal. An officer moved his patrol car long enough for Kerry to drive up to the action.

He parked near Curtis's massive rescue truck and greeted his crew, who were busy implementing the tasks their captain had assigned them. Curtis had broken their men into two teams—one to rescue the driver and the other to haul the vehicle safely back onto the bridge. They probably wouldn't have needed Kerry at all if not for the bit about someone dangling over the side of the bridge to rescue the driver. Kerry had a lot of experience with rappelling, climbing, and skydiving, so heights didn't usually bother him. He'd never hung from a harness over the side of a bridge, but he trusted his crew implicitly. Awareness made his scalp tingle, and Kerry knew without looking that Chuck was nearby. He'd felt the weight of the man's hateful stare enough to pick it out of a crowd, but it seemed especially malicious beneath the floodlights his crew had rigged to illuminate the scene.

"Are you about ready for me?" Kerry asked Curtis.

"Almost, boss." He glanced up from double-checking the rigging on the harness Kerry would wear. "I thought ole Frank and Chuck were going to come to blows."

Kerry grinned and clapped him on the shoulder. "Can't wait to hear all about it. I think this rescue calls for a trip to the Greasy Spoon after we leave here." It would be hours before they cleared the accident, so their options would be limited. The Greasy Spoon catered to long-haul truckers, emergency responders, and anyone unfortunate enough to work the night shift. It might not be his favorite place to eat, but they served strong coffee, crispy bacon, and waffles the size of Kerry's head. "My treat," he added.

"Even better." Curtis gave the rigging a solid tug and extended it to Kerry. "It's ready for you, boss."

Kerry quirked a brow as he accepted the gear. "Would you send your mother over the side of the bridge in this harness?"

Curtis scrunched his face in concentration. "Absolutely." His captain was the king of mama's boys, so that boosted Kerry's confidence.

"That's good enough for me," Kerry said before donning the harness and safety equipment. The crew overseeing the driver's rescue checked his rigging one last time. Curtis handed him a safety helmet and earned a snarl. "What good is that going to do me if I plummet into the river?"

"He's just afraid the helmet will obscure his face from the news cameras," Curtis told the crew. "You can put it on the driver's head during the ascension," Curtis said. "Give them a good view of your face."

A cop approached them with a cell phone pressed to his ear. "The rescue team is suited up and getting ready to come down, sir. I need you to stay calm just a while longer." So he'd been tasked with keeping the driver calm. The cop lowered the phone to mid-chest. "We almost ready here? The driver has been stranded for nearly forty minutes now."

"We're good to go," Kerry said, though he wanted to point out that there wouldn't have been a big delay if they'd contacted his rescue crew in the first place instead of Chuck the Fuck Up. "I'm doing a last check, then I'll head over." The cop walked away, and Kerry faced his crew. "Let's do this. Nice and steady, fellas."

A loud metal creak came from the big rig, and the trailer gave a violent shake. Hysterical screaming came from the side of the bridge as the trapped driver panicked. And who could blame him? Semitrailers weren't built to withstand this kind of pressure. They were built to haul things, not anchor heavy semi cabs.

"Scratch that," Kerry said. "Get me down there as fast as you can before this guy loses his cool and makes things worse."

Kerry crossed to the side of the bridge and assessed the distance down to the driver's door. Broken sobs came from the truck, and Kerry realized that keeping the driver calm might be the biggest challenge. "Hang on, buddy. I'm coming down for you right now."

He swung a leg over the barrier rail and then the other. He carefully turned around so he could keep his eyes on the truck cab while his crew lowered him down. Beyond the reach of the spotlight, the world was completely black. Kerry couldn't see the river, but he heard the rushing water below. He kept his breathing nice and even as he began his descent. The first few feet were the most nerve-racking. Kerry enjoyed skydiving at sunrise, but dangling over a river took a toll on his brain. He battled back his fear with deep breaths and by communicating with the driver.

"Not much longer now. Only about five more feet," Kerry called out. "What's your name?"

"R-r-r-onnie," came the nervous reply. "Ronnie Pettigrew."

"It's nice to meet you, Ronnie," Kerry said. "Here's what's going to happen. In a few feet, I'm going to tell you to open your truck door."

"N-n-no w-w-way," Ronnie stammered. "I'll fall out."

Kerry understood his hesitance, but he needed to move him past his fear. "I either pull you out and up through an open door, or I pull you out through the window. The first way is much easier and won't shake the truck cab nearly as much. You heard that creaking, Ronnie. That trailer is what's holding you in place. We need to avoid unnecessary vibrations." By the time he finished his spiel, Kerry was almost to the door. "Look in your side mirror. Do you see me?"

Ronnie turned his head and met Kerry's gaze in the mirror. "Yeah."

"I know what I'm doing, Ronnie. Listen to what I say, and we're both going home tonight. Okay?"

The guy nodded vigorously, then widened his eyes in alarm. Kerry could tell he was worried the jerky movement would be his doom. And it could be if they didn't act fast. "Yes."

The truck released another loud groan of protest that made Kerry very uncomfortable. "I have a crew working to stabilize the trailer, Ronnie. I want you to focus on what I'm saying. Okay?"

"Yes, sir."

"Is your seat belt on?" Kerry asked.

"Y-y-yes."

"Good. Leave it on. Open the door for me, Ronnie. You don't have to push it open wide. Just unlatch it and let me do the rest of the work."

The front end of the truck sustained a lot of damage, but the driver's door released without incident. "Good job. Just hang tight." Once he was level with the door, Kerry offered the man what he thought was a reassuring smile. Ronnie still held his cell phone to his ear, and Kerry asked him to disconnect and give his full attention to the rescue. "I've got some safety gear we're going to put on you, Ronnie. I'll attach your harness to mine before we release your seat belt." The driver shook his head, but Kerry kept talking. "My crew will pull us up together."

"Just haul the truck back up onto the bridge," Ronnie said. "That's what the cop said the other guy was going to do."

Kerry knew the identity of the "other guy" without being told. Chuck hadn't learned a damn thing from his previous mistake, but at least someone had been smart enough to stop him before he killed someone with his stupidity. Kerry carefully opened the driver's-side door and laid the harness on Ronnie's lap. The driver stared down at it and recoiled like Kerry had set a venomous snake there instead. Another metallic protest from above emphasized that Kerry didn't have time to coddle Ronnie or debate with him. He put a little starch in his voice and said, "Listen up, Ronnie. The first responders didn't go with the other guy's idea because it sucked. I'm down here for a reason, and that's because I'm the best at what I do. Do you want the best?"

Ronnie swallowed hard. "Yes, sir."

"Good." Kerry offered encouragements as he efficiently helped Ronnie put on the harness. The driver trembled with fear, but he didn't protest one time. Kerry double-checked the fit and security of the safety gear. He practically climbed into the cab so he could tether Ronnie to himself. The integrated seat belt kept Ronnie secure in the chair, but it was also in the way. There'd been no way to work around it unless Ronnie had wanted to take off the seat belt while donning the harness. That was a risk Kerry hadn't been able to afford.

"How are you going to get me out around this?" Ronnie asked frantically.

Kerry pulled the knife from his utility belt. "I'm not." He sliced through the polyester fabric with the razor-sharp blade. "I know this is scary and probably awkward, but our ascent will be easier if you wrap your arms around my neck and stay calm. Ready?"

Ronnie blew out a breath, and the alcohol fumes made Kerry's eyes water. The guy was facing a world of legal troubles, but he surely preferred that to the alternative. Ronnie eased closer and placed his arms around Kerry's neck. "Don't get any ideas."

"You're not my type," Kerry assured him.

That made Ronnie laugh, and Kerry gave his crew verbal and physical signals to pull them up. His passenger squirmed a little as soon as they cleared the cab, but he settled down with a stern admonishment.

"This is too high," Ronnie said, his voice sounding suspiciously queasy. "I might shit my pants."

"I can't believe you didn't do that when you went over the bridge," Kerry replied.

"I pissed a little, but my bowels held up."

*Let's fucking keep it that way.* "Don't look down," Kerry cautioned. "Either keep your eyes on me or look up at the bridge so you can gauge how close we are getting to it. Listen to the steady voices calling out commands and working hard to pull us to safety." As if the universe decided to have a little fun at Kerry's expense, a big gust of wind kicked up and made them sway from side to side.

"Oh no." It was the only warning Kerry got before Ronnie barfed all over him.

The hot, noxious fluid seeped into Kerry's clothes, and the stench made him gag. Bilious acid blazoned a trail up Kerry's esophagus, and he might've puked, too, if he'd eaten anything since lunch. Kerry swallowed the bitter bile back down and breathed through his mouth, hoping it would stave off a potential chain reaction.

"I'm so sorry," Ronnie said before bursting into sobs.

"Easy now, buddy. How are your bowels holding up?" Kerry hoped a little dark humor would take the guy's mind off his shame, but it only made him cry harder. Christ, Kerry hoped he hadn't shitted himself too. He didn't mean to make the guy feel worse than he already did. Would Ronnie sue him too? Accuse Kerry of verbally abusing him during the rescue? "Hang in there. It's almost over."

Ronnie looked up, his face covered in tears, snot, and vomit. His red eyes widened in surprise. "We're almost there."

A few more feet and they'd be even with the bottom of the bridge. A few more after that, and the crew would pull them up and over the railing. Kerry would've breathed an enormous sigh of relief if the stench of vomit wouldn't make him sick.

"Did I hurt anyone?" Ronnie asked solemnly. "I don't remember hitting anyone before I went over the side of the bridge."

"I just arrived minutes after I descended to you, but I didn't see any damaged cars on the bridge. I think you got lucky, man."

Ronnie sniffled and nodded. "This is the wake-up call I needed to get sober." He must've realized how it sounded and grimaced. "This must be the rock bottom I've heard so much about."

Kerry considered the rocky bottom of the river flowing beneath them and was grateful Ronnie hadn't literally hit it. He wasn't in a position to counsel anyone on their habits and coping mechanisms. Kerry's vice used to be engaging in meaningless sex to avoid forming attachments. And yeah, he thought about the habit in past tense because he would find healthier ways to deal with his childhood trauma. The harness jolted, and Ronnie's hold around Kerry's neck tightened. But first, he needed to survive the rescue.

"Ease up," Kerry groused.

"Sorry. Sorry." Ronnie loosened his grip but didn't let go until the crew grabbed their rigging and hoisted them both up and over the railing. "Holy fuck. We made it," Ronnie said when their feet landed on solid ground. Then, he promptly fainted and slumped against Kerry.

"This was not the cuddling I had in mind tonight," Kerry told Curtis.

The EMTs rushed in and checked on Ronnie's condition as Kerry's crew worked to separate the man from Kerry. Ronnie's pulse was strong, and he came around immediately, but the EMTs insisted he get checked out at the nearest hospital. Kerry wished the man well and walked away on trembling legs. There was a ton they still needed to do to secure the truck and haul it back on the bridge. Kerry wouldn't do that soaked in Ronnie's vomit. He walked to his truck and removed a spare change of clothes. Not caring who was watching, Kerry stripped down to his boxers and used the sanitizing wipes to clean himself off. The stringent alcohol smell was a welcome reprieve.

The same officer who'd approached him earlier walked toward him, carrying a red bag with a hazardous material symbol all over it. It reminded him that one round of wipes wouldn't be enough. Kerry thanked him and placed his ruined clothes and wipes into the bag. The cop was young, handsome, and didn't hide the interest in his light blue gaze. Kerry had met more than a few of his hookups this way, but those days were over.

He completed his second round of wipes, tossed them in the bag, and sealed it. "Appreciate it." Kerry returned the bag with a neutral smile that diffused the interest in the other man's eyes. The cop offered a polite nod and left Kerry to get dressed.

Adrenaline took control of his nervous system now that the worst of the danger was behind him. Kerry hadn't dwelled on all the things that could've gone wrong while dangling over the side of the bridge. His complete focus had been on rescuing the truck driver. Kerry's hands shook as he stepped into a clean pair of pants and fastened them around his hips. They still had to haul the rig up and back over the side and clean up the debris, so he cycled through deep breaths to settle his nerves and steady his limbs.

Heavy footsteps rapidly approached, and Kerry knew who they belonged to without looking. He'd felt a not-so-sudden disturbance in the force. Those weighted feet belonged to a man who'd bitten off more than he could chew…again, but the burdens Chuck wore around his neck like an albatross weren't Kerry's fault. And his days of playing Mr. Nice Guy were over, though Kerry had no intention of allowing Chuck to draw him into an argument with news crews loitering around and the freaking lawsuit hovering over his head.

"Always gotta show your ass, don't you?"

Chuck's sneering voice nearly canceled out Kerry's good intentions, so he thought of the way Keegan looked sitting in his kitchen, his lips swollen from their kisses. He bought himself a few more moments by slipping on a long-sleeve thermal shirt with his company logo on it. The temperature was dropping, and Kerry didn't plan to leave until the rest of the crew did. He snagged a clean service shirt and slid his right arm into it as he turned to face Chuck.

"I think what you meant to say was that I'm always coming along to clean up your mistakes. At least someone got smart enough to stop you this time." Kerry slid his left arm through the other sleeve and met Chuck's menacing gaze as he buttoned the front. He'd rather miss a buttonhole than react slowly to a sucker punch from his former employee. Frank Tallus approached them, but Kerry kept his gaze on Chuck instead of acknowledging the trustee. "I'd appreciate it if you and your crew would clear out so my guys can finish our work," Kerry said.

Chuck took two more steps forward and jabbed the air with his finger. "Listen here, hotshot. You didn't call me down to the scene, and you won't ask me to leave it." Chuck got in Kerry's face and opened his mouth to say more, but Frank slapped a hand on his shoulder and forcefully pulled him back.

"I called you here," the trustee said, "and I'm telling you to leave. You could've killed that guy tonight, Chuck. I can't believe I considered giving your company an exclusive contract. Temporary insanity is the only logical explanation."

"Bullshit," Chuck snarled. "In the time it took this asshole to arrive and suit up, I could've safely hauled the truck and driver to safety."

Frank pointed toward one end of the barricaded bridge. "I want you out of here now, and I won't hesitate to call an officer over here to make sure it happens."

Chuck spat a glob of tobacco juice at Frank's feet before turning his glower at Kerry. "This isn't over."

"Actually, it is," Kerry replied calmly. "You had a chance at redemption but shot yourself in the foot at the first opportunity. You have no one to blame but yourself. I'd like to offer a piece of friendly advice, Chuck. Be very mindful of what you say about me, my company, and my business practices. I won't hesitate to take legal action to protect my reputation."

"Fuck you," he snarled before stomping away.

"Not my type," Kerry said under his breath before he turned his attention to the trustee. "Don't wait too long to send over my signed contract, Frank. I'm starting to think I don't charge enough for my services."

"It's already sitting in your inbox," Frank said. "I'd already gathered the necessary signatures at the last budget meeting before Chuck approached me. I thought I'd give the idiot a trial run." He huffed out a breath before scrubbing a hand over his face. "I knew I'd made a mistake within the first five minutes of his arrival. I emailed your signed contract as soon as I had to call your dispatcher and grovel."

Kerry checked his phone and saw that he had an email from Frank in his inbox. "We all make mistakes. At least this one wasn't fatal."

Raised voices from across the bridge caught his attention. His crew was hard at work attaching cables to the rear of the truck cab. They'd positioned heavy-duty service vehicles at both corners and hooked the thick winching cables to the corners. The teams worked in tandem and communicated with the winch operators at the rescue rigs. Kerry was immensely proud of his team and excused himself from Frank to join them. The semi cab was heavy, and the first several moments were wrought with tension as metal and fiberglass protested the rescue attempt. Gravity was a hellacious beast to battle, but the tide turned in their favor once they got the truck's rear tires onto the asphalt. The truck worked with them instead of against them. Metal and debris broke off the damaged front end of the truck and fell into the river below, but everyone cheered when the mostly intact truck rolled to a stop on the bridge. Both the semitruck and trailer had sustained too much damage to be roadworthy, but his heavy-duty tow trucks could safely haul them away.

The cleanup was a massive effort, but his guys worked fast and efficiently. The promise of a hearty breakfast probably didn't hurt things. By the time they reached the Greasy Spoon, his tow truck drivers had already unloaded the wrecked truck and trailer and beat them to the small diner. The place was practically empty, so they pushed two tables together and settled in for one hell of a tasty meal. The server approached their tables, and Kerry had to do a double take because he had a build like Keegan's and even had a similar coloring. The eyes assessing Kerry were a cool green and not the warm hazel he craved.

"Hello, fellas." The server gazed around the group before stopping at Kerry again. "I'm Joey, and I'll be taking care of you tonight." Kerry didn't miss the sly grins and exchanged glances between his crew. This wasn't their first rodeo, but the outcome would differ vastly from what they expected. Joey tore his gaze away from Kerry and gave the other guys his attention again. "Are you familiar with the menu, or would you like recommendations?"

"We're ready," Curtis said, rubbing his hands together in glee. "This is going to cost ya, boss."

Kerry chuckled and shook his head. "Money well spent."

Joey watched their byplay and started taking orders at the opposite end of the table. He quickly learned that they were Greasy Spoon experts by the time he reached Kerry, who he'd saved for last. "And you, handsome?"

117

By this point, it had been over twelve hours since his last meal. "I'll have the trucker's breakfast platter and a side of biscuits and gravy."

Joey looked up from jotting down the order. "That's a lot of food."

"He's a lot of man," Curtis said.

Kerry threw him a warning glance before smiling at Joey. "And a large orange juice, please."

The server blinked a few times before he continued making notes. He took a few steps back and crashed into the empty table behind him. Joey's cheeks turned pink, and he laughed nervously. "I'll just turn your orders in. It won't be long."

The crew waited for Joey to leave before they started razzing Kerry in low voices. He took their good-natured teasing but steered the conversation to the pending lawsuit, Chuck's blustering remarks, and Frank's change of heart about the contract renewal. This was the first they'd heard about any of it, and they hung on to his every word until the food arrived. Joey brought a young lady from the kitchen to help him pass out the plates. Her gaze bounced between Kerry and Joey as the pair worked in tandem around the table. The attention wasn't subtle, but Kerry didn't acknowledge or encourage it. Keegan might not be waiting for him at home, but his little lamb had one hell of a death grip on Kerry's battered heart.

The servers shared a giggle as they left the crew alone to devour their food. Kerry's plate was overflowing with bacon, sausage, scrambled eggs, hash browns, grits, and two split biscuits smothered in sausage gravy. He second-guessed his ability to eat it all until he bit into a crispy strip of bacon. Next thing he knew, Kerry was using a stolen piece of toast to mop up the last bit of gravy. He shoved his empty plate away and held up his hands like a victor in a major battle. Kerry's digestive system was probably going to punish him for his wicked ways, but he was going to savor the meal until then.

Joey returned with the check and a smile for Kerry. The crew watched expectantly as Kerry pulled cash from his wallet to cover the bill and a generous tip. He didn't write his phone number down on the slip or attempt to get Joey's. He simply thanked him for a wonderful meal and scooted his chair back from the table.

"Wow," Curtis said once they reached the parking lot. "Is your eyesight going bad? It's not like you to miss all those signals."

"I didn't miss anything," Kerry replied. "Just not interested."

The crew stopped and gaped at him as if he'd confessed to being a vampire. They looked among each other, their confusion etched on their faces, before awareness dawned slowly.

"Who is he?" Curtis asked.

Kerry shook his head as he walked to his truck. "Good night, fellas."

He could hear their excited chatter as they tried to figure out who had snagged Kerry's attention. They'd find out soon enough, but until then, Kerry wanted to have Keegan all to himself. The toll of the past few days caught up to him during his trip home. Kerry sighed in relief when he pulled into his driveway and wasted no time heading upstairs to his room. He took a scalding hot shower and tried not to recall the driver getting sick on him, especially with such a full stomach. A shower usually woke up his deprived dick, but even it was too damn tired.

Kerry dried off and slid between the sheets. He closed his eyes and allowed his brain to play a new set of what-ifs, this time imagining what might've happened if the emergency phone call hadn't interrupted them. Kerry got as far as stripping Keegan down to his underwear before he crashed.

*Chapter*
# NINE

**K**EEGAN WAS USED TO KERRY OCCUPYING HIS WAKING thoughts each morning, but he typically starred in carnal roles. Those lustful feels were still there, but they'd taken a back seat to Keegan's concern about his well-being. He checked his phone to see if he'd slept through a text, but he hadn't missed a notification. Kerry had said he wouldn't call or text if the rescue ran late, but Keegan would've preferred interrupted sleep to wondering if Kerry was okay.

He'd never fretted like this before, at least not on a nauseating scale. Was it because he was on the cusp of achieving his impossible dream after months of pining, wishing, and hoping? Doubt, small but persistent, urged caution. Kerry's swift attitude reversal could spin out of his favor just as quickly. Maybe a part of Keegan would always wait for someone to yank the rug out from under him, but that wasn't how he wanted to live.

Instead, he focused on the sincere expression in those dark eyes and the blatant arousal Kerry had felt for him. An answering heat stirred low in his belly, but he would not fuck his fist if there was a chance he could have the real thing soon. Keegan debated on a reasonable time to text Kerry. He didn't want to wake him up, but he didn't want to come across as inattentive either. What was the correct level of eagerness and concern?

Groaning, Keegan threw back the covers and swung his legs out of bed. "Pull it together, Kee. You barely made it to first base with the guy, and you're ready to rush over there and check him for cuts and bruises." He snorted so hard it hurt. "Yeah, that's the reason I want to wake Kerry up." Keegan looked in the bathroom mirror and noted the smirk on his face. "Two things can be true at the same time," he told his reflection.

If that fucker talked back to him, Keegan would check himself into the nearest hospital. His sanity might be in question, but the sentiment rang true. Keegan wanted to assure himself that Kerry was safe and wrap himself around the man like a second skin. He decided ten o'clock was a reasonable time to text Kerry and went about his morning routine. Keegan spent longer on his hair than he normally would, but he liked the result.

His gaze landed on a message he'd printed and taped on the wall next to his mirror. Keegan had found the unicorn-themed graphic in a queer support group on Facebook. The bright colors might've caught his attention, but it was the words that touched his soul. *I am queer. I am worthy. I am beautiful. I am loved.* These affirmations had been a game changer and a lifesaver, and he repeated them every morning. Keegan looked in the mirror, adjusted his posture, and said the words out loud before he left his bedroom.

Rory and Harry were sipping coffee and looking at something on a laptop when he entered the kitchen. The ingredients for an amazing breakfast were spread before them on the kitchen island. The smell of baking bread or pastry tickled Keegan's nose and made his mouth water. He detected hints of berries and citrus, and that piqued his interest even more. Harry and Rory looked up at the same time and wore matching curious expressions. He'd mistakenly told a few of the guys that he was going on a date, which meant everyone on the ranch knew it. Harry and Rory looked especially bright-eyed and bushy-tailed when they noticed him.

Harry set her coffee cup down and rounded the island to reach for his arm. "Tell me. How'd it go?"

"The date was a complete disaster," Keegan replied without preamble.

"Oh no," Harry said with a frown. "I'm so sorry."

Rory took another sip of coffee as he assessed him. "You don't seem very upset about it."

Keegan shrugged and said, "He's not the one for me."

Harry rubbed his arm. "That's a great attitude to have, honey. The right guy will come along and scoop you right up."

Rory set his cup down and narrowed his eyes. "Our sweet Keegan isn't upset because he knows he's already met his special guy."

Keegan silently implored his body not to betray him and give away his thoughts, but it didn't listen. The telltale heat started in his chest and spread up to his face. His kitchen cohorts noticed and responded with the standard *oohs* and *aahs*. "The night wasn't a total bust, and that's all I'm willing to say right now."

Harry's delicate features formed an angelic expression, but Keegan didn't buy it. "I'm making the blueberry and lemon crumble muffin recipe you found." Her right brow arched up slightly. "Maybe you'd like to be the first to try them."

Keegan was a real tramp for anything with blueberries and lemon and would absolutely sing for his pastries. The words flew from his mouth so fast that Harry and Rory barely had time to process the horror of his date before he was gushing about Kerry's heroics. He didn't give them time to swoon over the sexiness before he had them laughing about Sven's antics. But then he reached the part in the evening where he followed Kerry home, and his words came to an abrupt halt. Keegan reached up and touched his lips. His mouth hadn't looked different in the mirror, but it felt changed. He hadn't just shared simple kisses with

Kerry. They were…they were…transformative. Was this how a butterfly felt after breaking free from its cocoon?

"Oh, honey," Harry said, throwing her arms around Keegan. "I was only teasing you. I'd never force you to talk about anything before you were ready."

Rory looked worried too, and Keegan wondered what he'd said to evoke these reactions. He sidled up and hugged Harry and Keegan, forming a small huddle in the kitchen. "If that Danny ever bothers you again, you won't need to wait for Kerry to ride to your rescue. Ivan and I will fuck him up. Have you seen my man? He's built like a Viking, and the littlest sneer renders a person useless." Rory pulled back, and malice shimmered in his light blue eyes. "And then I will use my cyber skills to destroy Danny."

"I know you will, Ro." Keegan squeezed his arm and kissed Harry's cheek. "Tell me what I can do to help with breakfast."

That seemed to prod the two back into action. Harry ran the kitchen like a general who prepared for every eventuality. She put Keegan in charge of making the Denver scrambled eggs and assigned Rory the home fries and breakfast meats while she went to work on a crêpe batter. With the three of them working in tandem, breakfast came together quickly and without a hitch. Harry handed him a blueberry muffin from the pastry basket, and he didn't bother with token resistance. He pulled the biggest crumble off the top and popped it into his mouth. Brown sugar, cinnamon, and a subtle hint of lemon made him do a happy dance right there in the kitchen. Harry giggled at his antics and encouraged him to take an actual bite. Keegan's phone chimed with an incoming text just as he lifted the muffin to his eager mouth.

Harry waggled her brows. "Someone is eager to talk to you this morning."

"Better not be Danny." Rory crossed his arms over his chest and looked prepared to do battle.

Keegan hoped Kerry had texted him, but it seemed awfully early for that, unless he was just finishing the job. But that seemed doubtful.

Keegan sighed and retrieved his phone instead of biting into his muffin. "It's a text from Sven. What's he doing up so early?" His friend was a night owl who wouldn't see his first salon client until late morning. Sven should still be dreaming of all the beautiful men he hadn't kissed yet.

"Only one way to find out," Harry said, adding a gentle elbow nudge to go with the verbal one.

Keegan tapped on the message and frowned as he read, *You better talk to your man about setting thirst traps.* A video link popped up beneath the message. The caption read: Jaw-dropping heroics from a local hottie. Keegan's stomach cramped, and he debated playing the video. The clip came from a social media page and not an affiliated news channel, though the cover image showed a reporter standing on a bridge with a semitruck partially dangling over the side of a bridge. The local hottie part rubbed Keegan the wrong way, but it was the jaw-dropping heroics part that gave him pause. He knew Kerry's job was dangerous without watching video proof. He must've stared at his phone too long because his kitchen comrades moved closer to see what he was looking at.

"Are you going to watch the video?" Rory asked.

Keegan chewed on his bottom lip as he considered his options. Curiosity got the better of him, and he tapped the link to play the video.

"Thank goodness," Harry whispered. "Saves me from finding it later."

Rory and Keegan chuckled, but their merriment turned to gasps when the video zoomed in on the truck's perilous position on the bridge. In the background, a reporter gave her viewers a summary of the timeline, starting with the accident and what she described as a major disagreement between law enforcement and the first rescue crew that responded. The camera panned to the right, and the reporter's arm came into view as she pointed at the newest arrival.

Keegan would've recognized Kerry without seeing the logo on the vehicle or hearing it from the reporter. The video cut to a different scene, one where a man in a harness went over the side of the bridge and the reporter again stated the obvious perils. The camera zoomed in to capture the intensity in Kerry's expression as his crew lowered him closer to the truck. He was saying something to the driver, but the microphones were too far away to capture his words.

"He's so brave," Harry said.

"And smoking hot," Rory added.

Metallic grinding and groaning noises came from the truck, and Keegan squeezed his eyes shut. "I don't think I can watch this."

A small hand rested between his shoulder blades and rubbed soothing circles. "You know there's a happy ending, or Sven wouldn't have sent it to you," Harry said.

Keegan nodded and opened his eyes again, but his heart raced a mile a minute as he watched Kerry rescue the driver and haul him up to safety. Harry had to remind him to breathe a few times as they watched the action unfold. The trio groaned in unison when the rescued driver vomited on Kerry. "There goes my appetite," Keegan complained.

But then the footage skipped forward to a view of Kerry stripping down to his underwear at the side of his truck. Heat and want flared to life inside Keegan.

"Oh my," the reporter said breathlessly.

Rory snorted. "Someone sounds thirsty."

"Indeed," Harry said, though she sounded a little breathless too.

Video proof of Kerry's survival wasn't enough. The urge to see, touch, and taste him grabbed Keegan by the heart in an unrelenting grip. He swiped up to dismiss the text thread and tucked his phone away. "I need to go."

Rory hummed approvingly while Harry burst into frenzied motion, wrapping food in foil or placing it in storage containers. She darted into the pantry and returned with a picnic basket.

"Going somewhere?" Rory teased.

"I'm not, but Keegan is." She looked up from her work and smiled at him. "I don't want you showing up on his doorstep empty-handed."

Rory snorted. "Your cooking is incredible, but it will be the last thing on Kerry's mind if Keegan shows up on his doorstep looking like that." He circled his forefinger in Keegan's direction.

"Look like what?" Keegan gazed down at his jeans and red hoodie. There was nothing enticing about his chosen wardrobe.

"Oh honey," Harry said. "It's your expression, not the clothes on your body."

Keegan darted around the corner of the kitchen and studied his reflection in the hall mirror. His cheeks looked flushed, and the expression in his hazel eyes was… Well, he didn't know. He'd never really noticed it before now. His pupils seemed bigger, and he looked…hungry. Keegan blinked, but the yearning was still there. Acknowledging the hunger only intensified the sensations elsewhere, as if his body had truly come alive for the first time. Was he crazy to get in his truck and drive to Kerry's house? And to do what? Feed him breakfast? Keegan cocked his head to acknowledge it was a good icebreaker. He turned back toward the kitchen before he could talk himself out of it and nearly ran into Harry as she rounded the corner with the basket in one hand and a thermos of coffee in the other.

She handed both things to him and rose on her tiptoes to kiss his cheek. "Drive carefully, and do not hurry back." She winked cheekily. "I'll be mighty disappointed if you do."

"Should I leave a note for Cash?" Keegan was eager as hell to get to Kerry's house, but he didn't want to let down the man who'd gone to bat for him in ways no one else ever had. He cycled through the things he'd planned to do but couldn't think of anything so pressing it couldn't wait a few hours.

"I'll tell him when he comes to breakfast." She gave Keegan an impish grin. "The boss knows a thing or two about living in the moment. I promise he won't be upset with you."

"Thank you for this," Keegan said, lifting the basket and thermos. "I don't know how any of us would make it without you."

Harry dismissed the idea with a wave before turning back toward her kitchen. "Don't forget your boots, honey," she called out.

Keegan glanced down at his socked feet and laughed. He absolutely would've walked straight out the door in his haste to get to Kerry's house. Keegan stopped at the door long enough to slide his feet into his boots before heading outside. A cacophony of distant voices warned that the rest of the crew was walking to the ranch house for breakfast, so he moved his feet faster to avoid them and their probing questions. He made it to the truck and was backing out of his parking spot before his friends emerged from the shadows and stepped into the circles of light cast from the porch sconces. He gave them a quick wave before driving away. He met Rueben on the long driveway and kept going instead of stopping to talk. His best friend would want to know where he was going before the sun was up, and telling Rueben might force Keegan to reevaluate his actions. He'd spent two years analyzing everything he'd ever said or done, and for once, he just wanted to follow his instincts.

Later, Keegan wouldn't remember the rest of the drive to Kerry's house. His next vivid memory was of standing on the porch and trying to decide if he should just ring the bell or call Kerry. Keegan set the thermos and basket down on the porch and fished his phone from his pocket.

"Hey, Kee." Kerry's sleepy voice sent a zing of longing straight to Keegan's groin. His breath hitched, and Kerry sounded more alert when he said, "Is everything okay?"

Keegan willed his racing heart to calm down. "That depends."

"On?"

"How you feel about me showing up on your porch unannounced… with a basket full of goodies?"

"Like Little Red Riding Hood?"

"Well, I drove over a creek and through the woods." Keegan considered for a second. "But there's nothing grandmotherly about you."

"Wait! Are you here now?" Rustling fabric came through their connection, followed by hasty footsteps on a hard surface.

"That depends," Keegan repeated.

Kerry's dark and delicious chuckle rumbled through the connection and down Keegan's spine. "This Big Bad Wolf is going to devour you." Then, he disconnected the call.

Keegan nearly lost his nerve when a light came on inside the house. The etched oval glass in the center of the door and the skinny panels on either side of it had a frosted design that blocked prying eyes while allowing light inside the house. A large, flesh-colored shape moved beyond the door, and footsteps grew louder as Kerry approached. Keegan tucked his phone away before picking up the basket and coffee but nearly dropped them again when Kerry opened the door stark naked. His hair was messy and wild around his face, and Keegan could feel the heat radiating off his hard body.

"Oh damn." Keegan sounded as breathless as the reporter from last night, and he would've clutched imaginary pearls if his hands weren't full. Too bad they weren't holding Kerry's taut balls, which were on full display. Kerry's dick hardened beneath Keegan's hungry stare. Christ, the guy was hung.

"You kind of look like Red in that hoodie," Kerry teased.

Keegan forced himself to meet Kerry's gaze, then swallowed hard at the stark hunger burning in his dark eyes. His mussed hair wildly framed his face, and his desire for Keegan was as naked as his gorgeous body. It was the exact moment that Keegan shed his doubts and embraced his instincts. "You definitely look like the Big Bad Wolf." Keegan's gaze drifted down to the dark, trimmed curls and the fully erect penis jutting forward. "Oh my. What a big dick you have."

Kerry hooked a finger in the top of Keegan's hoodie and tugged him inside the house. "The better to fuck you with."

"I brought breakfast," Keegan said nervously.

Kerry closed the door behind them and crowded Keegan against it, pinning his impressive erection between them. He cupped Keegan's face and pressed a brief kiss to his lips. "I ate enough food after the rescue to feed ten men. If you want to eat first, we can—"

"No. You're the only thing I want in my mouth right now."

Kerry's wicked smile promised Keegan wouldn't regret his decision.

He reached down and relieved Keegan of his burdens and took a few steps back. "I'll just set these in the kitchen. You can go on up."

It would feel strange, possibly intrusive, to enter Kerry's room for the first time without him. "I'll wait."

The detour to the kitchen didn't take long, and Keegan got the chance to ogle Kerry's superior ass as he walked away. He leaned against the banister at the foot of the stairs and soaked up the view—coming and going. Keegan had heard the term "size queen" but had never associated it with himself. The length and girth of Kerry's dick should concern him, but Keegan was too eager to stretch himself around it.

"You'll make me blush," Kerry said when he joined him.

Keegan rolled his eyes and headed up the stairs. Kerry's tread sounded heavy and eager behind him, and it spurred him to move faster. As if sensing a chase, Kerry increased his pace, too, until they both jogged up the stairs. Keegan would've bolted for Kerry's room if he knew the direction. When he asked, Kerry lifted him up and over his shoulder, giving Keegan a close-up view of that rounded, muscular ass. If Kerry could take some liberties, so could he. Keegan smoothed a hand over one firm cheek and earned a hard slap against his own.

"I'm trying so hard to be good," Kerry growled. "I wanted to take you right on the stairs."

"I wouldn't have objected," Keegan said.

Kerry stopped and deposited Keegan's sweet ass on the foot of his bed. He took Keegan's face in both hands. "Do you remember what I said about consent?"

Keegan nodded vigorously. "Yes. I want this, Kerry. I want you more than I've wanted anyone or anything in my entire life."

Kerry inhaled slowly and searched Keegan's face. "I'm so far out of my depth, but I'm done fighting this." He dropped his hands and stepped back. "I'm going to brush my teeth, and I'll be right back."

Keegan reached for his hoodie, but Kerry stilled him with a growl.

"I want to do that."

Keegan dropped his hands in his lap and looked around the room.

Kerry had turned on a bedside lamp before coming downstairs, but the low-wattage bulb only illuminated a small circle near the top of the bed. He should be grateful since the darkened space would make him feel less insecure, but it also meant he wouldn't get to see as much of Kerry. Would it be presumptuous to turn on the overhead lights? A fireplace was centered on the wall opposite Kerry's bed, with a television mounted above it. Spring had arrived in Colorado, but the mornings were still chilly and damp. Keegan imagined the play of shadows and light on Kerry's body when he—

The fireplace made a soft whoosh before flames licked along the fake logs. Keegan looked over and caught Kerry watching him. He stood next to his nightstand and held a small remote. "Handy little thing," he said. "My interior designer droned on about how romantic it would be to have a fireplace in the bedroom. I told her it would be a waste of money, but she persisted. The damn fireplace is my favorite feature in here, even though I've only used it for practical purposes until now."

Kerry dropped the remote in the drawer and closed it. He stalked around the bed and stepped between Keegan's thighs. Reaching down, Kerry lifted the red hoodie up and over Keegan's head. His T-shirt followed next and landed on the floor next to the bed. Static crackled in the air, and Keegan wasn't sure if it came from his clothes or resulted from the passion surging between them. Kerry kissed him, sliding his minty-fresh tongue inside Keegan's mouth to tease and explore.

The frenzied energy from the prior evening was gone. There was no "will they, won't they" deliberation happening behind closed lids. They kissed and touched each other with the confidence of two men who'd accepted the moment had been a long time coming. Keegan might not have been a virgin, but this was the first time he embraced the carnal urges guiding his hand to wrap around Kerry's hard length.

Kerry broke their kiss with a lusty moan and rested his forehead against Keegan's. "You're still wearing too much." He stepped back long enough to remove Keegan's boots and socks, then took stock of Keegan's bright pink toenails. Kerry lifted his right leg, and Keegan fell onto his back. Kerry stroked his thumb along the arch of his foot, then nipped the big toe before sucking it between his lips. Keegan gasped at the sensual intimacy and fell deeper under Kerry's seductive spell. He slowly withdrew the toe from his mouth and grinned wolfishly as he lowered Keegan's leg. "I told you they were made for sucking."

Keegan smiled at the memory. He'd been so insecure about wearing toe polish until Kerry showed up at Lucinda's salon and pronounced his toes were made for sucking. He'd proudly showed them off with flip-flops after that.

"But now I want to suck other parts of your beautiful body." Kerry dropped to his knees between Keegan's parted thighs.

Warm lips pressed a series of kisses on Keegan's belly, and a wet tongue dipped into his navel. Kerry angled his face to brush his beard over the sensitive skin, and Keegan squirmed. Big hands landed on Keegan's thighs to hold him in place, but in a way that drove Keegan mad with desire. Kerry nuzzled his nose along Keegan's stomach, then over the front of his jeans. The pressure against his thighs eased because Kerry shifted his hands up to Keegan's waistband, where he made the simple act of slipping buttons through holes the sexiest thing Keegan had ever seen. Kerry spread the placket open to reveal Keegan's pale pink briefs with a telltale wet spot. Then he held Keegan's gaze as he leaned down and inhaled deeply.

"You smell better than I ever imagined." Kerry's husky voice turned Keegan's insides to jelly. "I don't just want to imprint your body with mine. I want to devour you until there's no you or me, just us." Kerry personified the Big Bad Wolf in that moment, but Keegan would not play the meek Little Red Riding Hood.

He reached into his underwear and pulled his dick free. The swollen head was slick with precum when he pressed it to Kerry's lips. "Get to eating, wolf."

Their gentle exploration ended in a hungry growl as Kerry sucked his dick down to the root. Keegan arched his hips up off the bed, and Kerry tugged his underwear and jeans down to mid-thigh to bare more of him. Kerry angled his head so he could watch Keegan's expression as he worked his cock up and down. Keegan's entire body shook as pleasure threatened to blow his circuits. Instead of slowing Kerry down, Keegan fisted his luxurious, wavy strands and thrust his hips, driving his dick into the eager mouth. The wet, sloppy noises Kerry made were filthy, but instead of being repulsed by his reaction, Keegan embraced the carnal desire it stirred within. The only thing Keegan resented was the denim prison surrounding his legs. He wanted to spread them wide and offer all of himself to Kerry, but he didn't want to lose Kerry's wicked mouth.

Keegan started to squirm and push his jeans down a little farther. Kerry got the hint and shifted enough to strip Keegan bare without slowing his suction down. Warm hands massaged his thighs, inching closer and closer to his groin. Kerry's thumbs brushed over his taut balls and below to Keegan's taint. The blow job continued in earnest until a curious digit brushing over Keegan's puckered entrance earned a needy whimper.

Kerry lifted his head, wet lips curving into a wicked smile. "Feel good?"

Nodding, Keegan said, "Do it again."

Kerry placed his hands under Keegan's thighs and pushed his legs up and open. His hungry gaze fell to Keegan's most intimate parts. "Look at you," Kerry said. "So fucking perfect. So pink. I want to taste you here too." Their eyes met again, and Keegan saw the unspoken question in Kerry's gaze.

Did he want this? To know what Kerry's tongue felt like against his hole? The tight clinch in his core was a resounding affirmative. "Hell yes," Keegan said.

Kerry lowered his head between Keegan's legs again, stopping to place ticklish kisses on his inner thighs. Beard hair rasped over delicate skin as Kerry inched closer to Keegan's center, making him feel alive in a way Keegan had never experienced. He nearly came out of his body when Kerry pressed a kiss just to the right of Keegan's quivering pucker. Anticipation strung him tighter than a bow when Kerry lifted his head.

Waiting for his lips to land where Keegan wanted them most made the moment drag out insufferably long.

Kerry blew over the sensitive flesh, and Keegan released the neediest whimper. And then his mouth was there, licking, teasing, and sucking Keegan's entrance. Kerry held his hips in a bruising grip as if he feared Keegan would take his treat away. A wicked, wet tongue circled his rim and wiggled into his puckered entrance. Kerry wedged his broad shoulders under Keegan's thighs and lifted him into the air. He clutched Kerry's hair in surprise, then cried out in ecstasy when Kerry wriggled his tongue and breached Keegan's hole with a savage growl.

But that was just the beginning of Kerry's erotic onslaught, and Keegan's mouth fell open in a silent scream as Kerry tongue-fucked his hole with wild abandon. His nose bumped relentlessly against Keegan's taint, and Kerry's bristled jaw rasped against Keegan's spread ass cheeks. The onslaught of sensations brought him to the precipice of climax much too soon. He wanted to feel the euphoria of an orgasm with Kerry, but not yet. That's when his guilt and recrimination could make an appearance, and he was desperate to hold on to this joy for as long as possible.

"I'm going to come if you don't stop," Keegan warned. He didn't sound nearly as panicked as he felt, but Kerry must've seen the truth in his gaze.

He withdrew his tongue and lifted his head. "Then I'll just make you come again." The simple response made Keegan smile. Kerry held his gaze, waiting for his decision.

"Well, if it's that easy..." Keegan tugged Kerry's head back down to where he wanted it.

This time, Kerry sucked his middle finger deep into his mouth and made a show of slowly dragging it from his mouth. The digit was long and slick, and Keegan knew exactly where Kerry planned to put it. Soft kisses drifted across his pelvis, and Kerry's nose nudged against Keegan's cock. The wet finger pressed against his entrance at the same time Kerry wrapped his lips around Keegan's cockhead. He held his breath in anticipation, but it whooshed out when Kerry penetrated his ass and sucked his dick down to the root at the same time. The finger stretching Keegan open curled and nudged his prostate.

"Oh fuck," Keegan said. He tensed his body, fighting the sensations to make the pleasure last. Maybe he could've held off if he'd closed his eyes and hadn't witnessed the wicked joy in Kerry's dark eyes as Keegan thrust his hips, fucking Kerry's mouth while riding his finger. Suddenly, chasing a climax like this wasn't enough. He laid his hand on a broad shoulder, and Kerry stopped and stood up. Keegan scooted farther up the bed to give them room for what he really wanted. "I want you inside me when I come."

"Yeah?" Kerry truly looked like a powerful wolf stalking his prey as he crawled up the mattress at a slower pace.

"Yes."

Kerry didn't stop his momentum until he hovered over Keegan on all fours. He captured his mouth in a long, deep kiss before he leaned toward his nightstand to get supplies. He rolled on a condom with economical movements that betrayed his familiarity with the practice. Keegan didn't have time to get insecure over their varying experience levels because Kerry moved between his legs once more. Maybe he saw a flash of something in Keegan's eyes anyway because Kerry paused for a kiss. "This is the first time I've ever invited a guy to my home and into my bed. No one compares to you. Do you hear me?"

Keegan nodded eagerly and rested his hands on Kerry's shoulders. "Let's see what you've got."

He took his time working Keegan open before slicking up his erection and pressing it against his entrance. They kept their gazes locked on one another as Kerry entered him slowly. Keegan's breath hitched as his body burned and stretched to accommodate Kerry's girth and length. He didn't mean to tense, but Kerry was attuned to his every nuance. "Do you need me to slow down or stop?"

Keegan tightened his legs around Kerry's waist. "Don't you dare."

Kerry leaned over Keegan and kissed him hungrily until he relaxed, then pushed the rest of the way home. "Just give me a minute." He rested his forehead against Keegan's as a tremor racked his powerful body. "I talked a big game earlier, but I'm ready to come."

Keegan fisted his hands in Kerry's hair. "Go ahead. I'll just make you come again."

Kerry snorted and raised his head. "I'm insufferable, aren't I?" He pulled back a little and thrust back in, as if testing himself. Just that little friction made Keegan gasp.

"I wouldn't change a single thing about you." He tightened his clinch around Kerry's dick. "Except for you holding back right now. Move your sexy ass."

Kerry's response was a low growl, but he complied, slowly at first but gaining intensity with each thrust. He snapped his hips forward, his balls slapping against Keegan's ass as his dick nailed his prostate with precision. Kerry lowered his torso, trapping Keegan's dick between their bodies and applying the perfect amount of friction to heighten Keegan's pleasure. "Come for me. Come around me. Come all over me." Kerry grunted and dug his knees into the mattress for even better purchase. He lowered his head and nuzzled against Keegan's neck. "Just come."

As if on command, pleasure detonated in Keegan's body. The intensity stole his breath and made it impossible for him to do anything but hold on as Kerry fucked him mercilessly, using Keegan's body for his pleasure. Kerry lifted his head and locked his gaze on Keegan's at the moment he found his release. It felt like a full surrender to their strengthening bond and was easily the most vulnerable moment Keegan had ever shared with another person. He didn't shy away from it. He cupped Kerry's face and pulled him down for a kiss. Kerry braced his weight on his forearms, but even that distance was too much. Keegan ran his hands up and down Kerry's damp back, mapping out his muscles and bumping his fingertips along his spine.

Kerry eventually eased out of him and rolled over, bringing Keegan to lie on top of him. "I weigh too much."

Keegan tucked his head under Kerry's chin and sighed. "You can pin me to the mattress anytime." The significance of the moment fully hit Keegan. The afterglow used to turn into his freak-out moment, with bliss giving way to panic and shame. Not this time. Not with this man. Keegan raised his head and met Kerry's sleepy gaze. "How much rest do you need before round two?"

# Chapter
## TEN

"I worried about this." Kerry sighed dramatically, formed his features into a resigned expression, and gave his head a little shake. He had a hard time staying in character when Keegan's drowsy gaze turned sharp and alert. Kerry's mouth quivered at the corners and threatened to give him away. "I believe I even warned you this might happen during our locker room chat at the Feisty Bull."

Relief softened Keegan's gaze again, and he rolled his eyes. "So arrogant. The only ring I'm thinking about is the asshole you just stretched around your dick." Keegan pushed up to a sitting position and straddled Kerry's hips. His torso was slick from where they'd smeared his release between them. Kerry became aware of the stickiness on his stomach, too, but couldn't be bothered to wipe it off when the fireplace crackled behind Keegan and cast gorgeous shadows over his body. He was beyond grateful his interior designer hadn't let him override her decision to install it in his bedroom. "I can't wait to ride you like this." Keegan undulated his hips and triggered a fluttering response in Kerry's core.

Maybe he'd rebound quicker than usual and make both their fantasies come true.

Tucking one arm under his head, Kerry watched the play of muscle under Keegan's skin, the hypnotic movements pulling him under Keegan's spell. The glistening smears caught his attention again, and he reached up and swirled his finger through it, wishing it was his cum painting Keegan's golden skin. "I've never wanted to mark anyone or claim them for my own." Kerry had never resented using condoms during sex. He'd never yearned to tuck someone against his heart and hold on for dear life. Everything changed when he met Keegan. The impossible not only seemed possible but plausible. Inevitable?

Kerry cut off the train of thought before veering too far off track. He cupped the back of Keegan's neck and pulled him down to bring his lips within kissing range. He'd meant to keep things light between them, but the situation called for raw honesty. "I expected to feel a surge of resentment if I gave in to my attraction to you, but you've brought me a level of warmth and peace I've never known."

Keegan swallowed hard and blushed a little, but he kept his soft gaze locked on Kerry. Not that long ago, he would've broken eye contact. "And I expected to feel a surge of self-hatred and shame after sex." His eyes filled with tears, but Kerry didn't see sadness shimmering in his hazel depths. "This liberation and joy is something I couldn't have dreamed for myself." He blinked, and a few tears spilled down his face. Keegan groaned and pulled against Kerry's hold to sit up again. "Damn it. I vowed I'd never cry again after sex."

Kerry hadn't wanted to let him go, but he'd vowed to honor Keegan's choices. He lifted his hand and brushed the tears away instead. "Tears of joy and liberation are welcome anytime."

Keegan looked away then and stiffened. Kerry followed his gaze and found Betty sitting in the doorway, watching them.

*Meow.* Her orange eyes bored into Kerry's, and her twitching tail betrayed her annoyance.

Keegan chuckled. "Is your perverted cat rating our performance?"

"She's demanding breakfast." Kerry looked at the clock. "I'm seven minutes past her usual mealtime."

*Meow.* Betty's complaint got louder and would only continue to rise in volume and shrillness the longer he delayed. "I better meet her demands or suffer the consequences." He sat up and kissed Keegan before he could slide off Kerry's lap. "She's definitely giving you a ten out of ten. So bossy and sexy."

Keegan looped his arms around Kerry's neck and smiled. "Tell me more."

All thoughts of getting out of bed were gone. "How about I show you instead?" Kerry rolled and pinned Keegan beneath him once more and captured his bossy mouth in a kiss that left them breathless. He'd be more than willing to stay just like this for the rest of the day, or at least until he recovered enough for round two. The mattress bounced at the foot of the bed, and Kerry broke the kiss to glare at his cat. "There's dry kibble in your dish. Eat that. I'll give you tuna soon."

Betty narrowed her eyes and made no move to leave them alone. She didn't yowl at him, so he took that as a good sign to resume kissing Keegan, whose lips trembled with barely contained glee. "Don't encourage her," Kerry warned. His mouth barely grazed Keegan's when Betty's sharp teeth sank into his foot. She'd only warned him and didn't break the skin, but it hurt enough to make him yelp and sit up.

Keegan slapped a hand to his mouth to muffle his reaction, but his body shook with restrained laughter. Betty jumped off the bed and darted into the hallway. Kerry was tempted to shut the door and resume their activities, but she'd only make a pest of herself. And he still wore the condom.

"I'm going to take care of this." He pointed to the latex covering his dick. "Then I'm going to feed my nagging cat. How do you feel about taking a shower to clean up?"

Keegan stopped laughing and jackknifed into a sitting position. "Together?"

"The same woman who talked me into installing a romantic fireplace also convinced me to put a shower big enough for—"

Keegan launched himself off the bed and hauled ass to the nearest door.

"—two," Kerry continued.

When Keegan yanked the door open, he must've only seen the clothes hanging to the left and right because he turned, put his hands on his hips, and glared. "Really? You're just going to let me make a fool of myself?"

Kerry chuckled and crossed the room at a much slower pace. "It has showerheads on both ends and multiple nozzles along the sides for massaging." He stopped when he reached Keegan, took his hand, and led him into the closet. Kerry reached out and flipped on the switch. Light flooded the space and revealed a closed door on the other end. "I haven't tidied the bathroom, so it might be a little messy." Kerry opened the door, flipped on the light, and winced. His clothes from the previous night were in a pile next to the hamper instead of inside it. He'd flung his towel across the vanity instead of hanging it on the rack to dry.

Keegan stopped beside him and took his time examining the space. He lifted his head and sniffed the air. "Smells just like you." Before Kerry could ask if that was a good or bad thing, Keegan turned, pressed his nose against Kerry's neck, and sniffed him. He followed that up with an almost purr-like noise, which then reminded him of his furry beast.

*Meow!* Betty's insistent tone let him know she wasn't playing around. He'd better move his ass or risk losing a toe.

Keegan eased to the side and gestured to the cat. "You better take care of your girl." He eyed the shower with a skeptical eye. "I could probably figure this out."

"Just one more minute, Betty," Kerry told her. She flounced off with a low growl, and Kerry reached into the tiled enclosure and cranked the faucet handle. Only one showerhead came on, but that was his intention. "I don't want you on the other side of the shower if it means I can't hold you against me."

Keegan assessed the massive structure where steam already billowed toward the ceiling. "That bench is sure going to come in handy, though."

The comment drew Kerry's attention to Keegan's sweet ass. "Yes, it will."

Keegan looked over his shoulder as he stepped inside the shower. "Go feed the cat." He stepped under the spray, sighed, and tilted his head back to get his hair wet. "I'll be right here when you get back."

"Don't touch anything," Kerry groused.

Keegan considered him with a quizzical expression. "Do you ration your shampoo or something?"

"I want to be the one who does the touching and washing."

"Hurry back, then."

Betty was licking her ass on the center of his bed when he stepped through the closet door.

"We need to work on your manners, young lady," Kerry said as he strode out of his room.

The carpet muffled Betty's launch behind him, but he knew she was in hot pursuit. As soon as he put his foot on the first step, Betty zoomed past him like the hounds of hell were after them. In her eyes, being late for tuna was far worse than having slobbering dogs. He paused in the kitchen and stared at the picnic basket and coffee thermos as if they were apparitions. He'd forgotten all about the food Keegan had brought with him. Betty yowled her displeasure at his tardiness and got him moving again. He found her in the laundry room, sitting beside the empty tuna dish.

Kerry pointed to the bowl beside it filled more than halfway with her dry kibble. "You have plenty to eat."

*Meow.* Which sounded like Betty speak for "you have plenty of other toes."

Kerry didn't know why he wasted time arguing with his cat when Keegan was naked and wet upstairs. He yanked the can's pull tab so hard it snapped off before it broke the seal. "Damn it."

Betty swished her tail scornfully as she watched him through narrowed eyes. He put the can back on the shelf and grabbed a different one. That time, he opened the tuna and dumped it in her dish without incident. Betty attacked the fishy flakes with gusto, and he smoothed his hand over her back. Things didn't bode well for him when she ate her tuna too quickly, and she was mad enough to puke it up in the worst possible locations.

"Easy, girl. You're not starving, and there's plenty of tuna where that came from."

Betty glared at the interruption before continuing to eat, but thankfully at a slower pace.

Kerry dashed back upstairs and found Keegan in the same spot Kerry had left him in, and he turned and met Kerry's gaze when he reentered the bathroom. He opened the shower door and stepped inside. Kerry wrapped his arms around Keegan and pulled him against his chest.

"Ready to go again?" Keegan asked.

"My little lamb has turned into quite the minx."

Keegan fisted a hand in Kerry's hair and brought their mouths together. They kissed hungrily as their hands roamed all over slick skin. When they parted to catch their breath, Keegan traced the lines of a tattoo on his chest. "Your body makes a beautiful canvas." He looked up and met Kerry's gaze, but his fingers continued exploring. "I started taking art therapy classes to help work through stress and trauma. It looks like you've been working through yours with ink therapy for a while now."

Kerry looked down at his chest and watched Keegan's fingers as they traced over one dark line, then another. "I've never considered my compulsion to add tattoos is a form of releasing pain. I'd just heard they were addictive." He pointed to a set of initials over his heart, and Keegan traced the *NJH*. "This was my first one. I got it as soon as I turned eighteen to honor Natalie." He'd been so proud to show it off to his family. "My mother teared up when she saw it, but my uncle teased

142

that I wouldn't stop with one tattoo." Kerry grinned wryly. "He wasn't wrong, but I have zero regrets. Each tattoo memorializes something or someone important."

Keegan looped his arms around Kerry's neck and kissed him. "I didn't mean to bring up distressing topics." He smiled sheepishly. "Seems I could use some work on my after-sex techniques. First, I cried, and then I reminded you of the worst time of your life."

Chuckling, Kerry pulled Keegan tightly against him. "Until now, my after-sex techniques comprised of disposing a condom and zipping up. I'm the last one to criticize."

"Did you at least slap them on the ass as you walked away?"

Kerry laughed harder. "I was that douchebag on some occasions." He latched onto Keegan's ass with both hands. "We can learn proper afterglow techniques together."

They kissed and explored again. Kerry felt the welcome zing low in his belly, but it wasn't enough to overcome the effects of little sleep, an explosive orgasm, and hot water. He broke the kiss and rested his forehead against Keegan's, who correctly read the signs.

"We're clean enough for now." Keegan twisted his torso to shut off the water.

They remained in the enclosure until chilly air penetrated the steam and made them shiver. Kerry pressed a kiss to Keegan's forehead before he opened the door and pulled two towels off the rack. He draped one around Keegan's shoulders and rubbed his body with the other.

"This is warm," Keegan said as he toweled off.

"I didn't put up a fuss when the topic of a towel warmer came up. It turns on automatically when the shower starts."

Kerry ogled Keegan's fine ass as he followed him into the bedroom. The alluring view gave him a zing of energy, but it fizzled quickly when Keegan headed for his discarded clothes.

"You can borrow one of my shirts," Kerry suggested. "And stay a little longer."

Keegan froze with his briefs in midair. The desire to do just that was clear in his expressive eyes, yet the set of his mouth told Kerry his answer before Keegan could respond. He sighed longingly and said, "I can't. I have things I need to tackle at the ranch before I work a shift at the Feisty Bull tonight." Keegan stepped into his underwear and pulled them up his long legs. He turned and smiled at Kerry. "And you need to get some sleep. You look exhausted."

"I am." But it didn't negate his disappointment that Keegan wouldn't be there when he woke up. "Will you eat breakfast with me before you leave?"

Keegan's brilliant smile made the sun look like a slacker. "I'd love that."

Kerry tugged on a pair of sweats but didn't bother with a T-shirt. He sat on the bed and watched Keegan redress, resenting each new article of clothing that covered his gorgeous body. This was completely fresh territory for Kerry, and it felt like navigating uneven terrain. It would take him a while to find his footing, but he was determined to do this right. He stood up when Keegan finished and crossed the room.

"You're not going to put on a shirt?"

Kerry cocked a brow and tugged Keegan close. "Do you need me to?"

"Won't you get cold?"

"I'm hot-blooded." He playfully nipped at Keegan's throat. "Like a wolf." He added a growl when Keegan laughed at his antics. "And you still look tasty."

A scraping noise came from downstairs. "What's that?" Keegan asked.

It took Kerry's sluggish brain a few seconds to figure it out. He bolted out of the bedroom and yelled, "Betty! Don't you dare!" The ominous sound occurred again when Kerry was halfway down the staircase. He took the remaining treads two at a time and vaulted onto the hardwood floor. The kitchen came into view when he rounded the corner. Betty sat on the island with her paw pressed against the basket. She'd already scooted it so half of the basket hung over the side of the marble countertop. One more good push and it would topple over. Betty's expression could only be described as spiteful when their eyes met. Kerry had seen this look at least once a day since he brought her home as a kitten, and he ran faster. "Don't you—"

Betty gave the basket a shove, and it toppled off the counter. Kerry lunged forward and snagged it seconds before the basket crashed to the floor. He stood up to address his dastardly feline, but she was nowhere in sight.

"Betty!"

"Hello, beautiful," Keegan cooed. "Why is your daddy yelling at you?"

Kerry spun around to find his cat winding around Keegan's legs. She purred loud enough for him to hear it across the house. Betty stood on her haunches and placed her paws on Keegan's upper thighs. She didn't do a full stretch with Keegan because he was still a stranger to her, but she was making a big overture. Keegan reached out a hand and let her sniff it. Betty seemed to check out each finger before she head-butted his palm. Keegan glanced at Kerry as if seeking encouragement, and he nodded, knowing Betty was on the verge of adding another adoring member to her fan club.

"Oh my goodness," Keegan gushed. "You are so beautiful, Betty. Your fur is so soft, and your eyes are so pretty."

Kerry snorted and earned reproachful glares from both Keegan and Betty. "She's a tyrant. Don't let her fool you. We were mere seconds away from having our breakfast destroyed."

Betty purred louder and kept pressing her head against Keegan's fingers. She closed her eyes in a blissful expression that made Kerry jealous. *What the fuck was happening?* Getting jealous of other men was one thing, but his cat?

"I don't believe him for a second, sweetheart," Keegan cooed.

Kerry turned his attention to unpacking the food from the basket instead of trying to persuade Keegan. Besides, he hoped Keegan would spend a lot of time here, and he wanted Betty to like his favorite human almost as much as Kerry did. The food aromas made his mouth water. "Do I smell blueberries?"

Arms slid around his waist seconds before Keegan pressed his body against Kerry's. "Mmhmm. Blueberry lemon crumble muffins. I found the recipe, and Harry made them this morning."

"You eat like this all the time?" Kerry asked, gesturing to the bounty.

Keegan poked his head out from under Kerry's arm. "Yes, but we work it off. Well, the crew does. I mostly push paper around and fill in where I'm needed. I'd pack on the pounds if I didn't work out and box regularly." He dropped his arms and stepped back. "Where do you keep your plates?"

"In the cabinet above the dishwasher." Kerry opened the drawer in the island where he kept the silverware and serving utensils. "There are insulated packs in here to keep the food warm, but I can heat it up more if you'd like."

Keegan set two plates on the island. "Nah. Liberating sex and a joyful orgasm has made me famished."

Gesturing to the food, Kerry said, "You go first. My crew went out for a big breakfast at the Greasy Spoon after we cleared the accident."

Keegan didn't put up an argument. He loaded his plate and scooted a stool back from the island.

"Don't wait for me," Kerry said when it looked like he would do just that. "Do you want coffee from the thermos, or would you like something else? I have milk, orange juice, and water."

"Orange juice, please."

Kerry filled two juice glasses, then filled his plate. He sat down beside Keegan and smiled at his half-empty plate. Damn, he hadn't been teasing about his ravenous appetite. Pride swelled in Kerry's chest, and he leaned over to kiss Keegan without thinking about it.

Keegan turned wide eyes on him. "Hi."

Kerry ducked down for another kiss, this one longer. He tasted blueberry, lemon, and a hint of salt from the bacon. He deepened the kiss, claiming Keegan in ways he didn't fully understand yet. "When can I see you again?"

Keegan's eyes remained closed, and he swayed a little as he sighed. His lashes fluttered open, and dreamy hazel eyes locked on him. "You're still here."

The question amused Kerry. "Where else would I be?"

"I keep thinking I will wake up and find this has all been a wonderful dream."

Kerry brushed the back of his fingers along Keegan's jawline. "This is real, and I want to take you on a proper date. Just you and me. No Sven tagging along. No family members watching our every move."

Keegan smiled. "So, I didn't mistake the matchmaking attempts at the family dinners or Sven's interference on Saturday night."

"Nope, and they don't get to take credit for us getting together," Kerry said stubbornly.

"Good luck with that." Keegan broke off a piece of muffin and popped it into his mouth. "I'm working tonight."

"I am too," Kerry said. "I'm filling in so Curtis can attend his kid's ballet recital."

Keegan practically melted. "That's so sweet. What a lucky girl."

"Boy," Kerry corrected. "The little guy dances like it's no one's business. Curtis will send me a video, and I'll show you."

Keegan covered his heart. "That's even sweeter."

"What about tomorrow night?" Kerry pressed.

"I have a therapy appointment, but it should be over by four or four thirty at the latest."

"I'll be home by five," Kerry said. "Why don't you pack an overnight bag and head here after therapy instead of going back to the ranch? We can leave from here."

"You want me to stay the night?"

Kerry kissed his luscious mouth. "If it were up to me, neither of us would leave this cabin for several days. You wouldn't have to worry about clean clothes because we wouldn't wear them."

"Whoa," Keegan whispered.

Kerry thought the same thing as soon as the words left his mouth. "Too much?"

Keegan swallowed hard. "Not for me, but what about you?"

"Honestly?" Kerry asked.

"Of course." Keegan set his fork down and seemed to brace himself for Kerry's response.

"It feels like not enough. I have eighteen months of stupidity to overcome."

Keegan shook his head. "Not on my behalf. I wasn't ready for you when we first met. I might not have been ready for you six months ago either. I think this happened when it was supposed to and not a second sooner."

"That sounds too easy," Kerry said. "Like something you've made up to make me feel better."

Keegan shrugged his shoulders and lifted a forkful of eggs. "Doesn't make it less true."

They ate in companionable silence until Keegan pushed his plate away several minutes later. He'd made a hellacious dent in his food, but there were some scrambled eggs left over.

"Want to make Betty your best friend forever?"

"Of course," Keegan replied.

"Give her a few pieces of scrambled eggs."

Keegan imitated the clicking sounds Kerry had made the previous evening. Betty trotted over and stretched up to sniff his offering. She swiped them out of his palm and devoured them off the floor. Then she purred and rubbed against Keegan's stool, begging for more.

"That's enough, my darling hellcat," Kerry said. He picked up the plates and carried them to the sink. "Want me to pack this back up so you can take it home?"

"Nah," Keegan said. "You can eat it after you wake up."

Kerry yawned as if on cue.

"I can take a hint," Keegan teased. "Text me later."

Kerry snagged his waist and held him in place but kept his grip light. "One more kiss before you go."

One more kiss stretched on for another twenty minutes. Keegan's phone chimed, and he snarled adorably.

"A work calendar reminder," he said. "I better take off."

Kerry walked him to his truck but kept their last kiss short. "Be careful."

"You too," Keegan replied. "And try not to strip down to your underwear in front of news cameras."

Kerry grimaced. "They caught that?"

"Caught it?" Keegan asked. "Hell, they zoomed in and broadcasted it live. There are so many thirsty videos and memes out there now."

Kerry buried his head in his hands and groaned until a thought hit him. "Is that why you came over here? To stake a claim?"

"Hell yes."

Kerry laughed. "This bossy side of you is sexy." He pressed one last quick kiss to Keegan's lips, then stepped away from the truck. "Better go before the wolf takes over again."

Keegan expelled a shaky breath and climbed into his truck. Kerry watched him drive away before returning inside, where Betty waited for him on the back of the couch.

"We need to work on your manners," Kerry said. A big yawn stopped him from naming her most egregious crimes. Damn, he felt good. Tired, but in the best possible way. The warmth he felt in Keegan's presence was still there, a silent blanket wrapped around him. "Damn it," Kerry swore. "Am I on the cusp of turning into a sap like Seth?"

Betty's *meow* seemed like a resounding yes, and Kerry decided he was okay with it. He went upstairs and fell into the deepest sleep of his life. When he woke a few hours later, Kerry found a text from his mom. Lucinda wanted to meet for lunch at the diner during her break at the salon. Kerry recognized a summons when he saw one and agreed to the meeting. It was better to conserve his energy for the interrogation ahead than waste it resisting Hurricane Lucinda.

He arrived at the diner first and chose a corner booth in the back. Kerry caught several heads turning in his direction as he walked by and remembered what Keegan had said. Had all these people seen him in his underwear? One elderly gentleman at a neighboring table gave Kerry a thumbs-up, and a woman at another winked at him. Kerry decided they approved of the mission and not the fit of his underwear and turned his full attention to the menu. He stared at the damn thing until his mother arrived, even though he could recite each item by memory.

Lucinda's radiant smile had him reaching for the menu again to shield his retinas from permanent damage. "Turn that down a notch, will you?"

She snagged the menu from his hand and laid it on the table. "Just let me have this."

He'd said something similar to Seth not that long ago when his cousin caught him during an unguarded moment. Kerry had been observing Keegan with his family and admiring the way he fit. *Belonged.* It hadn't been the first revelation of the sort, but it was the one that rocked Kerry the hardest. He'd allowed himself a moment to wonder what a future with Keegan could look like if he weren't so messed up.

Kerry's face must've betrayed the joy he'd glimpsed and had drawn Seth's attention. Kerry had zero intentions of acting on his attraction at the time, so he'd waved off Seth's concern for Keegan's heart and told his cousin to just let him have the moment. Kerry might resemble the Harts, but Lucinda's influence ran deep. He didn't need to rely on their mother-son bond to know the source of her happiness. "Let me guess. Sven called you when he got home last night."

His mother responded with an indignant snort. "It's like you don't even know your brother, Ker. Sven called me before you even pulled out of the parking lot." Her smug expression turned somber. "Sven promised you didn't kill anyone. Was he telling the truth? Do you need me to help hide Danny's body?"

Kerry chuckled. "The asshole is still among the living, as far as I know."

"Sven told me that Keegan followed you home to *talk*."

He didn't miss the emphasis she'd placed on the last word. "And I received an emergency phone call before we could get to our conversation."

Lucinda leaned forward and said, "Conversation or *conversation?*"

Kerry shook his head at the innuendo she'd bled into the word the second time around, but he kept his expression neutral. "I'm not discussing this with you."

She studied his face for only a few seconds before her lips twisted into a knowing smirk. "Your body language tells me everything I need to know, and you're welcome that I insisted you include the fireplace and fancy shower in your bedroom suite." She held up her hands before Kerry could respond. "Again, just let me have this moment."

"Did you call me here to gloat?"

Lucinda placed a hand on her chest and batted her eyelashes dramatically. "Me?"

"Careful," Kerry cautioned. "You'll lose an extension."

His mother rolled her eyes. "You don't know what it's like to be lash impaired. Both you and Natalie inherited Graham's eyelashes. All the Harts have long, black eyelashes that don't require curling or mascara. It's just not fair."

"I admire how easily you can say their names." Kerry hadn't intended to take their conversation in a heavy direction, but maybe that had been his problem all along.

Lucinda reached across the table for his hands, and he obliged her. "It hasn't always been this easy, but you know that."

"You put in the time and hard work to heal," Kerry said.

"One step, one hour, and one day at a time. I didn't have a choice. You'd lost your sister to a violent death and your father to grief. I wouldn't leave you alone in this world. You were my reason for fighting every single day."

Damn, how he loved this woman. "You started fighting for yourself at some point. You opened the salon, and you fell in love with Steven." Kerry shook his head. "I don't know how you learned to love again."

Lucinda took a deep breath and looked like she was considering her words. "I couldn't stay mad at Graham. I wanted to, but he hadn't left us because he didn't love us anymore. He blamed himself for Natalie's death and never recovered."

The discussion between his parents on the morning their lives changed forever was as clear as if it had happened yesterday instead of twenty-five years ago. Natalie had just gotten her license and wanted to drive to the river to hang out with friends. Lucinda had said no, which prompted a rare argument between mother and daughter. Graham had intervened and worked out a compromise. Natalie could take Seth and Kerry to the ice cream parlor in town and meet up with her friends there. He couldn't have known Natalie would drop off the boys in town and catch a ride to the river with a guy she'd been secretly dating.

"Graham's protective instincts became so severe that he wanted to shut us in against the world so no one else could hurt us. The isolation only deepened his depression until he became unrecognizable, Kerry. I urged Graham to get help. I wanted him to see a therapist to talk through his grief and paranoia. He just couldn't live in a world without Natalie." She shook her head sadly and squeezed Kerry's hands before releasing him. "He lost out on watching you grow up to be an incredible man who risks his life to save others. I'd like to think Graham and Natalie are watching over us. They'd be so proud."

Maybe on some level, Kerry realized he'd followed in his father's footsteps. He'd built a protective wall around his heart and rarely let new people in. His close friendships were all ones he'd formed before Natalie died. He respected and liked his crew, but he only knew them professionally. Kerry had made space in his life for sexual pleasure with willing partners who knew the score, but he never permitted physical comfort. That changed when he met Keegan. Somewhere along the way, he realized he'd been existing instead of living. "I don't want to close myself off to love anymore."

"Then don't," Lucinda said firmly. "You've had countless examples of the truest love within our family alone. Everything you need is right here" —she pointed to her temple, then to her heart—"and right here. It's never too late to start therapy to work on the things that are holding you back from the rich life you deserve."

Kerry exhaled a shaky breath. He'd seen firsthand what a good therapist could do for people who'd bought into the process. "I'll think about it, Ma." He grinned wryly and shook his head. "I'm thirty-eight years old and about to go on my first date. I don't want to mess this up with Keegan."

"Sweetheart, don't overthink this. Keegan isn't a guy who needs grand gestures."

"He deserves them. I thought about watching some rom-com movies to get ideas."

Lucinda giggled and gestured for him to stop. "Don't do that. Keegan is crazy about you, not Hollywood's version of the perfect man. Keep it simple. Start with a nice dinner. Then, you need a nonsexual activity. Bowling, a movie, or something you know he enjoys." Lucinda leaned close and waggled her brows. "Then you get to the really good stuff." She sighed wistfully and got a faraway look in her eyes. "I remember when Steven and I first started *dating*." Her emphasis on the word made him cringe.

"Got it," Kerry said. "Dinner and an activity." They could do both those things at his house, but he wanted to make Keegan feel special. "Anything else you want to recommend?"

"Don't screw this up."

*No pressure.* "Yes, ma'am."

## Chapter

# ELEVEN

"WE'RE HAVING A SPRING FLING AT OUR VINEYARD NEXT month, and I'd love for you to come." Darryl's voice boomed through the speakers on the desk phone as he rattled off a date in May. Keegan and Cash were a good thirty minutes into the phone call with the vintner, though the conversation was mostly one-sided. Every time Cash opened his mouth to speak, Darryl was off and running again. "It's an annual event to kick off our wine season. Folks get cooped up after the winter months, so we always have a good turnout. We invite top regional chefs each year to wow us with their culinary skills, and guests enjoy live music. Does that sound like the kind of shindig you're thinking about hosting once you've established your alehouse?"

"What you've described sounds wonderful. We're still trying to decide on what kind of vibe we want for Hooch and Honey."

"Perfect," Darryl said. "The Spring Fling is sold out, but I can leave two tickets for you with my event coordinator."

"I will be in Denver that weekend," Cash said, "so I'll send Keegan and his plus-one in my place." The boss waggled his brows, and Keegan had to fight back a laugh. By the time he returned from Kerry's house the previous day, everyone had seen the video of the big rescue and Kerry stripping down to his underwear. The crew had guessed the source of his *errand* and had shot knowing smirks and lecherous winks at him ever since, but this was the first time the boss acknowledged Keegan's rendezvous at Kerry's house.

"Terrific!" Darryl boomed through the connection and jolted Keegan from his thoughts. "I'll just put down two guests from Redemption Ridge. No need to overcomplicate things."

"Sounds great, Darryl," Cash said. "I appreciate you taking the time to speak with us today. I admire your business model and your ethos."

"It's my pleasure, Cash," the jovial man said. "I'm not one of those guys who thinks every person on this earth is his competition. The table's big enough for everyone. I think it's pretty cool that you'll produce your mead and craft brews from ingredients you grow on your ranch. I want an invite to your grand opening."

"Sure thing." After a few rounds of niceties, Cash disconnected the call and gave Keegan his full attention. "What do you think?"

"Me? I've only worked two shifts at the Feisty Bull. I've barely dipped my toes into hospitality."

Cash chuckled. "What do you think about having events like Darryl described? Live bands and special cuisine to celebrate occasions?"

"I love that idea," Keegan admitted. "I just don't know how to implement any of that." Just thinking about it made his chest tighten.

"You don't have to," Cash replied. "I'll hire architects to design the layout of the spaces in the vineyard. An event planner will organize the celebrations from top to bottom and book the best chefs. You'll be the charming one who works the front of the house and assures our guests are happy."

Keegan exhaled. "I really want to make something special of this opportunity." His heart raced whenever he thought about it. Not as much as when Kerry was near, but fast enough to let Keegan know this was something he wanted. "I just need to work through my insecurities."

"And I'm here to help you do that," Cash replied. His cell phone rang, and he checked the caller ID. "It's about time he called me back."

Keegan took that as his cue to go.

"Hey, Kee," Cash said before he reached the door. "Your potential is limitless. You're intuitive, kind, and smarter than you realize. I'm determined to help you believe these things about yourself someday."

Keegan was too choked up to speak, so he just nodded before he stepped into the hallway and closed the door behind him. He wanted to have the same faith in his abilities as others did, but he hadn't achieved that level of confidence yet. Keegan saw glimpses of his promise occasionally but still considered those instances to be flukes. Maybe he would bring it up with Brendan during therapy later.

Someone had placed a stack of mail on his desk while he was in the meeting. He was used to seeing business correspondence, but the top envelope was addressed to Keegan. There was no return address on the plain white paper, but he would've recognized Miriam's loopy handwriting anywhere. He'd expected this day ever since he filmed the web series interviews about the abuse he suffered from his mother and the monsters at Salvation Anew. Keegan wasn't sure how long it would take for word about the interview to cycle to her. Miriam had fled with the other rats when the ship started to sink. He had no idea where she'd landed, but he would've bet money that some of the most fanatical ex-members would've formed a secret faction to keep the movement alive.

No one was more zealous than Miriam Scott, who manipulated her gay son into conversion therapy by threatening to disown him after reading text messages between Keegan and his secret boyfriend. People who'd never been abused would question why Keegan didn't walk away from him. He was glad they couldn't comprehend his choices because it meant they weren't caught up in a vicious cycle of abuse. It meant they hadn't faced homelessness and starvation because their only parent thought they were an abomination. Keegan could've gotten help if he'd been brave enough to ask his boyfriend for help at the time, but he'd been too scared to defy Miriam.

And he'd paid dearly. Starvation was the kindest form of abuse he'd survived. He had begged her for help, but she turned her back on him. When the leadership decided the only way to cure Keegan's *sickness* was to force him to have sex with one of the ladies in the cult, Miriam had chosen the woman and expected Keegan to thank her. He'd refused and had suffered more physical and verbal abuse than he'd believed possible. But he had survived her. He got to live in the sunshine while she had to hide in the shadows. He surrounded himself with love while she festered with hate. He broke the cycle. He won. Keegan needed her to know it.

The former Salvation Anew members had too much hate in their hearts to not keep an eye on things happening at Redemption Ridge and in Last Chance Creek. Keegan had known his interview would draw her ire, but he did it anyway. His association with Redemption Ridge was public knowledge, making it easy for people to find him. He did it anyway. Miriam would never miss an opportunity to berate his failings and for speaking out against the men she deemed godly. He did it anyway. Keegan knew he'd never get the apology he deserved. But he did it anyway.

Keegan picked up the envelope and bounced it in his hand. The correspondence weighed next to nothing, so she couldn't have said much. Acid churned in his stomach as he debated opening the letter or just putting it through the shredder so that he could have the last word. If he didn't open the envelope, he'd wonder for the rest of his life. With a heavy sigh, Keegan removed his letter opener from his desk drawer and sliced it open. After a few deep breaths, he pulled the sheet of paper free and read it.

*I wish you'd never been born.*

Two years ago, Keegan would've agreed with her. Hoping for a merciful death seemed like the only opportunity he'd had for freedom. But he'd escaped that hellhole. He'd learned the beauty of found family. Keegan had people who championed his recovery every step of the way. And he'd danced with Kerry that fateful night eighteen months ago, and those three minutes changed his life. He hadn't just survived the monster; he was fucking thriving despite her.

Keegan turned his chair and fed that toxic vitriol through the paper shredder. He watched until the last of the note disappeared and the high-pitched *whir* of the motor stopped. "Never again, Miriam."

The cycle was over.

"What's going on with your face?" Brendan teased.

Keegan raised his hands and felt around his mouth, cheeks, and chin. "What do you mean?"

Brendan circled his finger in the air and gestured to Keegan. "I asked what else is new with you after you told me about the letter from Miriam, and you gave me Joker lips."

That made Keegan laugh. "You've heard me mention Kerry before, right?"

"Once or twice," Brendan teased.

Keegan suspected the number was much higher. "Well, he and I… we, um…" The inability to express himself was interesting. Sexuality had been a major part of their conversations. Keegan had talked about his loneliness and horniness and other humiliating things with relative ease. Why couldn't he tell Brendan that he'd not only had sex but had it with the guy he'd been pining after for nearly two years?

"I won't judge you," Brendan said.

"I know." But he might suggest it was a bad idea or urge caution.

"You don't have to earn my approval," Brendan added.

"I know that as well." Keegan took a deep breath, then said, "We had sex. Fantastic sex. And I didn't feel shame afterward. I wanted to do it again." A rush of emotions surged inside him, pushed against his ribs, and filled his eyes with tears. "He sees me. Really sees me. Kerry understands how fiercely I need to be in control of my destiny, and he supports that. I've never wanted anyone the way I do with him." Keegan frowned as he considered his next words. "I don't think anyone has ever wanted me as intensely as he does."

"And it's scary?" Brendan asked.

Keegan nodded. "It's terrifying. What if it doesn't work out? I could lose Sven too. What if I swing and miss and end up back where I was before?"

"Before you met Kerry or before you started therapy?"

Keegan shook his head. "I'll never be the person you first met."

Brendan's expression was neutral, but his words held a lot of gravity when he next spoke. "You're the same person, Keegan. Therapy didn't erase all the misery you've endured. It's helped you process what you've been through and provided you with tools to build a stronger future. A failed relationship or heartbreak might set you back a little, but no, I don't think you'll end up in the same headspace as when we first met."

"I'm stronger now."

"You are," Brendan agreed. "Being frightened is natural. Trying to create a life where you're never scared or challenged isn't feasible. It's better to identify your concerns and work through them, but you don't want to start off any new relationship or journey with a defeatist attitude." Brendan glanced at the clock. "We don't have a lot of time left, but I'd love to hear how your relationship with Kerry has grown. The last I heard, you were hopelessly pining after him."

Keegan chuckled. "The story will probably take longer than we have."

"So hit the highlights," Brendan encouraged.

"Just remember you asked for it." Keegan began with Sven's botched matchmaking, and Brendan got a huge kick out of Sven's method. He listened stoically as Keegan described the locker room conversation and their family dinner confrontation, but his lips twitched a few times as if he found them amusing. Brendan didn't find anything to laugh about when Keegan recounted his date with Danny. He interrupted a few times to ensure that Keegan wasn't harmed—physically or emotionally—before encouraging Keegan to continue. The timer went off, signaling the end of the session, but Brendan gestured for him to continue. He seemed charmed by Keegan's reaction to the news story and the thirsty reporter's comments.

"And I had an 'oh my' moment of my own when Kerry answered the door naked." Keegan's face heated when he realized what he'd said. "I didn't mean to get that descriptive. But yeah, we had sex. I didn't hate myself afterward. And we're going on our first date after my session with you."

"I'm really happy for you, Keegan," Brendan said. "And I have to wonder why you're still talking to me if you've got a hot date."

Keegan laughed and stood up. "I'm out of here. See you next time." He was still smiling to himself as he exited the building and walked to his truck. Even though his session had run over, he finished earlier than he'd told Kerry. He pulled his phone out and texted Kerry to see if he needed anything from town before he headed over.

Kerry replied immediately. *Just you. I'm home now so come over. I can't wait to start our date.*

*On my way!*

To touch Kerry, to taste him, and have those muscular arms wrapped around him. To embrace his queerness and go on his first real date. Keegan shifted the truck into Drive and pressed the gas. "I am queer. I am worthy. I am beautiful. I am loved." Keegan smiled as he pulled out of the parking lot. "And I get to see Kerry naked! Talk about thriving."

# Chapter
## TWELVE

"HE'LL BE HERE ANY MINUTE," KERRY SAID AS HE PACED IN his living room. Betty raised her head and glared at him for disturbing her slumber. "I'm not sorry, but you should be for trying to sleep instead of offering emotional support during my freak-out." Betty lowered her head, closed her eyes, and sighed loudly. "Why am I so nervous?"

Keegan had put him in charge of their date arrangements and had assured Kerry that whatever he chose would be perfect. He'd remembered the advice his mother had given him: dinner, an activity, and then sex. Lucinda hadn't come out and mentioned sex specifically, but she had implied it. Kerry had trouble deciding between two restaurants, two activities, and there were a dozen sexual activities he was eager to try with Keegan. Then he got an idea from a TikTok video he watched while procrastinating on his admin tasks at work. Kerry had found a partial stack of index cards and a black Sharpie in his desk, then set out to make this a night neither of them would forget.

But doubt dimmed his excitement as he waited for Keegan to arrive. Just because something was popular on social media didn't mean it translated well to real life. A car door sounded from the front of the house, and Kerry looked out the window to see Keegan strolling to the porch with a backpack slung over his shoulder. Keegan's lips curved into a coy smile, and he walked with confidence and purpose. Kerry's nerves settled when he realized he was the purpose Keegan was so certain about.

"He's here, Betty. Please be—" Kerry's words died off when he saw that Betty wasn't in her favorite spot on the back of the sofa. He found his cat waiting by the front door to greet Keegan. "Good," Kerry finished as he joined her. She spared him a disdainful scowl before her ears perked up. Her superior hearing detected Keegan on the porch before Kerry did. He opened the door before Keegan could knock or ring the bell. "Hey—"

Keegan pressed eager lips to his, cutting off Kerry's greeting. When he moved to pull back, Kerry snaked his arm around Keegan's waist and deepened the kiss. "Hi," Keegan said when they finally separated.

"Hi." Sharp teeth pierced his left sock, and Kerry yowled and hopped on one foot. "Damn it, Betty."

The cat moved in once Kerry was out of the way. She purred obnoxiously loud and wove around Keegan's legs before she rose to greet him. Keegan scratched her ears just right, and Betty closed her eyes in blissful happiness.

"Is he being mean to you, pretty girl?" Keegan asked.

"Me?" Kerry limped along dramatically, hoping to get a fraction of the attention Betty received. He wanted to feel Keegan's magic touch too. "She bit me to clear a path to you. Betty wants all your attention."

"Well, it's only fair since I'll be spending most of my time with you." Keegan added a second hand to rub her chin, and she revved up her purrs like a small engine.

"I'm nervous about tonight." Kerry hadn't meant to admit it out loud, but Keegan's softening gaze made him glad he did.

Keegan gave Betty one last scratch before straightening and crossing to him, placing a hand over Kerry's heart. "You have nothing to worry about tonight. Wherever we go and whatever we do will be wonderful."

Kerry captured Keegan's sweet lips in a brief kiss. "Do you think we're doing things kind of backward, though?"

"How so?"

"Traditionally, you go on dates and get to know each other before having sex," Kerry said.

"It seems like dating is nothing more than people putting their best foot forward so they can get the other person in bed. A less cynical theory is that people go on dates to test their compatibility. We already know one another. Heck, we've already seen each other at our worst and still want to give this a try." Keegan's lips curved into a wry smile. "And I mean, we *know* each other."

Kerry nuzzled his nose against Keegan's neck and kissed a path up to his lips. "I adore everything I've learned so far, but I want to know more."

"How much more?" Keegan asked huskily.

"Everything. You fascinate me like no one ever has." Kerry brushed a thumb over his full bottom lip. "I think I'll treat our date as Keegan appreciation night."

"Color me intrigued," Keegan replied. "And where will this event occur?"

Kerry worried his bottom lip between his teeth. What if Keegan thought his plan was lame?

"Now I'm even more curious," Keegan said. "Whatever you've decided will be perfect."

"We'll see about that." Kerry reached behind him and pulled two index cards from his pocket. He held them up so he saw what was written on them while Keegan saw the blank side. "I came up with a few ideas for our date but couldn't settle on one. I'm going to present a series of options to you throughout our date, and you will blindly choose what we do next."

Keegan's eyes glowed with delight. "Oh, this is fun."

"I'm glad you like it." Kerry bounced the cards in front of him. "Round one is a choice of where we will eat." Kerry had written Saucy Bones Barbecue Joint on the left index card and Eleanora's steak house on the right card. "Which do you choose?"

Keegan squinted like he was trying to see through the card stock. Kerry had already tested that out and knew he couldn't read the options. Keegan cocked his head to the side and nibbled on his lips as he considered. He reached for the card on the left but pulled back at the last minute. He stroked his fingers over the top of the card on the right but didn't grab it. Keegan squared his shoulders, snatched the left index card, and flipped it around. He whooped and did a little shimmy that might've been a happy dance. "I love Saucy Bones." He looked at the remaining card in Kerry's hand. "What's that one?"

Kerry shook his head, folded the card, and tucked it away. "Nope. I'm saving this idea for our next date."

"Feeling pretty cocky that you'll get another one, huh?" Keegan teased.

"A man can hope." Kerry removed Keegan's backpack from his shoulder and placed it on the sofa. "Ready to get our night started?"

"Absolutely." Keegan spun and headed to the front door, and Kerry followed.

Kerry opened the door for Keegan. "And just what do you consider my worst behavior?"

Keegan waggled his brows and headed onto the porch. "Why don't you tell me what the other restaurant option was first?"

"Eleanora's." Kerry could tell by Keegan's expression that he didn't expect him to give in. "But you can't tell Debbie and Rick." Eleanora's was their stiffest competition, though the Feisty Bull was the superior steak house. "So, how bad was my worst?" Kerry raked his memories to see how badly he'd shown his ass in front of Keegan.

His minx marched toward the truck as if he didn't plan to answer him, but he turned at the passenger door and smirked. "The family rummy tournament earlier this year."

Kerry threw his head back and laughed. "Things got a little intense."

"A little intense? I thought someone was going to get hurt." Keegan shook his head. "And I thought the poker nights at the ranch got wild."

"Hey, I've heard about Saturday night poker on the ranch. I'd like to get in on the action."

"I can make that happen." Keegan opened the door but paused before climbing into the truck. "The crew has taken their role as my found family very seriously, so be prepared for them to flex their brotherly concerns."

Kerry patted his shoulder. "I got broad ones and can take it."

"You've got big everything," Keegan replied. "I plan to enjoy every inch of you." He hopped into the truck and shut the door.

Kerry debated hauling him back out of there and going back to the house, but Keegan deserved a fun night out. Kerry did too. They'd have plenty of time for exploration later. Kerry got in the truck and fired up the engine. "Just out of curiosity, what do you think your worst behavior was?"

Keegan groaned and briefly buried his face in his hands. "The way I acted on Sunday at the family dinner. I was so obnoxious."

"You were hurt," Kerry countered. "And it's my fault for baiting you because I was jealous."

"No," Keegan said. "I grew up with a woman who blamed everything on everyone but herself. It would be too easy for me to fall into the same trap, so it's important that I own up to things when I mess up."

Kerry reached over and took Keegan's hand. "We'll have to agree to disagree about family dinner on Sunday. What you see as bad behavior, I see as the kick in the pants I needed." He felt Keegan's gaze on him and glanced over with a smile.

"I want to believe that," Keegan said.

"Then do."

They kept the conversation light on the way to the restaurant, catching up on their day. Kerry sensed Keegan was holding something back, but he didn't push. They'd talked on the phone after Keegan's shift the previous evening, and Keegan had mentioned that he sometimes gets lost in his thoughts after a therapy session. He made Kerry promise to pull him out by his legs if that happened. Kerry wouldn't do anything of the sort, but he could sit beside Keegan and be there when he needed him.

Saucy Bones was a happening place for a Wednesday night. Smoke billowed from behind the restaurant. If someone didn't know better, they might think the place was on fire. Kerry tilted his head back and inhaled. "Smoked meat is the best," he announced.

"Period," Keegan agreed.

Kerry's mouth watered, and his taste buds danced when he stepped into the restaurant. The interior wasn't much to look at, but no one there cared a plug nickel about decor. Roy "Saucy" Jones kept his restaurant as spotless as his reputation. They found a small table for two open at the very back of the restaurant, and Kerry led Keegan to it. Neither of them reached for a menu, proving how familiar they were with the offerings.

"Why didn't I know you loved this place?" Kerry asked.

Keegan shrugged. "Guess it never came up."

They shared a smile before the server came over to get their drinks. Keegan only wanted water, while Kerry chose a diet soda. When asked if they knew what they wanted to eat, the guys started talking at the same time. The server laughed, pointed his pen at Keegan, and directed him to go first. Kee ordered the saucy trio with macaroni and cheese and baked beans as his sides.

"I'll have the same," Kerry said. "Could I get an extra mac and cheese and a double portion of cornbread?"

"You got it," he said. "Your drinks and dinner will be right out."

Kerry looked at Keegan when they were alone again. "The trio, huh?"

"I can never decide if I want brisket, pulled pork, or ribs, so I get the trio," Keegan said.

"Double mac and cornbread, huh?" Keegan raked his gaze over Kerry's torso. "Where the hell do you put it?"

"I need a lot of food to fuel this body," Kerry replied.

Keegan's eyes glazed over, and his nostrils flared with his next inhale. Kerry had no doubts about where his mind went.

"But I try to balance things out with exercise and a healthy diet most of the time." Kerry looked around the crowded restaurant and noted the happiness on everyone's faces. "Life is too short not to eat the things that bring you joy."

The server returned as quickly as she promised with their food and drinks. The macaroni and cheese arrived just how Kerry loved it. Some people liked buttery breadcrumbs on theirs, but Kerry was all about the golden-brown cheesy top. The moan he made with the first bite got everyone's attention at the nearby tables. Keegan watched him for a few minutes without taking a bite. Kerry swallowed his bite, washed it down with cola, and pointed his fork at Keegan's plate. "You've got ribs, pulled pork, and brisket to eat."

Keegan's cheeks turned pink. "Sorry. I got distracted by how much pleasure you got from eating the mac and cheese."

Kerry leaned forward, lowered his voice, and said, "Wait until I eat you later." He slathered a thick layer of butter on a thick square of cornbread and set it on Keegan's plate.

Keegan's mouth parted on a silent "Oh," and he swallowed hard. He sampled his sides and took a bite of the cornbread before moving on to his meats.

Kerry watched in awe as Keegan ate everything on his plate. "I can't finish this second mac and cheese. Do you want it?"

"I'm full." Keegan reached for his wet wipe packet but stopped and lifted his hand to his face. He licked a spot of sauce off the tip of one finger. He glanced up and caught Kerry watching. Wickedness danced in his hazel eyes as he angled his body just enough so only Kerry could watch him roll his tongue around the tip of the next finger. "Where are my next set of cards?" When Kerry only blinked, he added, "For the next part of our date."

"Oh, um, they're in the truck."

Keegan nodded to his plate. "Are you done eating?"

Kerry tapped his knuckles on the table and sat back in his chair. He signaled for their server so he could settle their bill. They went through two wet wipes each, and Kerry still didn't feel clean. He'd smell like woodsmoke for at least a day, but that didn't bother him. Once in the truck, he opened the center console and pulled out the two index cards. One offered Keegan a night of axe throwing, and the other would take them to a wine and guided painting session at the art center. Kerry didn't have an artistic bone in his body, so he definitely had a preference, though he'd give painting his best shot if that was Keegan's choice.

"Wow," Keegan said.

Kerry thought he'd gotten a peek at the writing on the cards, but Keegan's attention was focused on the box of condoms and lube packets in his console. His active sex life hadn't been a source of shame until that moment.

"Looks like you have a big appetite everywhere," Keegan teased.

"This stash has been in here a long time." He closed the console and angled in the seat to present the cards to Keegan. "I haven't needed the supplies and forgot they were there."

"Kerry, you don't owe me an account of your sexual history. I know the score."

He shook his head. "You know what it used to be," Kerry amended. "Random hookups stopped appealing to me the night I met you."

Keegan searched his expression for several seconds before he smiled. "Don't get rid of them now. Who knows when the mood will strike us?"

"Like back there," Kerry said, hooking his thumb toward Saucy's. "I thought you were going to deep-throat your finger."

"I wanted to," Keegan admitted. "Turning you on drives me crazy too." He reached over and stroked a finger over Kerry's forearm. "Maybe we should just go back to your place and save these date options for another night."

Kerry was damned tempted, but he shook his head. "This is your appreciation night." Kerry cut him off with a kiss before Keegan could express that sex was the best kind of appreciation. "Let's go have some fun and digest our food a little. Then I'll worship every inch of your body right down to your adorable toes."

Keegan inhaled slowly and snagged the right card. "Axe throwing," he said.

Kerry pumped his fist and turned the truck on. "This is going to be a blast."

"I've never been before, but it sounds fun," Keegan said. "What's the other one?"

Kerry opened the console enough to toss it inside. "Wine and a guided painting class at the art center."

"You'd do that for me?" Keegan asked.

"As long as you don't show anyone my painting. I don't have an artistic bone in my body."

"Doubt it," Keegan said, "But your secret will be safe with me." And Kerry knew it would. "I don't think I've ever seen you drink wine. Do you even like it?" The question seemed fair considering the alternative date option, but something about Keegan's tone and his expression led Kerry to believe it was more significant than mere curiosity.

"I like wine okay, but I prefer beer."

Keegan nodded, then looked out his window. Kerry had been ready to pull out of his parking spot, but something seemed off. It felt like Keegan was wrestling something around in his mind, and that seemed more important than checking off the next box on his dating agenda. Kerry reached over the console and took Keegan's hand.

"What's going on in that gorgeous head of yours?" He knew Keegan enjoyed an occasional glass of wine and thought he enjoyed art. "Did I mess up somehow?"

Keegan turned and looked at him with wide eyes. "God, no. This night has been perfect so far. I couldn't ask for a better first date." His lips curved into the sly smile Kerry adored. "And I don't even have to wonder if I'm going to get lucky."

"I'm a sure bet," Kerry agreed. "So, where'd your mind go just now?"

"Well, it seems the world is conspiring to throw us together as often as possible." Keegan told him about the Spring Fling vineyard event in May and their invitation to attend to get a feel for the atmosphere. "Cash suggested I take you with me since he will be out of town."

"And you didn't want to invite me?" Kerry teased. "Afraid I'll embarrass you?"

Keegan's eyes widened. "What? No? I just wasn't sure if it was something you'd enjoy."

"But then you learned I put the wine and painting on the table. Where'd your thoughts go from there?" Kerry asked.

"I wanted to be sure you weren't doing the art and wine thingy just for my benefit," Keegan said. "This can't be a one-way street where we always do what I like. I want to experience the things you love, even if it's something I might not choose on my own. I'll get joy from seeing you happy."

"How can either of us know if we like something if we don't try it?" Kerry challenged. "Truth is, I don't know how to feel about a vineyard event until I attend one. I'd be honored to attend with you, if that's what you want." Kerry considered the situation a little longer before adding, "And I don't want you inviting me to things because someone else says you should. I won't be upset if you'd rather take Sven or someone else from the ranch."

Keegan shook his head. "I would love for you to go with me."

"It's a date." Inspiration struck, and Kerry added, "In fact, why don't we make a weekend out of it? I'll find a hotel or bed-and-breakfast nearby."

"That sounds perfect." Keegan inhaled a shaky breath. "But if you change your mind—"

"I won't."

"The event is a month away," Keegan said.

And Kerry understood the source of his turmoil. He didn't want to set his hopes too high and have them crash and burn. "I am so freaking into you, Kee. I will spend every day between now and then proving just how much I want you."

The tenderness in Keegan's expression made Kerry's heart flutter. He claimed a quick kiss before setting off for part two of their date. There were only a few cars in the parking lot when they arrived, but it was the middle of the week, and Lumberjack's Axe and Ale was new. The rustic, Western-themed decor was pretty standard in their part of the world, and the owners leaned into it without going too far. Country music drifted through hidden speakers, and a full-service bar took up one side of the building. Kerry questioned the wisdom of combining alcohol and sharp weapons, but what did he know?

A woman named Karen greeted them at the checkout counter with a friendly smile and chipper voice that declared she alone was going to take back the name for all the good Karens in the world. She put a ton of personality into her presentation of the rules of axe throwing. Basically, they didn't want their patrons to throw those axes all willy-nilly. Again, Kerry wondered why they'd introduce alcohol onto the premises because that would never go sideways. Karen slid a waiver across the counter for them to sign after her presentation. "Follow me, guys," she said.

Keegan leaned close and said, "Personal injury waivers on a first date. Man, you sure know how to show a fella a good time."

Kerry placed his hand on the small of Keegan's back. "Wait until you see the waiver waiting for you back at my place."

Keegan stiffened, and Kerry wasn't sure if it was his hand placement or his reference to potentially rough sex. He was about to withdraw his hand and apologize, but Keegan smiled up at him. "This night just keeps getting better." He stopped and spun around to face Kerry. "Sorry I tensed. I'm not used to PDA, but I like it."

"Me too."

Keegan rose on his tiptoes and pressed a quick kiss to his mouth.

"I like it a lot," Kerry amended.

Keegan laughed, took him by the hand, and led him to find Karen. She waited patiently for them around the corner. Each range looked like a fancy horse's stall but without the bedding on the floor. The targets were set up on the rear wall, and stagecoach lights provided the perfect amount of illumination without ruining the Western vibe. Old-timey wanted posters hung on the walls, and other decor like whiskey barrels filled the space. The rules they'd just agreed to also hung on the wall as a reminder. Karen demonstrated the proper axe-throwing technique and posture. She struck the target at dead center of the bullseye.

"Wow," Keegan said. "You must practice a lot."

Karen smiled and shrugged. "It was just a really lucky throw."

Kerry doubted that very much.

"I'll work with both of you to make sure you're comfortable before I leave you to it," Karen said. "Who wants to go first?"

"He does," Keegan said, pointing at Kerry.

"I will," Kerry agreed.

It looked much easier than it really was. Kerry focused on his footing and balance first before bringing the axe over his head with both hands. He went through the motion without releasing the axe once before he let it fly. The weapon soared through the air, smacked into the target, and fell to the floor.

"You've got brute strength on your side," Karen said. "You'd knock an enemy out cold with that blow. You might want to take a little off the velocity and work on the finesse part." She waved a hand for Keegan to join her. "Let me show you what I mean."

She directed Keegan's movements with his steps, the pull back and the release of the axe. His throw struck the target but at the farthest ring from the bullseye, though you'd never know by his jubilant celebration.

"I did it!" Keegan cheered before leaping into Kerry's arms.

His joy was contagious, and Kerry caught him up in a hug. "You sure did. That was a solid throw."

Keegan sobered a little and considered him. "You're not about to turn this into another Hart family card night, are you?"

"No," Kerry said defensively.

"That's where I know you from!" Karen said, pointing at him. "I saw you on the news when you rescued the truck driver on the bridge."

Kerry scratched behind his ear. "Yeah, that was me."

"You were very brave," Karen told him. Her expression grew serious, and she glanced between Keegan and Kerry with narrowed eyes. "What happens at the Hart family card nights?"

"Nothing," Kerry replied.

Keegan snorted and leaned toward Karen. "It's a testosterone-filled night of chest thumping and silliness." Realizing what he said, Keegan added, "No one gets intoxicated, stupid, or violent. There's just a lot of teasing."

Karen nodded. "Teasing is good." She gestured for Kerry. "Come on over here, and let me see if I can help you hone your skill a little better."

"She means land the axe *in* the target," Keegan teased as he stepped aside. His hazel eyes looked more brown than green in the stagecoach lighting, and they glittered with a challenge.

"Big talk for a guy who barely stuck the landing."

"This isn't gymnastics," Keegan quipped. "And I'll take barely over nada anytime." He swept his arms to the range. "Let's see what you've got, big guy."

Karen grimaced. "Strong man, sharp weapon."

"He'd never hurt me," Keegan replied.

Kerry had never wanted to kiss that smug mouth more than he did right then. He loved that Keegan knew he'd always be safe in his presence. He winked at Keegan and said, "Damn right." Kerry turned his attention to the target, pictured Chuck's stupid face in the center of it, and threw his axe. "Bullseye!" Kerry cheered when the blade struck the target with a loud *thud*.

Karen gave him a high five, and Keegan celebrated with an exuberant but all-too-quick kiss.

"I think you guys have the gist of it," Karen told them. "I'll leave you to it, but let me know if you need some help."

The lane rental was like a bowling alley, allowing them to play as many rounds as they could squeeze into their time limit. Scoring was all done by hand instead of a computer, and they didn't have any fun graphics when they landed an axe. Kerry found their jeers and reluctant congratulations much more stimulating than dancing cartoons. The first game went to Kerry, but he knew the next would be much tighter since Keegan's accuracy improved with each throw.

"How much time do we have left?" Keegan asked as he approached the thrower's mark on the floor.

"Forty-five minutes."

"It only took you fifteen minutes to pound me into the…" Keegan's words trailed off as he realized their secondary meaning. "To win," he amended.

Kerry waggled his brows. "I like the first remark better." He tilted his head and reconsidered as he closed the distance between them. "Though I'm not sure if that was a complaint or a compliment. Are you suggesting I slow things down or speed them up?"

Settling his hand on Kerry's chest, Keegan gave a playful push. "Get back over on your side of the stall until it's your turn. Don't make me call Karen over here to remind you about the rules."

Kerry took a few steps back and pointed to the sign. "No need to get me in trouble. I can see the rules."

"Then obey them," Keegan replied. He squared up against the target and pulled his arms back over his head, but he looked at Kerry instead of releasing the axe. "Fast, slow. I don't care how long it takes as long as you pound me." With that, he returned his attention to the target, took a deep breath, and let it fly. The axe landed dead center in the bullseye. Keegan turned and strode toward him with an extra swagger in his step. "Top that."

Kerry lightly cupped Keegan's jaw to hold his mouth in place for a hard kiss. "I'm going to top you."

Keegan sighed, and his eyelids lowered to half-mast. "Promise me that both of the cards will lead to life-affirming orgasms?"

"Not earth-shattering?" Kerry asked.

Keegan snorted. "Why would I want the world to break apart when I finally get my hands on you?" He swatted Kerry on the ass and tipped his head to the throwing line. "Now, get over there and wow me."

Kerry complied, but his throw was off a little. He turned narrowed eyes on Keegan. "You got me all flustered."

Keegan rolled his eyes, but it was true. "I'm sure my last shot was pure luck."

Except it wasn't, and neither was the next one or the one after that. His throws didn't all land in the center of the bullseye, but close enough. Kerry had some excellent throws, but they weren't enough to beat Keegan. They set their axes down and exchanged congratulatory hugs and kisses.

"We have some time left," Kerry said. "Do you want to—"

Keegan took him by the hand and led him out of the range. "Where are you hiding the third set of cards?" He stopped by Kerry's truck and faced him. "Are they somewhere on your person? Because I wouldn't mind a thorough body search."

Kerry wouldn't mind that either, but not in the parking lot of Lumberjack's Axe and Ale. "The cards are up in my bedroom."

Keegan was around the truck and opening the passenger door before he finished his sentence. "Let's go."

"I feel kinda cheap," Kerry teased.

"Just wait until I'm through with you."

Kerry almost asked what he had in mind but decided against it so they could arrive safely at his house. They chatted about random topics during the short drive, but the conversation ceased the moment he pulled into the driveway. Keegan was practically out the door before his truck came to a complete stop, and he sure as hell beat Kerry to the front porch. They kissed while he fumbled with his keys to unlock the front door. Their clothes started coming off as soon as they shut themselves inside the house. Keegan shivered hard when Kerry trailed kisses down his neck and gripped his bare ass with both hands.

"Cold?" Kerry asked.

"Horny. I don't think I can make it upstairs."

Kerry hoisted him into the air, and Keegan wrapped his legs around Kerry's waist. "I got you." He took the steps two at a time and hurried down the hall to his bedroom. He deposited Keegan in the center of the bed and followed him down, crawling between his spread thighs. "In order to get the cards, I have to let go of your body." Kerry thrust forward, rubbing their erections together.

Keegan whimpered and dug his heels into Kerry's ass to encourage more frotting and friction. "Just tell me what my options are."

"And take the fun out of guessing?" Kerry extracted himself from Keegan's hold long enough to fish the cards out from his nightstand. He held the cards over Keegan's gorgeous face. One card granted him a ride on Kerry's cock and the other a ride on his face. A total win-win situation.

Keegan grabbed the card on the left, which was the cock ride, and pumped his fist in the air. "Hell, yes!" He flung the card across the bed and reached for the other one, but Kerry pulled it out of his reach and flung it away too. "What's it say?"

"It was a ticket to ride my face," Kerry said.

Keegan's eyes widened, like he was trying to figure out how that would work.

"I'd eat your ass while you use my face like a bicycle seat," Kerry told him. "Or, you could blow me while I—"

"Yes," Keegan said. "That's the appetizer. We'll get good and primed for me to sit on your dick."

Kerry rolled to his back fast enough to make the room spin. He turned his head to look for Keegan when a scrumptious ass didn't immediately settle over his face. "Second thoughts?"

"Well, I mean, do I just crawl up there and literally sit on your face? How will you breathe?"

Kerry crooked his finger. "Come over here, and I'll show you." He patted the mattress just above his shoulders. "Put your knees here and place your hands down by my knees."

"Doggy style."

"Yeah," Kerry said. "You'll lower your head to suck my dick while I raise mine to fuck you with my tongue."

They'd experimented with rimming the other night, which was Kerry's first attempt. Random hookups didn't invite that kind of intimacy, but he didn't want to leave anything unexplored with Keegan. He was going to make a feast of that sweet peach. Keegan got into position, putting his round ass in the air and his dick pointing due south. Kerry gripped Keegan's cheeks and spread them apart, wasting no time before diving in. He licked, sucked, and teased Keegan's pucker and felt confident about his command until firm lips wrapped around Kerry's cock and sucked him into a hot, wet mouth. Keegan was tentative at first, keeping his suction light and his strokes shallow, but it was enough to throw Kerry off his rhythm. Keegan kept taking his dick deeper and deeper with every downward trip, and he might've levitated off the bed without his sexy tormentor holding him down.

Kerry doubled down on his efforts to drive Keegan just as wild, and he knew his shallow tongue fucking was working when warm, sticky precum dripped onto his bare chest. He drew his head away enough to see a trail of it leaking from Keegan's cock. He wanted a taste of that sweet syrup and scooted down a little.

"Hey! Where are you…oh!" Keegan exclaimed when Kerry rolled his tongue around his cockhead and sucked the tip into his mouth.

"Fuck, you taste good," Kerry growled. He repositioned his body so he could get more dick in his mouth. Keegan's legs shook, and he pitched forward but caught himself before he fell.

"Your mouth is a weapon," Keegan moaned. He gave himself over to the joy of Kerry's mouth working up and down his length before he resumed blowing Kerry.

As with the axe throwing, they spurred each other on, knowing there would be no losers this round. Keegan pulled his mouth off Kerry's dick, panting heavily as he climbed off Kerry's body long enough to open the nightstand drawer and find Kerry's supplies. He straddled Kerry's thighs and opened the condom wrapper with his teeth. Keegan's hands shook as he rolled the latex over Kerry's erection before grabbing the lube.

"Give me," Kerry said.

Keegan shook his head. "I'm primed to go off the second one of your thick fingers pushes inside."

Kerry wanted to accept that challenge, but he saw the desperation in Keegan's gaze and in his hectic motions. He rested his palms on Keegan's quivering thighs and said, "Watching you open yourself up for me is no hardship. Spread your legs wide and give me a good show, baby."

"Christ," Keegan moaned. "Apparently, your voice is enough to make me come." He gripped the base of his dick, closed his eyes, and cycled through a few breaths.

Kerry was dangling on the edge of the cliff, too, when Keegan slicked his dick with lube. "Option three," he husked. "You come up here and fuck my face."

Keegan's pupils expanded until only a thin band of hazel showed. "But I want to feel you inside me."

"Then you can sit on my dick if you won't be too sensitive after coming."

Keegan crawled up Kerry's body and straddled his face again, this time with his dick lined up perfectly to Kerry's mouth. "Open up." He obliged, and Keegan pushed in slowly, not stopping until his balls brushed against Kerry's beard. "Sexy bastard," Keegan groaned as he gripped the headboard and fucked Kerry's mouth.

Hearing his cries of ecstasy and watching Keegan chase his pleasure was almost enough to detonate Kerry's orgasm. Keegan's eyes closed, and his head tipped back as he lost himself in the moment. It was the sexiest thing Kerry had ever witnessed. Keegan's body stiffened suddenly, and he looked stunned as the first splash of release shot down

Kerry's throat. "Oh shit." Keegan pulled his dick free, and his release shot all over Kerry's neck, beard, and mouth. "That happened so fast. I didn't mean to come in your mouth."

Kerry lifted his head and licked the dripping cum off Keegan's fingers, sucking them into his mouth one at a time before swiping the remnants off his lips. "I just had my tongue in your ass. What's a little jizz down my throat?" He gripped Keegan's hips and scooted him down toward his eager dick. "You good for this?"

Keegan wrapped his fingers around the base of Kerry's dick and lined it up to his hole. "Are you?" He sank down on Kerry's erection and rode him for all he was worth. Kerry watched in awe as Keegan completely owned his body. Keegan placed a hand in the center of Kerry's chest and rolled his hips back and forth, driving Kerry out of his ever-loving mind. He gripped Keegan's hips when the pleasure reached a climax, then thrust his hips to go deep with his release. He resented the barriers between them and wished he could bathe Keegan's channel with his spunk.

Keegan collapsed onto his chest in a warm, sweaty heap. "Best. Date. Ever."

# Chapter
# THIRTEEN

THE SETTING SUN BATHED THE VINEYARD AND THE ROLLING hills and mountains beyond it in a golden light that stole Keegan's breath. "Utter perfection," he whispered.

But he'd been thinking that a lot over the past month, existing in a blissful dreamlike state. Keegan finally understood what it felt like to flourish professionally and personally. Debbie had taken him under her wing and taught him so much about what hospitality means in the restaurant industry. Cash had included him in the process of choosing an architect and scouting potential locations. His mentor listened and encouraged his ideas. Keegan no longer felt like an aimless extra on the ranch who just filled in wherever the crew needed a body. He had a purpose and a future that made him proud.

And the universe was finally easing up on Kerry. Chuck the Fuck hadn't made a nuisance of himself since the night of the semitruck accident on the bridge. As for the lawsuit, Vinny told Kerry not to worry about it, so Kerry didn't. The deposition was coming up on Monday, and Vinny expected Bozeman to drop the lawsuit when he saw the evidence they had on him. Without those stressors, Kerry had more free time to give to Keegan. The dates, overnight stays, and the long phone calls when they couldn't be together just entrenched Kerry deeper and deeper into Keegan's heart. Yet a not-so-small part of himself waited for someone to pull the rug out from under him or to jump out from a hiding spot and declare this had all been a colossal practical joke.

His next inhale hurt, and Keegan realized he'd been holding his breath…again. It happened every time he basked in the new joys he'd discovered about himself and the man he fell harder for every day. *This is too good to be true.* The thought would invade his happiness like an infectious disease, tainting his joy and killing his mood. And like with any sickness, the side effects were often just as painful and, in his case, took the form of additional mean thoughts. *You're being too clingy. Careful, your desperation is showing.*

All the things he feared attacked him when he seemed to be happiest, like cuddling against Kerry after sex. He'd move to give Kerry space, but a big hand would haul him back and tuck Keegan tighter against his body. That should've been an antidote to cure his fears, but it felt more like slapping a bandage on a bullet wound and hoping for the best. Keegan tried the techniques he learned in therapy to silence the negative voices, but he'd only turned down the volume so far.

"Yes, you are." Kerry's husky voice caught Keegan by surprise, and he turned from the wall of windows to find him standing there with a wineglass in one hand and a bottle of water in the other. Kerry had switched to water after a glass of wine since he was driving. His responsibility was almost as sexy as the rocking body he'd covered with slacks and a white dress shirt for their vineyard date.

"I'm what?" Keegan asked in confusion.

Kerry studied him for several seconds with a wry smile that dragged Keegan's attention to his mouth. "You don't even know, do you?"

"Apparently not."

Kerry set the drinks on the table beside them. He settled one hand on Keegan's hip and cupped his face with the other. Keegan leaned into his caress, much like Kerry's beloved cat did, and relished the warm palm against his cheek. Then Kerry moved, a gentle sway to the live music at the opposite end of the large room. The slow dance didn't make his turbulent musings vanish in a puff of smoke, but the remaining tendrils were faint enough for Keegan to pretend they weren't there. Kerry leaned in close for what Keegan thought was a kiss, but he put his mouth to Keegan's ear instead. "Just now, you were gazing out the window at the beautiful sunset, and you called it utter perfection. And I said, 'Yes, you are.'"

"Oh," Keegan said breathlessly. "I didn't realize I'd spoken out loud." How often did he do that? And did he talk in his sleep? His insides curdled at the thought because that's when the insidious thoughts lashed at him the hardest, invading his dreams and putting Keegan back in his place after he'd dared to climb too high. "I'm not perfect."

The joy in Kerry's gaze dimmed a little, and two lines formed between his brows when he narrowed his eyes. "You are perfect for me." Kerry leaned in and softly kissed his lips. "I think we're perfect for each other." He rubbed his nose against Keegan's. "Your courage is the reason I've decided to seek therapy. I still have so much shit to work through, and I want to give you the best version of myself."

Keegan pulled back and stared into Kerry's dark eyes. "I'm so proud of you, and I will support you however I can. Always."

Over the past month, they'd spent hours sharing their deepest, darkest traumas and fears. Kerry talked about losing his sister and father with a naked vulnerability that stole Keegan's breath. He understood why Kerry had protected his heart so fiercely. And Kerry never shied away from Keegan's trauma. He didn't back away from the tears or express pity or disgust. He sometimes had to work through anger on Keegan's behalf, but that usually ended with them getting naked in the home gym. Kerry made him feel cared for and seen for the very first time in his life, and it was both exhilarating and so fucking scary.

Keegan closed his eyes and savored the warmth of Kerry's body pressed to his. He allowed himself to get lost in the music as they swayed in the fading sunlight. Soft lips pressed against his, and he parted to let Kerry in, and they kissed until they were breathless. When Keegan stared into Kerry's beautiful brown eyes, he vowed never to take beautiful moments like these for granted.

"Do you think you've taken enough notes for Cash?" Kerry's husky tenor left no doubt about some alternative activities he had in mind.

He took Kerry by the hand and led him across the floor. "Let's get out of here."

"I had a wonderful time," Kerry said once they stepped outside. "I'm trying all kinds of new things with you, and I really like it."

"Glad you feel that way because I packed an impulse buy in my bag. It's for couples, and you might think it's lame."

"Sounds intriguing," Kerry said. "Give me a hint."

"It involves nudity."

Kerry tugged his hand and walked faster. "I'm tickled pink anytime I get you naked."

Keegan smiled at a reference Kerry wouldn't understand until they got back to the hotel room, and he revealed the couple's activity he'd purchased on a whim. They were strapped in and heading down the vineyard's long gravel drive in record time. Keegan watched the venue fade into the side mirror through a small cloud of dust stirred up by Kerry's tires. He wasn't driving fast or reckless, but the man was definitely on a mission.

"Can I have another clue?"

Keegan considered it and shook his head. "It will be too easy to guess." But he had something else on his mind that he finally felt brave enough to broach. "I don't want to use condoms with you anymore."

Kerry had reached the end of the drive and stopped the truck.

There wasn't another vehicle in sight, but he didn't pull onto the road. He turned to look at Keegan, eyes blazing with an intensity that sparked a response low in his belly. "I've wanted that since the first time our lips met. I hate anything separating us, but are you sure? I've always used condoms, and I get tested regularly. I could undergo another round if it makes you feel better."

"I had a full round of screenings during my hospital stay after I escaped the compound. I've maintained the testing, even though I wasn't having sex until recently. I started taking PrEP after discussing my readiness for intimacy during therapy. I...um, didn't intend to have unprotected sex with strangers. I wanted a backup." Keegan swallowed nervously. He'd stepped this far out of his comfort zone and didn't want to stop now. "I need all of you, and I want to get downright filthy with you tonight."

"Hold on." Kerry faced the road and punched the gas hard enough to make the rear tires spin. He whooped like a wild man as he fishtailed out of the driveway and sped down the deserted road.

Keegan threw his head back and laughed at Kerry's antics.

"Told you I was a mess," Kerry said, but he sounded proud of it for the first time. "And we're about to get a lot messier." He glanced over at Keegan with a quirked brow. "I believe you said downright filthy."

"You have no idea," Keegan replied.

They made it back to the hotel without incident, crashing through their room door and slamming it shut behind them. Kerry paused from undressing Keegan long enough to engage the locks. "Where's the couple's surprise?"

Keegan tripped over his pants as he walked backward, but Kerry snatched him before he fell. "In my bag."

Kerry divested Keegan of his clothes and laid him out on the bed. He stripped naked in record time before he unzipped Keegan's bag. It didn't take much rifling to find the rectangular box he'd tucked under his clean clothes and toiletry bag. Kerry grinned wickedly as he studied the exterior photos. He tore one end of the package open with the enthusiasm of a kid on Christmas morning, then tipped it so a plastic pot with pale pink liquid fell into his palm. Kerry held it up and read the label at the top. "Tickled Pink body paint."

Keegan sat up and stroked Kerry's erection, eliciting a throaty moan from his man. Kerry closed his eyes and tilted his head back. Keegan continued to stroke him until a bead of precum gathered at his slit. Keegan swiped his thumb over it and used the moisture to massage Kerry's frenulum.

"So good," Kerry moaned.

Keegan released his cock and waited for those dark eyes to open before he licked Kerry's essence from his thumb.

His big man inhaled shakily, and his expression promised Keegan retribution. He set the pink pot on the bed and read off the other five pastel colors, all of them with playful names. "Blue no more," he said with a snicker as he held up the light blue paint. Keegan had told him all about the blue ball painting he'd created during his first attempt at art therapy, so the paint color put an extra gleam in his dark eyes. "Got that right." Kerry unfolded the canvas that came with the kit and shook it out. It was a fraction of the size of a drop cloth painters would use, but it was large enough to cover the hotel bed so they wouldn't ruin the linens.

Keegan got off the bed and spread the canvas over the duvet. "A sexier version of wine and painting night at the art center." Something wet and cold landed on his ass before he could straighten up.

"Pink is definitely your color." Kerry's large hand warmed the paint as he spread it all over Keegan's right cheek. He braced himself with a hand on the bed and enjoyed the massage. "Fuck, art is fun," Kerry said with a sexy growl. "Too bad it's not edible because I want to lick you everywhere."

"And I want your tongue everywhere." Keegan made a mental note to find or create an edible version of body paint that wouldn't stain their skin for all eternity. Before he finished the thought, Kerry dropped to his knees behind Keegan and buried his face between his ass cheeks. "No fair." His protest was as weak as his knees, but Keegan twisted out of reach at his first opportunity and reached for the lime paint color.

"Come back here," Kerry demanded. "I wasn't done." The pale pink smears on Kerry's face and in his beard were a sensual work of art that made Keegan's pucker quiver in anticipation of more, but he wanted to get in on the action.

Keegan shook his head and stood up. "I need to spread some of these paint colors on your gorgeous body to paint the canvas. He swiped a finger through the pink paint on Kerry's face and showed it to him. "Unless you want me to shove you face-first down on the bed."

Kerry randomly selected a paint pot and handed it to Keegan. "We haven't tried that yet."

"Have you ever..."

"Bottomed? No." Kerry snaked a hand out and hauled Keegan up against him. "I'd try it with you, though."

Keegan had considered himself a dedicated bottom, but he might like to try topping someday. He dipped two fingers into the plastic pot and scooped out a generous amount. "I'll keep that in mind." He smeared the lime-green paint over Kerry's tight pec, lingering on his nipple before dragging his fingers lower to create a wiggly line over taut abs. "This is a great color for your skin tone."

"Looks too much like the slime from the Nickelodeon channel," Kerry said.

"Oh, I'm going to slime you all right. Downright filthy, remember?"

Kerry playfully tackled Keegan to the bed, and the festivities began in earnest. They kissed and smeared paint all over each other without getting it all over the bed and floor. They rolled and played, being sure to thoroughly decorate the canvas with their passion. Kerry wisely kept one hand clean so he could slick his bare dick with lube and slide deep and snug inside Keegan. They stayed like that for several moments, holding on to one another while staring into each other's eyes. Kerry shuddered and groaned when he moved inside Keegan.

"Feel different?" Keegan whispered.

"So intense. Hotter, tighter, and so fucking sweet." He inhaled sharply. "I probably won't last long."

"Don't hold back." Keegan used his heels to spur Kerry into action. "Give me all of you."

Kerry snapped his hips forward, scooting Keegan up the bed with his thrusts. "Like that."

"Yes. Fill me up. Make me yours."

"You are mine." Their bodies slapped together loudly, and the bed squeaked as Kerry set about proving it. Despite his doubt, he lasted much longer than he predicted, working Keegan into a shattering climax before Kerry joined him.

"I feel you," Keegan whispered in his ears as Kerry pinned him to the bed and rutted through his climax. "So hot and slick inside me."

Kerry eased out and sat back on his haunches. He pushed Keegan's knees toward his chest to raise his ass up. Kerry eased a finger inside and growled when he felt his release inside Keegan. He came back down on top of Keegan, and they kissed until they were breathless. Kerry rolled off Keegan, and they looked at the mess on their bodies. Keegan's release had rehydrated the drying paint and smeared the colors into a hue neither of them could name. "Kinda looks gray?"

"I was thinking beige," Keegan said. "What's the color that looks both gray and brown in different lighting?"

"Taupe, I think, but I'm the last one you should ask about colors." Kerry laughed and ran a hand through Keegan's hair before he realized his mistake. "Oops. Sorry about that." His cheeky grin said otherwise.

"Sven will kill you if you've messed up his handiwork. He spent hours making my highlights look natural."

"Hours?" Kerry scoffed. "You don't have that much hair."

"It's this entire process of separating the strands with a comb, then bleaching some and wrapping it in foils. He uses toners and hair masks, and it's just an extensive process." Keegan rolled his eyes upward as if that would allow him to see Kerry's damage. He snorted at his silliness and asked what color paint was in his hair.

"Well, it's like the color on your stomach but darker since it wasn't diluted with your spunk."

Keegan slapped Kerry's shoulder, signaling for him to move. "I better wash this off."

Kerry nestled closer, nuzzling his nose in Keegan's neck. "But this feels so good."

And he groaned because it was better than good. "Amazing." His shower was all but forgotten when Kerry kissed him deeply. Their phones both went off at the same time with incoming FaceTime calls. If one of their phones rang, they could ignore it, but both? Kerry rolled to the side, and Keegan fumbled through the pile of clothes until he found one of their ringing devices. "Sven is calling me," he said as he searched for Kerry's phone. He snagged it off the floor and tossed it to Kerry.

"And Dom's calling me, but that's Sven's face."

Mindful of the phone's angle, Keegan accepted the call. "Sven, what's up?"

"Oh good," he said breathlessly. Kerry's phone immediately stopped ringing, so Sven was calling both of them from his and Dom's phones. "I was afraid neither of you would answer." He squinted into the phone and leaned closer. "Why is it so dark there? Are you in a cave?"

A snort came from nearby Sven, and then Dom said, "They're at a hotel during a lover's getaway, Stevie. Why do you think it's dark?"

"Oh. Ohhh. I didn't expect you to do it with the lights off," Sven replied. "Turn on a light and cover your bits. This is an emergency."

"What are the two of you doing together?" Kerry asked while

Keegan turned on the bedside lamp. He joined Kerry on the bed and positioned the phone so they could both see the screen.

"Wouldn't you like to know?" Sven teased and batted his eyelashes.

"Quit teasing him, Stevie," Dominic growled. "Sven is helping me with a case, which is why we're calling."

"But first," Sven said, "what's smeared all over your skin? Why is Kerry's beard pink, and what's in Keegan's hair? What kind of freaky getaway are you two having?"

"Let me see," Dom demanded. Sven moved the phone over, and Dom's handsome face came into view. It was clear he was driving, but he glanced over long enough to see what Sven had described. "Holy shit. You kinky little fuckers."

"The nature of the call, please," Kerry demanded. "Maybe we weren't done getting our freak on."

Sven sighed. "Unfortunately, you are."

Kerry and Keegan sat up straighter. "What happened?"

"Vinny put me on another case with short notice," Dom said. "I started my investigation last night and already asked questions around the bar. I didn't want to make any of the regulars suspicious, so I called Sven to help me."

"Sven?" Keegan and Kerry said at once.

The man in question snarled at them. "Neither of you recognized me when I trailed Keegan on his date." They conceded his point graciously and encouraged them to talk. "So, I went into this bar to get pictures and details for Dom's case. I looked so hetero that some hot ladies tried to pick me up."

"Focus, Sven," Dom said.

"Hang back," Sven told Dom. "He's going to notice you're following him. Put more car lengths between us."

"I'm the professional here," Dom replied dryly. "You just bring Kerry up to speed."

Sven sighed heavily. "While I was gathering evidence for Dom, which I bagged in record time, I noticed Chuck the Fuck ranting and raving at a nearby table. His dumb ass wouldn't recognize me if I'd come in my usual fabulous attire, but I took advantage of my disguise to secure a table close to his so I could eavesdrop and snap a few discreet photos."

"Sven, you shouldn't have risked your safety," Kerry said.

"You'll be singing a different tune when you find out what he overheard," Dom replied.

Sven preened for a few seconds. "As soon as I heard him say your name, I turned on the video recorder on my phone. The quality probably isn't great with all the bar noise in the background, but I caught every word of his plot."

"What plot?" Keegan and Kerry asked.

Sven made puppy dog eyes and covered his heart. "Could you guys be any cuter?"

"Sven!" Dom growled.

"Right! The plot. I recorded a lot, but the gist is that Chuck told his buddy that you ruined his career twice, and he was going to get even. The fool is planning to sabotage the vehicles in your lot so that the crew can't respond to emergencies. He plans to ride in and save the day."

"How do you want us to handle it?" Dom asked.

Kerry ran a hand through his hair. Luckily, the paint had dried. "Is he headed to my station now?"

"Seems so," Dom said. "But we're thirty minutes away. Plenty of time to get someone in place and catch him red-handed."

"That's what I want to do," Kerry said. "I'm willing to sacrifice minimum damage if it results in an arrest that will forever get this asshole out of my life. Do you mind calling the local police?" Kerry asked. He would prefer to call Seth, but Kerry's station was situated in an incorporated zone patrolled by the township cops. The county boys would provide backup if needed, but the township officers needed to make that call. Kerry would make some enemies if he went over people's heads to involve his cousin.

"No problem," Dom said.

"Then I'll call the guys at the station and give them a heads-up. I don't want any of you confronting Chuck. He's clearly not in a good headspace, and there's no telling what he's capable of doing."

"Fair enough," Dom said.

"Now, if he tries to light the building on fire or something, then maybe you take him down as best you can," Kerry said. "What do you know about the guy he was talking to at the bar?"

"I haven't seen the pictures or heard the recordings yet," Dom said.

"The conversation sounded like it was about a business deal that had gone wrong," Sven said. "The guy just kept yelling at Chuck and reminding them they had a deal. There was a lot of money on the line, and he'd put himself out there for Chuck. It was pretty loud in the bar, so I didn't hear everything. I'm not so sure how great the recording will be either. Do you have software to clean up the background noises, Dom?"

"Somewhat," Dom told him. "We suspected that Chuck had a silent partner, but I couldn't legally get my hands on bank records and transactions," Dom said. "Only Chuck's name is registered to the business."

"I think we all know who the mystery man is," Kerry said. "It's Keith Bozeman."

"I called it," Sven said. "The timing of Chuck's new business was too suspect."

"The timing of this confrontation is more so," Kerry agreed.

"Bozeman doesn't have money to invest in Chuck's business," Dom said. "That dude is dead broke."

"Maybe he knows somebody," Keegan said.

"We could guess all night long, or you can send me the picture," Kerry said.

"Will do," Sven said. "Sorry if we ruined your weekend, Ker."

"You probably saved me a lot of headaches," Kerry replied. "In fact, I might not even need to come back if things don't get out of control."

"We'll get everyone in place," Dom assured him.

"Catch you in a bit," Kerry said before he disconnected the call and called his station. "This won't take long."

Keegan kissed his bare shoulder and stood up. "Take as long as you need. I'm going to clean up. The paint is getting itchy."

"I'll join you as soon as I can."

Keegan turned on the shower and surveyed the damage in the mirror. Kerry's voice came through the door, but he couldn't make out what he said. He spoke for a few minutes before he ended the call. Keegan tested the water, but it was still barely lukewarm. He was just about to throw caution to the wind and step into the shower when he heard Kerry's phone chime with an incoming text.

"I fucking knew it!" Kerry shouted.

Keegan turned off the shower and ran into the bedroom. "Is it him?"

He looked up from his phone with a smug expression on his face. "Sven was right." He turned the phone around to show two men in a dimly lit bar. "That's Bozeman and Chuck."

Kerry's dark eyes glittered with fury. "This should make our deposition on Monday even more fun."

## *Chapter*
# FOURTEEN

"THANKS FOR COMING TO THE DEPOSITION WITH ME TODAY," Kerry said. Finding support hadn't been hard. He'd turned down several kind offers to join him, but Kerry reached over the console and laced his fingers with the only person he'd wanted by his side.

"There's nowhere else I'd rather be," Keegan replied.

"Hands at ten and two," Lucinda instructed from the back seat.

His mother was the only one Kerry hadn't been able to persuade to stand by for updates. Watching Keegan and Lucinda go several rounds of insisting the other sit up front with him had been amusing. The whole thing reminded Kerry of when he'd learned to drive. His mother had wanted to be included, but she'd been too nervous to ride in the front passenger seat. Lucinda volunteered Steven to ride shotgun and grip the oh-shit handle while she called out instructions from the back seat.

"Yes, Mother." Kerry exchanged a quick smile with Keegan lest he earn a lecture about keeping his eyes on the road. A glance in his rearview mirror earned an approving nod, but it would be hard to get on Lucinda's bad side after she noted Keegan's radiance when they picked her up. Steven had already left for work and would meet them at Bozeman's attorney's office for their noon deposition. Like Lucinda, Steven insisted on being there for moral support.

"How long do you think it will take Vinny to shred Bozeman and his ambulance chasers?" Lucinda asked. "I say fifteen minutes."

"I hope you're right," Kerry said, but he wouldn't bet on it. The opposing counsel wasn't up to Vinny's level of brilliance, but they weren't likely as inept as Lucinda hoped. Kerry didn't care how long it took, as long as Bozeman dropped the case against him. Vinny was confident of that outcome after their phone call on Sunday afternoon. He'd been just as impressed with Sven's sleuthing as he'd been with Dom's, and he'd started referring to Bozeman and Chuck as *Beavis and Butthead* by the end of the conversation.

Chuck was supposed to be deposed at the attorney's office, but he was still in county lockup. The least of the charges was the minimal damage he'd managed to a Hart's Creek Rescue vehicle. He might've been released the next morning for that, but he'd taken a swing at a police officer with a crowbar, and his breathalyzer test came back as over the limit. Good ole Chuck had an arraignment to attend instead of the deposition, though it was unclear if Bozeman and his attorneys knew that yet. He really hoped not. Kerry wanted to see their expressions when Vinny produced evidence that the primary witness for Kerry's supposed negligence was actually a coconspirator in the scam to fleece Kerry out of money. No matter the deposition's outcome, he would not offer a settlement. He'd take the case all the way to trial if necessary and put his financial fate and reputation in the hands of strangers before he shelled out a penny of his hard-earned money to those fraudsters.

Ryker, Free, and Halbert's office was in the newest commercial development that combined retail stores, business offices, and restaurants in a complex that mimicked a city within a city.

"Could they make these parking spaces any tighter?" Kerry groused as he dismissed one spot after another, looking for enough room to accommodate his vehicle.

"We're totally going to the Cheesecake Factory after this is over," Lucinda announced when Kerry finally found a spot he liked. "Good thing you parked three miles from the building, so I won't feel guilty about the carbs I plan to devour." The distance was a great exaggeration, but she raised him to have better manners.

Kerry met her gaze in the mirror. "I should've dropped you both off before looking for a spot. We're here early, so I can drive you back up."

His mother rolled her eyes and waved off the notion. "I'm just keeping you humble."

"We're attending a deposition because I'm getting sued," Kerry reminded her. "How much more humbling do you think this day could get?"

"But you woke up next to this one," Lucinda said, patting the back of Keegan's chair. "How much luckier do you think this day could get?"

Keegan's eyes went wide, and his cheeks turned a lovely shade of pink.

Kerry gathered his hand and raised it to his lips. "She's right, though she's only guessing about the overnight part." It was a safe bet since Keegan stayed over more nights than he spent at the ranch.

"No guessing necessary. Mothers know everything," Lucinda said as she unbuckled her seat belt and reached for the door. "Was I correct when I said you'd never let your special person go once you found them?"

Kerry smiled as he stared into Keegan's eyes. "You were."

She leaned forward between the front seats. "And didn't I tell you Keegan was your person the first time I saw the two of you together?" She made explosive gestures with her hands that made Keegan giggle. "Fireworks."

"Yes, and now who needs humbling?" Kerry grumbled.

"Oh, there's my honey!" Lucinda exclaimed like it had been months since she'd seen her husband instead of hours. "See you inside, boys." With that, she was out of the truck and heading toward Steven.

"Did she really say those things?" Keegan asked.

"Yes," Kerry replied. "When people expressed concern that I hadn't settled down by thirty, she pointed out that I hadn't met my person yet. And she pulled me aside the first night Sven brought you home to meet the family and announced that you were my person."

Keegan radiated so much joy that Kerry expected beams of light to shoot out of his ears. "Is that why you resisted even harder?"

Kerry tilted his head and considered. "But did I? Okay, maybe a little, but it's not like I made myself scarce every time you came around, and I could've easily used work as an excuse. You enthralled me then, and you do even more now." He cupped Keegan's neck and leaned into his space. "I can't touch you, kiss you, or hold you enough."

A tapping at the window behind Kerry cut him off. He turned and found his parents smiling like twin lunatics. Steven gave him the wrap-it-up gesture, then pointed to his watch. They still had a solid twenty minutes before the deposition, and Kerry could accomplish a lot in that span. But perhaps not in a public parking lot.

"Hey," Keegan said when Kerry moved to exit the vehicle.

Kerry held up a forefinger to his parents, asking for a minute, then made a shooing motion at them to get some privacy. He could tell by the slight quiver in Keegan's voice that he had something important to say. Kerry gave him his full attention again. "What, baby?"

"You're my person too. The night I met you, I came alive in ways I never dreamed possible. I wasn't ready for you—for us—then, and I'm still going to struggle with my insecurities for a while. Maybe a lifetime. But I want you to know something before you go into the deposition." He paused and cycled through some shaky breaths, but his hazel gaze never wavered. Kerry couldn't recall a time when Keegan had looked so certain.

"And you don't have to say it back now, or even ever," Keegan rushed to add. "You've demonstrated what I mean to you, and that's more important to me." His words came faster, breathier, and Kerry's heart raced in anticipation. "I love you. I don't care what anyone says about you in that deposition. You are the best man I've ever known. I know this sounds soon and maybe a little desperate. We've only really dated for a month, but—"

Kerry cut him off with a kiss that went from tender to fierce in a heartbeat. When he pulled back, tears trailed down Keegan's cheeks, and he fully understood what it cost to put himself out there. "I love you, Kee. Other people's opinions and timelines don't matter. The ones who love us the most have been encouraging our relationship for a while now."

Keegan smiled through a laugh. "They didn't bother with subtlety."

"It's not the Hart way."

The knock came back, more persistent this time. Kerry whipped around and found Seth and Rueben standing on the other side. Beyond them were Rick, Debbie, Sven, and Dom. Kerry sought his mother through the crowd, and she just shrugged when he found her.

"Looks like the cavalry has arrived," Keegan teased.

Kerry looked at him with a raised brow. "Did you know about this?"

Shaking his head, Keegan said, "No one told me they were coming, but are you really surprised?" He gestured to Kerry's family. "Show up and show out. That's the Hart way, and you're so lucky to have them."

"*We* are so lucky to have them." Kerry sighed and reached for his door handle. "Might as well greet the crowd and head into the deposition." It didn't feel like heading to the gallows, though he could think of a hundred different things he'd rather do. He stepped out of the truck and into a swarm of hugs from his loving family.

"Let's head on in," Steven told the gathering.

They looked like a small army as they entered the lawyer's office. The receptionist looked up from her task, and her dark blue eyes widened. "Um, can I help you?"

"I'm Kerry Hart, and I'm here for a deposition." He gestured over his shoulder with his thumb. "And this is my support system."

She recovered quickly and introduced herself as Mabel. "And is your attorney among them?"

"He's not here yet," Kerry told her.

"I'm afraid we don't have seats for everyone, but I can probably bring some out of a conference room."

"That won't be necessary," Lucinda said kindly. "There are plenty of shops to check out while we wait."

"I could use a good cup of coffee," Rick said. "Can you recommend a coffeehouse nearby?"

Mabel gave him directions to the place she visited every afternoon. The Kerry Hart Fan Club wished him luck and filed out the door, leaving only the president behind to wait with him. "Can I get either of you something to drink?" Mabel asked.

"I'm fine," Kerry said before checking with Keegan.

"Nothing for me either."

They settled into gray chairs in the waiting room, and Keegan reached for a magazine. Kerry knew he wouldn't be able to concentrate and let his gaze wander to the artwork hanging on the walls. He wasn't aware his knees were bouncing until Keegan's hand landed on his thigh. Keegan's warm gaze brought him immediate peace. Movement at the entrance pulled Kerry's attention, and he stood up as Vinny walked through the door. His attorney was dressed to kill in a navy three-piece suit and polished dark brown dress shoes that matched his leather briefcase. Kerry shook Vinny's hand and introduced him to Keegan.

"Steven has said so many wonderful things about you, Keegan," Vinny said when they shook hands. "It's nice to meet you."

"Likewise," Keegan said.

"Is this your attorney?" Mabel asked.

Vinny spun and introduced himself. The receptionist's eyes widened with recognition. "Will you let Mr. Ryker know we're ready to go, please?"

"Absolutely." Mabel picked up her phone and talked quietly into the receiver, darting a glance in Vinny's direction every few seconds. She hung up the phone and stood up. "I'll show you to the conference room."

Keegan stood up and hugged Kerry. "See you soon," he said. "Then we can put this whole mess behind us."

Kerry gave him an extra squeeze before he stepped back. "You can always track down my mom and Debbie."

"This is where I'm needed." Keegan resumed his seat and picked up the magazine he'd abandoned.

Vinny clapped him on the back as the two of them followed Mabel down the hallway to the conference room at the very back. Two women were already in the room. One was the videographer setting up a camera to record the depositions, and the other was the court reporter unpacking her stenography equipment. Vinny introduced himself to both women, shook their hands, and gestured for Kerry to have a seat. He reviewed with him again what he could expect and the conduct he'd need to adhere to. Kerry figured this was mostly for show because Vinny had a devilish twinkle in his eye that spelled trouble. He figured it was code for "sit back and behave because I've got this under control."

Two newcomers entered the conference room a few minutes later. The first man was tall, slender, with thick gray hair nearly the same color as his expensive suit. It took Kerry a second to recognize the second man, who somehow slouched while wearing a rigid back brace. The black device stood out against his untucked and wrinkled white dress shirt, which was likely the intended effect. Keith Bozeman raised his head and briefly met Kerry's gaze, but it was enough to show off his sallow skin and bloodshot eyes. He looked like he'd just rolled out of bed after a hard bender and threw on the first thing he could find.

"Roger," Vinny said, extending his hand to the attorney.

"Good to see you again, Vinny." Roger Ryker was cordial but tense. "Let's take a seat so we can get started."

Kerry didn't look in Bozeman's pitiful direction even once as the court reporter took control of the room and signaled for the videographer to record. She introduced herself as Selma Brown, then stated the date and time of the meeting before introducing the parties present, including the videographer.

"It looks like we're missing the deponent named Charles Dahl and his legal counsel. Is anyone aware of the circumstances there?" Selma asked.

And that was the opening Vinny needed. "He's being detained for driving under the influence, aggravated vandalism against my client's commercial property, and assaulting a police officer." Vinny turned a hard stare in Bozeman's direction. "The events occurred on Saturday evening after Mr. Dahl met with Keith Bozeman to discuss their scam against my client."

"Nonsense," Roger Ryker yelled. "How dare you sully my client with your accusations?"

Vinny pulled out a small stack of photographs from a folder and slid them across the table. "I believe this is your client with Mr. Bozeman."

"There's no date stamp on this photograph." Ryker looked over at his client and noticed the sweaty sheen on his pallid face. Bozeman kept his gaze down and didn't acknowledge what Vinny said about him. The attorney sounded less confident when he added, "It could've been taken years ago."

Vinny hit a button on his cell phone. Bar noises and angry male voices filled the room.

"You owe me, Chuck. I went to bat for you with my uncle and convinced him to invest in your company. If not for me, you wouldn't have the fancy new service truck." Keith Bozeman flinched when he heard his voice. "Lot of good that's done for you with your stupid stunt on the bridge. I thought you would've learned a lesson."

"Fuck you!" Chuck screamed. "I had everything under control, but those wimps weren't brave enough to listen to me. They called in Kerry Fucking Hart to save the day. The asshole has ruined my career twice now."

"This is no one's fault but your own," Bozeman yelled. "I did my part and got you the money you needed. Sober up and honor your part of the bargain on Monday."

"I'm going to hit that fuck boy right where it hurts the most,"

Chuck said. "His crew can't answer emergency calls if they don't have trucks to drive."

Vinny stopped the recording and sat back. "That's just the beginning of the damning evidence I have against you. Shall I continue?"

Keith Bozeman waved him off and then covered his face with both hands.

Ryker leaned toward his client. "I think it would be wise to drop the lawsuit, Keith. If you decide to continue, you'll need to hire new representation. You might reconsider the offer from Mr. Hart's insurance company."

Bozeman hung his head but nodded. Ryker assured Vinny that he'd file the dismissal paperwork by the end of the day. With that, Kerry and Vinny left the office. The reality of the moment didn't hit him until Keegan leaped to his feet upon seeing them.

"Well?"

The tension drained from Kerry's body, and he smiled at Keegan. "It's over."

"Yes!" Keegan threw his arms around Kerry's neck and hugged him tightly. "Now, we can celebrate with your family."

Pressing his lips to Keegan's ear, he said, "Or maybe we sneak off to someplace private."

"I need to head out, Kerry," Vinny said. The two men hugged, and Kerry thanked him profusely. "Are you kidding? Dom and Sven did most of the legwork. Let's do dinner sometime soon. I don't get to see you guys enough, and I'd like to get to know your guy."

"I'll talk to Mom and put something together."

"Sounds good. Take care." And then Vinny was off with his phone pressed to his ear.

Kerry hauled Keegan back into his arms. "About that celebration…" His voice drifted off when it sounded like a stampede of elephants, or possibly a zombie horde, was approaching the lawyer's office. After some pushing and elbowing, Lucinda came through the door first. "Hello, Ma."

"We saw Vinny leaving," she said as she rushed forward. "He looked especially smug."

"As he should be," Kerry said. Accepting there was no way he could sneak off now, he looped an arm around Lucinda's shoulders. "I'll tell everyone about it over lunch."

"To the Cheesecake Factory!" Lucinda called out in a near battle cry. "My treat." That earned clapping and cheers.

Kerry and Keegan joined hands and followed the group down the sidewalk toward the restaurant. "That poor staff doesn't have a clue what they're in for, do they?"

Keegan laughed and nudged him with his elbow. "Your family is wonderful."

"That's not in dispute," Kerry replied. "But you have to admit they're a lot to handle sometimes, especially to people who don't know them."

"Fair point." Keegan looked up at him with a coy smile. "So, do you have some free time after lunch?"

"I'm taking the entire day off," Kerry replied. "Have something in mind?"

Keegan smiled and nodded. "A few things. I didn't bring index cards with me, but I can still give you a choice."

"Okay, let's hear my options."

"We finally watch *Jurassic Park*, eat popcorn with M&M's, and then we engage in animalistic sex where I make you roar like a T-Rex."

Kerry nearly stumbled over his two feet. "Damn, that sounds like a perfect afternoon. Favorite movie, favorite snack, my favorite guy, and my favorite activity. I don't even need to know the second choice. I want that!"

"You're not even a little tempted to know what else I had in mind?" Keegan teased.

Kerry stopped a few feet away from his family since they'd nearly caught up to the horde. "Of course I want to hear it. Just know it couldn't possibly be as perfect."

Keegan slid his arms around Kerry's waist. "We fuck like animals until you roar like a T-Rex, then we watch *Jurassic Park* to rate your impersonation while eating popcorn and M&M's."

Kerry pursed his lips and pretended to think hard. That's when he noticed the rest of his family had disappeared inside the restaurant. "Let's go!" He grabbed Keegan's hand, and they ran for the parking lot.

"You didn't tell me which option you chose," Keegan called out as they ran.

"I will always choose to get you naked before anything else." And that's just what he did.

*Epilogue*

THE WEIGHT OF BETTY'S STARE WOKE HIM FROM A DEEP SLEEP, and Keegan cracked an eye open. It was still dark outside, but that hulking silhouette towering over him from his nightstand could only belong to one feisty feline. A white-tipped paw eased out of the darkness and booped him on the nose. When Keegan didn't immediately throw back the covers and leap from the bed, Betty lowered her head closer to his so that they were nearly eye to eye. Even in the predawn dusk, Keegan could see that she meant business. He did too, and he tried to convey that to her through telepathy. *Come on, Betty. It's Thanksgiving. Just another hour.* She booped him on the nose again, and Keegan knew she was seconds away from raising the dead with an ear-piercing yowl.

Keegan eased from the bed before that happened, not because he feared zombies or ghosts but to prevent Betty from waking Kerry, who'd had a deeply emotional therapy session the previous day and a late-night rescue. The cool air triggered goose bumps on his bare skin before he could don his robe at the foot of the bed. He slid his feet into his slippers and headed for the door. Betty didn't budge from her perch until she was certain Keegan's easy compliance wasn't a trick. Kerry had pulled that stunt with her more than once, but he'd never attempted it. Betty flew past him when he was halfway down the staircase, but he'd been ready for it. After four months of permanent cohabitation, Keegan was used to her shenanigans. And he didn't need it to be Thanksgiving to be grateful for his blessings—big and small.

He headed straight to the utility room and fed the queen her tuna and made sure she had plenty of dry kibble and water in the fancy fountain he'd bought for her fifth birthday. That was just one way Keegan made his mark on the house. Little by little, he put his touch in every room. Sometimes it was a seasonal throw blanket, a new coffee mug, or a piece of artwork for the bedroom, but he marveled whenever he came across them. It was the first time he'd ever felt a sense of home, and he understood it had more to do with the man upstairs than the walls and roof surrounding them.

Keegan hurried upstairs, hoping to slip under the covers and get another hour of sleep before they needed to get ready for the Thanksgiving festivities at Lucinda's. There'd be family overflowing in every room, food aplenty, football, and fights over rummy. Keegan was eager to enjoy every second, but maybe after a little more sleep. When he entered the bedroom, the fireplace was on, and Kerry had propped himself against the headboard, all sleep-rumpled and delicious. He lifted the bedcovers and beckoned Keegan with a wolfish smile that made sleeping the furthest thing from his mind.

Keegan stood at the foot of the bed and removed his robe. The heat from the fire warmed his backside as the hungry gaze from his man scorched his front. There was more swagger in Keegan's step these days, which Kerry enjoyed immensely. He climbed into the bed and slid over until their bare bodies touched. After a long kiss, Keegan pulled back to brush some of the wildest strands away from Kerry's face. "I'd hoped you'd get some more sleep after a rough day and late night."

Kerry's smile came easily as he ran the back of his fingers over

Keegan's cheek. "This is our first Thanksgiving together, and I didn't want to miss another second of it."

"It's barely six o'clock."

"Perfect time to have a little fun," Kerry said. "I have something special to mark the occasion."

Keegan reached under the blanket and trailed his fingertips over Kerry's dick. "Yes, you do."

"That comes next," Kerry said.

Keegan arched a brow. "What's first?"

"I'm so glad you asked." Kerry leaned over to turn on his lamp and adjusted it to the softest setting. Then he reached under his pillow and pulled out two index cards. They'd been playing this game for seven months, but they somehow kept it exciting and new. Kerry held them up and bounced them excitedly. "Which one?"

Keegan pressed his finger to his lips and hummed. Whatever he picked would lead to something he'd cherish for the rest of his life. Sometimes he could tell which option Kerry wanted him to pick, but his expression remained neutral as Keegan contemplated, and he didn't tighten his grip on the right card when Keegan tugged it free.

Kerry's lips spread into the biggest grin he'd ever seen. "Read it."

Keegan's heartbeat tripped over itself as he turned the card around. *Say yes and make love to your fiancé.* Keegan's hand shook so badly he dropped the card. "Kerry?"

They'd talked about marriage, so the proposal hadn't come out of left field. But it was another example of something Keegan wanted so badly it hurt to think about sometimes. Tears filled his eyes, and he blinked them away. He picked up the card and read it again. It definitely said fiancé. Keegan raised a hopeful gaze to Kerry and noticed the sheen in his dark eyes too.

"Really?" Keegan asked.

"Will you marry me?"

The air left his lungs in a shaky exhale. Of course he'd marry this man. He opened his mouth to tell him but said, "What's on the other card?"

Kerry burst into laughter as he turned it around to reveal a gold band taped next to a small sketch of interlocking hearts. "Your engagement ring and the tattoo I will wear on my ring finger."

Keegan let the tears flow this time. "You're going to ink your commitment to me on your body? That's permanent."

"So is my love for you." Kerry removed the gold band from the card and reached for Keegan's hand. "I found my special someone, and I'm keeping you." He stroked his thumb over Keegan's ring finger. "If you'll have me."

Keegan nodded at first, then cried, "Yes!"

Kerry slid the ring onto his finger, then pulled Keegan onto his lap. "You are the thing I'm most grateful for." And then he showed Keegan.

Lucinda's house was already bustling when they arrived, yet every person froze in place when Keegan and Kerry walked through the front door.

"Did you do it?" Lucinda asked.

Keegan arched a brow. That was bold, even for Lucinda. Then he realized what she'd really meant and raised his left hand to show off his shiny gold band. The room erupted in cheers as everyone rushed forward to congratulate them.

"Huh," Debbie said when she looked closer at the ring. "It's a little plain, isn't it, Ker?"

"I think it's perfect," Keegan said, cradling his hand to his chest.

Kerry chuckled. "That one is just for our engagement, Aunt Deb. His wedding band is blinged out properly."

Keegan quirked a brow in surprise. Two rings? He loved the simple band, but the blinged-out one sounded intriguing too.

"Attaboy," Debbie said before she let the next relative gush over them.

When it seemed like they'd never make it farther than midway through the living room, Lucinda carried out platters of appetizers. The family abandoned the newly engaged couple and pounced on the food like fleas on a barn cat. Kerry waded into the fray to grab them a bite to eat. Keegan breathed a sigh of relief and eased to the side of the room, where Sven greeted him with open arms.

"I'm so happy for you, honey," Sven said. "I knew this day would come, but I was worried I'd have to take desperate measures."

"I shudder to think what that might entail," Keegan said. When Sven didn't respond, he caught a faraway look on his friend's face. Keegan was nearly positive he knew the source of Sven's daydream and had his suspicions confirmed when he followed his friend's line of sight. Sven's entire demeanor changed anytime Dom was near. He dialed everything up to a hundred, and Keegan couldn't tell if he was ready to battle or—

"Fuck, why does that man have to be so damn hot?" Sven asked before he stomped in the opposite direction from Dom.

Keegan didn't miss the way Dom's eyes tracked Sven's movements.

Kerry joined Keegan and extended the plate of snacks toward him. He snagged an olive and nearly choked on it when Kerry said, "Dom and Sven just need to fuck already."

After Keegan recovered, he said, "Aren't you the one who cock-blocked them?"

"Yes, and I'm not sorry," Kerry said. "It wasn't the right time."

"And it is now?"

They watched as Sven kept inching closer and closer to where Dom chatted with Lucinda. A group of cousins plowed into Sven and nearly took him down, but Dom was there with a helping hand that lingered on Sven's bare midriff afterward. The two men locked eyes, and something electric passed between them.

"Yeah," Keegan said. "It's time."

As luck would have it, Keegan and Kerry would get their chance to play matchmaker when Dom expressed his dread about the upcoming Christmas holiday plans with his family.

"You don't get along?" Keegan asked.

"We got along great until I caught my husband in bed with my cousin," Dom told him. "You can imagine the explosive reactions in my family when I went to war with my cousin, and my mom took her sister to the mat."

"Oh, Dom," Keegan said. "I'm so sorry."

"I want to say it's all water under the bridge, but it would be a lie. I'm over the failed marriage better than I thought I'd be at this point, but I'm struggling with my cousin's betrayal."

"Who wouldn't?" Kerry asked. He tightened his grip on Keegan's hip and sent a scathing look in Seth's direction.

Keegan scoffed. "As if."

Kerry nuzzled his nose in Keegan's hair and nipped his ear.

"That's the shit I'll get to look forward to over the holidays, except it will be my ex loving up on a guy I loved like a brother." Dom sipped his beer.

"Why are you even putting yourself through that kind of heartache during the holidays?" Kerry asked.

"My nana isn't doing very well," Dom said softly. "You know how much I love her."

"I thought she'd outlive us all," Kerry said.

"I wish that was true, but Mom thinks this will be her last Christmas. She wants everyone to suspend their animosity for two weeks so she can have the most amazing holiday ever. My aunt and uncle rented a huge chateau in Vail, and Mom expects me to go. I can't let Nana down, but I don't want to be the only single loser getting pitiful looks every time my ex-husband and his new lover go up to bed for the night."

"Man, that's rough," Kerry said.

"Take Sven!" Keegan blurted.

Kerry's eyes glittered with glee. "That's a great idea."

Dom looked over at Sven, who made lounging on a couch look sexy. "I don't know." Dom turned back around and sipped his beer. "Some of my family members are pretty uptight. Sven's outfits wouldn't go over very well."

"I'm sure he'd wear something more conservative if you approached the subject in the right way," Keegan suggested.

"Hell no," Kerry said. "Sic Sven in his full glory on the pretentious assholes. No one who has been hurt as badly as you were would ask you to shack up with your ex and his lover for two weeks. That is selfish and inconceivable. Sven would love to help you teach them a lesson."

Kerry took out his phone and typed a quick message. Sven looked at his phone, quirked a brow, and headed toward them.

He raked an ardent gaze over Dom. "Kerry said you need me."

Dom's cheeks turned pink as he fidgeted with the label on his beer bottle. "I could use your help with a situation."

"Ohhh," Sven simpered. "Undercover for another case?"

Dom swallowed hard but held Sven's gaze. "This is personal."

"You'd get a two-week trip to Vail at Christmastime," Kerry said. "Dom, lead with the selling points first."

"Color me curious," Sven said. "Tell me more."

Kerry's teasing seemed to loosen Dom up because he didn't have any difficulty explaining the situation. Sven's interest was piqued with each new twist and turn.

"Sounds fa la la la fabulous, baby. I'm in." Sven hooked his elbow through Dom's and pulled him away. "Let's work out the details someplace quieter."

Keegan and Kerry watched them until they disappeared from sight. "Did we make a mistake?" Keegan asked.

"Hell no," Kerry said. "They both deserve this." Usually people uttered that phrase in a snide tone, but Kerry sounded blissfully happy. "What? You don't agree?"

"I'm trying to figure out what's behind your joy. Is it the chance for Dom and Sven to find genuine love, or are you anticipating the fireworks this will cause?"

"Both."

Kerry set the plate of food down and pulled Keegan into his arm. "Enough about other couples. I want to talk about us."

Keegan kissed his lips. "My favorite topic."

"When do you want to get married?" Kerry asked. "Lucinda will kill us if we try to pull a stunt like Seth and Rueben did with their wedding."

"I definitely want our friends and family with us, but I don't want something fancy."

"What if we decorate the Feisty Bull and get married there?"

"That sounds perfect," Keegan said. "But when?"

"Either before Sven and Dom leave for Vale or as soon as they get back."

Keegan's eyes widened. "That soon?"

"Why wait?" Kerry asked. "We pick out suits, string up some pretty decorations, and invite our friends and family. That won't take much planning."

"Surely, it's harder than that."

Kerry quirked a brow. "I'll take that challenge." He looked over at the living room. "Hey, Ma. Got a minute?"

"Oh, sure," she said. "I'm not trying to feed over thirty people."

Kerry snorted. "I might've fallen for that if I didn't know Keegan, Sven, and several others were all over here helping yesterday. But I understand if you don't want to help us plan a wedding."

Lucinda was nearly on them before Kerry finished his sentence. "You're not too big for a spanking."

"Yeah, but someone else doles them out now," Kerry said.

Lucinda clutched her chest and cackled. "Do you seriously want my help with the wedding?"

"Yes, but I want to get married before Sven leaves for Vail," Kerry said.

"Vail? What are you talking about?" Lucinda asked.

Kerry waved that off. "I'll let Sven tell you all about it." He looked at Keegan and smiled. "I want to marry the love of my life in two weeks." He told her the few things they worked out so far.

She patted both of their cheeks. "Consider it done." Lucinda left them alone to return to the kitchen, where a joyous whoop rang out.

Kerry kissed him until his toes curled. "Now I understand why the newlyweds skipped all the family gatherings for months to stay home."

Maybe they would've slipped away if one of Kerry's cousins hadn't called him over to watch a replay of a touchdown. Keegan followed too, though he didn't have the first clue about the sport. Instead, he sat beside Kerry and observed the amazing family he would soon call his own.

*This is thriving.*

The End!